MIRROR IMAGE

TRISH MORAN

Published by Accent Press Ltd 2017

The story contained within this book is a work of fiction. Names and characters are the product of the author's imagination and any resemblance to actual persons, living or dead, is entirely coincidental.

Paperback ISBN: 9781786153340

Ebook ISBN: 9781786152770

CHAPTER ONE

Morgan whistled softly as he walked along the white corridor. When he reached the double glass doors, he checked the cameras above his head and gave a satisfied nod. All seemed quiet.

'All OK on C block,' he said into a walkie-talkie.

'Acknowledged,' came the reply.

Turning, he continued along another corridor until he reached the second pair of double doors. Once again, he nodded happily and spoke into his walkie-talkie.

'Acknowledged,' came the voice again.

Morgan glanced at his watch; two hours until his first break. He yawned and turned into the third corridor.

Another guard was standing at the next set of doors.

'All quiet here,' he said.

'Double guards on tonight?' Morgan asked him.

'Just the manager putting on a show! Must be some new subscribers upstairs,' the second guard replied. 'I saw a stretch limo arrive in the south car park an hour ago.'

'This place is worth a fortune.'

'Yeah,' the man said. 'I wish a bit more of it came our way, though!'

He watched as Morgan continued along the corridor to the next set of double doors and breathed a sigh of relief as he disappeared around the corner.

'Quickly!' he whispered to a young teenager who was waiting outside the door.

'Is she here?' the boy asked.

'Yes. Come on. We don't have much time.'

They hurried into a small room filled with security screens. A teenage girl looked up. 'The security cameras will be on selected replay from eleven o'clock until midnight tonight. There will only be Morgan and one other guard in this area by then.' She pushed back her chair and stood up. 'Now to set the timers on the capsules.'

The older man went back into the corridor and signalled it was clear for the younger ones to follow him. Stopping outside a large set of doors, he swiped a card across the lock. 'Make it quick! Morgan will be doing his rounds on this side in five minutes!'

The youngsters nodded as they stepped into a large room bathed in an orange glow. There was a gentle humming of machinery in the background. The room was filled with rows of translucent capsules. They went straight to a panel on the wall where the girl keyed in a series of numbers.

'Numbers forty-five to sixty-seven set for 23:10.'

Her companion nodded curtly. 'We'll be here.'

'Abe, Sel, we have to get out of here now!' the older man urged them from the doorway.

*

In another part of the building, a surgeon pulled gloves on to his hands.

'Brain activity?' he asked as the medical staff rushed a stretcher into the operating theatre.

'Fifty per cent … forty-five per cent; falling fast!' one of the staff replied, reading a monitor at the head of the stretcher.

'Is the SP in place?' the doctor looked around.

'Yes, fully prepared, sir.' A nurse indicated the second bed on which a covered figure lay inert.

'Get ready to start the download as soon as possible – while there still *is* something to download!' the surgeon ordered.

The staff silently moved around the theatre.

'Download complete, sir,' a young doctor looked at the older surgeon. 'Thirty-eight per cent.'

'He'll have some catching up to do this time! Isolate the SP organ and ready the patient for surgery,' the surgeon continued as a nurse pulled on his gloves.

Once again the medical team worked quickly and efficiently together. It was several hours later when the surgeon pulled down his face mask and wiped the sweat off his forehead. He signalled to the younger surgeon. 'You can finish this off, OK?'

'Yes, sir. Same as last time. And the time before that!' He gave his superior a grin, 'He's becoming a regular customer!'

'Yes,' the older man nodded. 'Have you reclassified the SP, sister?'

‘Yes, sir. Discard. The porters are here now,’ she said looking up as the door opened.

The second bed was wheeled from the room.

‘Good,’ said the surgeon. ‘I’d better go and see his father now. Well done everyone! Great teamwork again! Gilshaw, are you down for this afternoon’s theatre?’

‘Yes, sir,’ the younger doctor replied.

‘Speak to the parents straight afterwards, Gilshaw. Customer service, remember?’

‘Right, sir.’

Four figures stood motionless in the darkness, watching the door.

‘That’s the signal!’ Abe whispered, hurrying forward followed by Sel and two other young people. The man they had spoken to earlier held open the door.

‘He’s just finished his check; you have about thirty minutes.’

Sel nodded as they slipped silently back into the room they had visited earlier.

CHAPTER TWO

Stella looked out of the window. She watched as a robin hopped around the lawn, now and then putting its head to one side and pecking at the ground before it moved to a new spot.

'So what do you think, Stella?' the teacher's voice broke through her reverie.

'*Does* Stella think?' a girl whispered. Several others sniggered.

'Is your book *open*, Stella?' the teacher sighed.

Stella opened it quickly glancing around to see if she could spot which page the others were looking at.

Delia, a rather large, ungainly girl, mouthed, 'Thirty-six,' from the other side of the room.

Stella gave her a quick grateful smile and flicked to the correct page.

'We are looking at the arguments for and against animals being used in medical research,' the teacher repeated. 'What's your opinion, Stella?'

'I don't think it's right,' Stella said. 'It's cruel.'

'But lots of medicines are tried out on animals first, then later they can be used on humans,' a girl suggested.

'It's still cruel though, isn't it?' a third girl said.

‘If someone you loved very much was dying and the scientists had developed a medicine that could save their life by using animal research, wouldn’t you be happy to use it?’ the teacher asked.

‘Oh, then I wouldn’t think twice about it!’ Stella nodded at her.

‘There are other ways to trial medicines without causing suffering to animals,’ another girl said.

‘Yeah, people who support animal research should try being guinea pigs themselves!’ said another.

‘Anyway, they don’t need to use animals now, do they? They’ve got places like the Centre where they’ve developed stem cell research, so no animals need to suffer,’ the animal supporter was saying.

‘Why don’t they catch those gang members that have been causing all the trouble round here this past year and experiment on them?’ suggested one.

‘That’s a bit harsh! My mum says some of them have had a tough start to life. They need help, not punishment,’ another girl said.

Stella quietly nodded in agreement.

The first girl sneered. ‘They’re just the dregs of society! They need shooting, not help!’

A heated debate continued until the bell sounded for lunch break.

‘That gang fight over at the old cinema last night was pretty vicious, wasn’t it?’ Stella said to Delia as they carried their trays to a corner table in the canteen.

Her friend nodded. ‘Two of the bikers ended up in hospital. One said he’d never seen a young boy with such strength before, like he was superhuman or something.'

'Well, he would, wouldn't he? He was probably embarrassed about losing the fight,' Stella said.

A group of girls and boys walked past them and giggled. One stopped at their table and smiled.

'Hey, Stella! New trainers? Reebok or Nike?' a boy called out.

'More like Charitybok!' a girl laughed.

'And Delia must spend so much time deciding what to wear! Do you buy all your clothes at Tents R Us, Del?' another girl sniggered.

'Just ignore them, Stella,' Delia muttered as they walked past.

Stella could see her friend was upset; two bright red spots lit up her cheeks.

'You're right, they're not worth it!' she replied.

'I don't know how you can bear to go to netball Monday evenings and put up with even more of their company,' Delia said.

'I'll get a few more credits; make it easier to pass PE. God knows I need some help if I'm to get my scores up to Standard level by the end of the year!' Stella sighed. 'I want to get onto a training scheme when I'm sixteen so I can at least earn some money to help Gran out, but I won't have that option if I don't get to Standard level. And I have to pass my manual driving test this time or redo the whole course! It's so unfair that we have to pass a manual test when we can only drive a Self-Drive car anyway until we're eighteen! The car drives itself and all we have to do is sit in it; so why on earth do we need the manual test?'

'It's just in case there's a power cut and the Self-Drive fails,' Delia pointed out. 'You have to be able to drive yourself to safety.'

'Hmm!' Stella scowled. 'It's just another worry for me as well as the other subjects!'

'I'll help you with English and Maths, Stella,' Delia offered.

'Thanks, Del,' Stella smiled at her. 'You're a real friend.'

My only friend, she thought.

That evening after netball practice Stella jumped off the bus and hurried up the road. It was starting to get dark and she felt a shiver go down her spine as she turned into the side road. She quickened her pace as she neared her house. Glancing around her, she caught a glimpse of movement in the bushes and started to run towards her front door. The movement continued while she fumbled with her key in the lock. Then suddenly she burst out laughing as a sleek black cat wound itself around her legs.

'Sooty!' She picked up the cat and hugged it as she opened the door. 'Gran!' she called, 'Guess who just scared the life out of me?'

She walked into the lounge to where her grandmother was seated on a reclining chair.

'I thought it was one of those street gangs after me!'

'Naughty Sooty! We haven't had any trouble round here, Stella,' her grandmother replied, stroking the cat Stella had placed on her lap, 'but I'm glad you're home. I don't like you to be out so late on your own. Can't you ask one of the other girls' parents to drop you off?'

'A couple of girls did offer,' Stella said without meeting the older woman's eyes, 'but I'd rather have a quiet time on the bus home. Did Margery come round today?'

'Yes, she made me a lovely stew and left some for you to heat up. She did a bit extra too, it's in the freezer for the next few days,' Gran replied as Stella came in from the kitchen with a tray.

'So she's not planning on calling round again this week then?' Stella's expression was stony.

'She has her own family to look after, Stella, she can't spend all her time on me! Anyway, I was talking to her again about you, when I'm not here anymore –'

'Oh, Gran! Don't talk like that! Charlie at the shop says you'll outlive all of us.'

'Stella, you've got to face it. I'm not going to live for ever. Dr Gregory told me I'm already on borrowed time, with my heart!' Gran continued. 'By State law you can't live independently until you're eighteen, so it makes sense that you stay with Margery and her family if anything happens to me before that.'

'But Margery and her family don't even like me!' Stella argued.

'Of course they like you! They're our only family left now. They'll look after you until you're able to stand on your own two feet in the world.'

'Did Margery say that?' Stella looked at the older woman's face.

'Not exactly, but I know she won't let family down,' Gran picked up her knitting. 'Well, tell me about your day. How did the match go after school?'

'I played attack and scored two goals!' Stella beamed.

'Well done! I bet all the girls want you in their team!' She smiled fondly at her granddaughter. 'You know, you should go out with your friends some evenings, maybe at the weekend when you haven't so much schoolwork to do.'

'Why would I want to spend my time listening to idle girl chat when I can sit here and have a grown-up conversation with you?' Stella quipped.

Gran shook her head. 'Oh you always make me smile, Stella! I bet you have all your friends in stitches at school!'

Stella busied herself with her food. She'd never let her Gran know what life at school was really like. The constant taunts about her shabby appearance. Even the teachers felt they could do little with her; she daydreamed during lessons, making few worthwhile contributions. She was just passing time until the day when she could leave and find work so she could look after herself and Gran and not depend on the condescending help from Margery. A sigh escaped her lips.

'A penny for them, Stella!' Gran said.

'Just thinking I'll make us a cup of tea, then finish

my homework before *Champions* starts. I wonder if Bill Blazer will win again?'

'Of course he'll win!' Gran snorted. 'The contest is rigged!'

'It's not, Gran. It's filmed live!' Stella countered, smiling. They had the same argument every time they watched the television programme.

An hour later they were both watching the end of the news before *Champions* started.

'US President Armstrong's son is making a remarkable recovery in hospital in London today after an accident that nearly cost him his life on the racetrack last night. His co-driver escaped with a fractured collarbone,' the announcer said. 'Both men are lucky to be alive, a spokesperson from the hospital told our reporter.'

A photo appeared of the young man sitting up and smiling in a hospital bed. His head was bandaged and there were several cuts still visible on his face.

'How many accidents has he survived?' Gran asked. 'You'd think his parents would stop him taking part in such dangerous sports!'

'Yes. He had three serious injuries last year and two this year!' said Stella. 'His guardian angel must be looking after him!'

Stella pushed her nails into her tightly closed fists to try to stop herself from crying. She didn't want anyone else giving her a hug and telling her she must be brave, or it was really all for the best. How could it be for the best that she had lost her wonderful grandmother, the only person she really loved and the only one left who really loved her? Despite her efforts, a tear slowly ran down her cheek as the vicar standing at the front of the church read out a solemn prayer for Brenda Wyatt, her gran.

The story replayed itself in her head:

It had started as a normal school day. She had got up as usual, had a shower, made her packed lunch, and a pot of tea and some toast for Gran. She had seemed fine when Stella took the tray into her bedroom. They had chatted for a few minutes before her grandmother had looked at the clock and told Stella not to miss the bus.

The morning passed uneventfully until morning break.

Delia and Stella were sitting in the canteen. Luckily, they had managed to get to a corner table without encountering any of the other students and their clever taunts.

As they sat together, Stella sipping a cup of coffee, Delia munching on a piece of toast, they chatted about the television programmes they had seen the previous night. The bell had sounded and the canteen was emptying when Stella felt a hand on her shoulder. It was Mrs Dunne from the office. She looked concerned.

'Can you come with me for a minute, Stella?'

Stella felt a wave of panic rising up in her. It was Gran. It must be Gran! She hurried to the office and sat, barely taking in what the woman was telling her.

Mrs Gardiner, her neighbour, had phoned the

school. She had rung Gran's doorbell that morning and, getting no reply, had got the spare key from Margery. They had entered the house and found Gran slumped on the staircase. An ambulance had taken her to hospital.

Now William, Margery's husband, was here to pick her up and take her there. On the way he explained that Gran had suffered another massive heart attack. It was unlikely she would pull through this time. At the hospital the doctors were amazed that the old woman managed to hold on until Stella arrived.

'Gran! You're going to be fine! I know it,' Stella had whispered to her, clutching her hand, but the old woman had shaken her head gently.

'Not this time, Stella, love. Margery will look after you now, until you're a bit older. And I'll always be looking down on you, wherever I am...' Her voice had trailed away at the end and slowly her eyes had closed.

Stella came back to the present as William patted her arm gently. It was time to go to the cemetery. She followed him and Margery outside the church. Their two boys were already there; one was laughing, but quickly composed himself with a look from his father.

The rest of the day went by in a haze. After the burial, a few friends and some distant relations that Stella didn't recognise had come back to Margery's house for tea, sandwiches, and cakes. The atmosphere was strained. Stella was thankful when she could finally crawl into bed and pull the blankets over her head. She felt exhausted, yet, lying in this strange bedroom, sleep was far from her. Finally, she pulled back the bedclothes and got up. She was tiptoeing silently to the bathroom past the top of the stairs when she heard voices. Pulling her dressing gown around her, she padded down and sat on the bottom stair.

'... Work it out for yourself, Will!' Margery was saying. 'The old woman didn't even leave enough to cover her own funeral, and now we're supposed to pick up the tab for bringing up her granddaughter! Just because I happen to be Brenda's niece doesn't mean I owe her anything. God knows I did enough for the pair of them when she was alive!'

'But, Marge, she's just a kid. She has no one to look after her,' William replied.

'How can we have her live here with our two boys?' Margery continued. 'Anyway, she's not even friendly; I find her quite hostile most of the time!'

'She's just lost her grandmother, Marge. What do you expect her to be like?'

'She never was friendly! It's no good, Will.She's not moving in here. A couple of nights, then the State Services will have to sort something out for her. They can foot the bill. I've done my bit!' Margery sounded firm. 'I made enquiries earlier today; there will be a place for her at the unit just outside Meersridge until she's sixteen. She can take her Standards there. Then she'll be put in one of those supervised houses while she continues work training until she's eighteen. Then she'll be considered independent and off everybody's hands.'

'It's a big wrench for her, Marge. Couldn't she at least stay here with us until she's sixteen and stay at the same school?' William suggested.

'That's another six months! It's not possible. We can't have our own boys crammed into one bedroom for that long!'

William made a few more weak pleas in Stella's favour, but Margery refused to budge.

Stella could see her face reflected in the hall mirror: eyes huge, the despair visible in her ghostly image. She silently crept back up to her bed and lay awake for hours. The worst thing possible was going to happen. She was going to be 'cared for' by the State for two and a half years! Finally, exhausted, she fell into a fitful sleep.

The next morning Stella came downstairs after the boys had gone to school and William to work. She told Margery that she didn't feel like going into school.

Margery gave a tight smile. 'I'm sure the teachers will understand, dear. I'm going into town. I've a bit of business to sort out.'

The State Services, thought Stella as the car drove off. She went to make herself a cup of tea, but found there was no milk in the fridge. She decided to walk to the nearby supermarket.

'Stella! So how are you today, love?' Mrs Gardiner, her old neighbour, appeared beside her. 'If you need any help, you know, sorting things out in the old house just let me know.'

Stella looked startled.

'Love, I'm really sorry. I didn't mean to upset you. I'm so sorry!' Mrs Gardiner looked flustered.

Somehow, Stella found her voice. 'No. Please, I would really like you to help me. It's just that I hadn't thought…'

Mrs Gardiner patted her arm, 'Just tell me when you're ready, Stella.'

'Now,' Stella stammered. 'I'd like to do it now.'

Mrs Gardiner looked surprised.

'If you have the time, of course. If it suits you,' Stella added.

'No time like the present. Pay for your milk and we'll go and have a cup of tea at my place before we make a start,' Mrs Gardiner nodded.

They had just left the supermarket when a loud cry made them look around. Two security men were struggling to hold a teenage boy. A police car drew up and a policeman jumped out beside them. He was speaking into a walkie-talkie.

'The security man said he's one of those street gang boys! Pinching stuff no doubt!' He grinned at his partner who had joined him. 'It's good to get at least one of them off the streets!'

Stella looked across at the boy who had now stopped struggling. He didn't look much older than she was. He glanced at her, his face full of despair, with no sign of hope. She shivered as she realised it reminded her of her own face reflected in the mirror the previous night. Mrs Gardiner tugged her arm.

‘Come on, let’s go! Looks like they’ve got one of those young street thugs.’

Suddenly Stella hurled the milk container she was holding across the car park, behind the police men.

‘They’re over there! Seven of them, no, eight! The gang! They’re coming for us!’

Amidst all the shouting and screaming, Stella noticed the boy slipping free and quickly disappearing into the surrounding woodland.

She kept on screaming until one of the security guards walked up to her and shouted in her face.

‘You know, you let a violent thug slip through our fingers there!’

Mrs Gardiner stepped in front of him, ‘Now, young man, it’s not her fault. She’s going through a distressing time!’

She whispered something to him in a low voice. He made a gruff reply and walked towards the police car.

‘Come on, love,’ Mrs Gardiner tucked her arm through Stella’s and led her past the crowd. ‘Are you sure you’re up to this today?’

Stella hunched her shoulders and nodded.

Two hours later, Mrs Gardiner pushed the last of the clothes into a plastic bag and tied it closed.

‘How are you getting on with those papers, Stella? I’m sure Margery and William will help you sort out bank accounts and things like that.’

‘I’ve put those ones in this pile,’ Stella replied. ‘I’ve found some photos of me and Gran when I was a baby. And one of Mum. None of Dad, though. Did you know him at all, Mrs Gardiner?'

'I met him once or twice when my Joe was still alive. He came round to visit Brenda with your mum, first when she was pregnant, then again when you were about a year old. He was a quiet sort, never said much,' Mrs Gardiner told her. 'Then the next time we saw you and your mum, you were about two and you were moving in with your Gran. Must have been just after he left.'

'Was Mum upset?' Stella asked her.

'At first she was, but she seemed to be getting over it. You were the light of her life. Then suddenly, she got sick. You used to come round here and have your tea with us on the days your Gran would take her to the hospital,' she sighed, 'A month later she passed away. Then there was just you and your Gran.'

'And now it's just me,' Stella said quietly.

'I'm sure Margery will look after you, love,' Mrs Gardiner stood up. 'You know, I made a fruit cake yesterday. I bet you could do with a slice and a cup of tea.'

Stella nodded. 'I'll just finish this cupboard, and then I'll join you next door.'

Soon two suitcases of her belongings stood beside the door.Not much to show for nearly sixteen years, she thought. She put the front door key in her pocket and went to the next house.

Stella sipped her tea and nibbled at a slice of fruit cake. 'Mrs Gardiner?'

'Hmm, love?'

'Was that really one of the street gang at the supermarket today? He didn't look like a violent thug, did he?' she asked.

'Well, he didn't look like it, but there's been a lot of stealing and some terrible fights over the last year. It would be good to get some of that sort off the streets; make the town a safer place like it used to be.' She patted Stella's hand. 'But don't you feel guilty about making such a fuss and him escaping; no one will hold you responsible for your reactions today, pet. No one will think you really wanted him to escape.'

Stella looked into her cup. She *had* wanted the boy to escape.

She thanked Mrs Gardiner for her help and set off for Margery's house shortly after that.

'I'm glad you've made a start sorting out the house,' Margery said as they sat down to tea that evening. 'The rent's paid up until the end of the month. I expect they'll have it lined up for another family then.'

William gave a slight cough and looked at his wife. She didn't seem to notice and continued.

'Tomorrow, Stella, I'll need you to come down to the council offices with me, to sort out your Gran's affairs. And things. They won't be expecting you back at school this week anyway.'

'I wish I could have a week off sch …!' her younger son started to say, but his brother kicked him under the table.

'Ow! What was that for?' he retaliated, glaring at him.

Stella pushed back the chair. 'I think I'll just read upstairs for a while.'

'Yes, go on, love,' William smiled at her.

'She doesn't even have to do the washing-up!' the younger son was complaining as she went up the stairs.

It was nearly midnight by the time Stella felt sure everyone was asleep. She had lain for the past few hours planning what she would do. The boy at the supermarket had helped her make her decision. She wasn't going to spend two and a half years in the care of the State.She was going to find the boy from the supermarket and join him and his friends. Slipping out of bed, she put a pillow under the blankets. It would look like she was still asleep if someone glanced into the room, giving her more time to get away.

Every stair seemed to creak loudly as she made her way downstairs. Several times she stood still, holding her breath, but no one stirred. She pushed open the front door then closed it as quietly as she could after her.

Hurrying along the pavement, she felt a mixture of fear and excitement. She glanced up at the dark windows of Mrs Gardiner's house as she let herself silently into her old home. She didn't dare risk having the overhead light on, so she pulled the curtains and put a small lamp on the floor near her. Opening her suitcase she selected two pairs of jeans, two jumpers, and some underwear. These she pushed into the rucksack she used for school. She went into the kitchen and put some tinned food, a tin opener, and a bottle of water into the rucksack. She rummaged through some of the cases Mrs Gardiner had packed until she found a sleeping bag. Finally, she found a torch and put in into her coat pocket. A lump filled her throat as she picked up the envelope containing the photos of herself, Gran, and her mother. She put them carefully into her rucksack.

'Goodbye, old home!' she whispered as she took one last glance around the room, turned off the light, and headed for the front door. She stood for a few moments, letting her eyes adjust to the moonlit street, then taking a deep breath, she set off. The place she had lived in for all of her life seemed strange and unfamiliar in the darkness. Window panes like blank eyes seemed to watch her as she walked by. She gasped and drew back into a narrow alley as a lone car went past. As the rear lights disappeared, she hurried on to the Green, the small patch of grass between the local pub, The Dragon, and the bus stop. The pub's dragon-shaped sign creaked in the wind as a tumble of litter and leaves blew across the road.

Stella gave a last sigh as she climbed over a stile into a muddy field. It became more difficult to make her way up the rough hillside as it gradually became steeper. Frequently she tripped over branches and rocks yet she was afraid to use her torch until she had put a good distance between the town and herself. Finally, she stood and looked down at the few lights on in the town. She was free of Margery and the State Services! Now she had to find the boy and his gang.

By dawn, Stella was high up on the mountainside. She had seen no one, just a few sheep. Spotting a small cave, she decided to rest for a while. As she hurried towards it she stumbled on a large rock, twisting her ankle painfully. Moaning with each step, she dragged herself the last few feet to the cave. She wrapped the sleeping bag around her shoulders and lay back on the rough ground. Despite her pain and discomfort, she soon nodded off to sleep.

'Who do you think she is?'

'A Lab?'

'No. They don't let newly freed Labs travel on their own.'

'Non-Labs don't come up here.'

'Maybe she's run away.'

'Or been thrown out.'

Stella stirred and opened her eyes. She sat up and looked around her. She was surrounded by a group of teenagers, all about her own age or a bit older. One girl was black with long hair in narrow plaits. There were identical triplet Asian girls and twin blond boys. All were looking at her curiously.

Stella climbed out of her sleeping bag and tried to stand up, wincing as her swollen foot touched the ground.

'Hi,' she ventured nervously.

'She's injured,' one of the girls said.

'We can't leave her here, can we?' one of the blond boys said.His twin shook his head in agreement.

'I think we should take her to Abe,' the first girl said.

'Yes,' the triplets agreed.

One of the boys scooped her up in his arms as the other collected her belongings.

'Who are you?' she asked, but was only given a nervous smile in return.

Soon they arrived at a cave high in the hills. The entrance was scarcely visible from outside, but once they had travelled for about a hundred metres down a narrow, dark tunnel they entered a larger area, lit by tapers. From the gouge marks on the walls, the chamber had obviously been dug out and enlarged. Stella noticed there were several other tunnels leading away from the main one. The boy sat her down on the floor in the centre of the area. Slowly, she found herself surrounded by other people – all teenagers like her. They seemed to be from all the different races and they seemed to be from all over the world. She was surprised at the number of twins and triplets there were, and there was even one set of quadruplets. All stood looking at her.

'What do you think she was doing up here?' a girl, one of triplets, asked. Her sisters gave a questioning look to all the others, as if they had all asked the question.

'Is it a Lab?' a boy asked. He and his twin looked expectantly at the group who had found Stella.

‘Don’t think so, but we can check,’ one of the Asian girls answered. She and her sisters looked nervous.

A boy stepped forward and grabbed Stella’s right arm. He pushed her sleeve up and rubbed her inside wrist.

‘No. Must be a Non-Lab.’

‘We can ask her,’ suggested one of the twin boys who had found her. His brother nodded and looked at Stella, ‘Who are you?’

‘I’m Stella.’

‘Are you a Non-Lab?’ the first boy ventured.

Stella frowned. ‘I don’t know what you mean. I’m just a girl, still at school. Well, until recently.’

‘What have we here?’ a loud voice sounded. Everyone stood back to let the owner of the voice come through. He was tall with a lean, muscular body, his straight black hair tied back in a ponytail. He wore the same type of old jeans and T-shirt that many of the others were wearing. And although he was probably about the same age as the others, Stella thought, he was obviously in charge. He scanned her face as he grabbed her arm and pushed up her sleeve again.

‘We’ve checked, Abe. She’s not a Lab,’ a girl told him.

‘Where did you find her? What was she doing up here?’ Abe gave Stella a fierce stare. He pulled her to her feet and turned her around. He ran rough, callused hands over her body, pulling money and the torch out of her pockets which he glanced over before tossing them down. Stella started to feel uneasy as his eyes bored into her.

'She was sleeping in the little cave up near the big pine tree,' one of the Asian girls said, while her sisters nodded in agreement.

'She's hurt her foot,' the girl with braids said, helping Stella to sit down again.

Abe had now tipped the contents of Stella's bag out onto the ground and picked up and shook each thing.

He turned to Stella. 'Who are you? What are you doing here?'

'I'm Stella. I've come to join you. You're the street gang, aren't you?'

Abe gave a laugh. 'And why would you want to join us, Stella?'

She rubbed her face. 'Because … I know how you feel … everyone around here is against you. I've got no one either. And I saw one of you yesterday, at the supermarket. He didn't look anything like what they say about you,' She looked around, 'None of you do.'

'It was me she saw,' a voice said. The others looked around and then stood back as the youth Stella had seen the day before came forward. 'I went into the town yesterday. I saw those bikers you had trouble with the other night and I ducked into the supermarket. But the security guy thought I was trying to steal stuff and he called the police. She helped me to escape.'

Stella smiled at him and watched him slowly

smile back at her.

'Ket!' Abe turned on him. 'You know it's forbidden to go into the town during daylight! And only those with permission can go at night. Your permission is suspended as from now. What do you think you were doing? You could have put us all in danger!' He swung around to face the twin boys who had brought Stella to the cave. 'And what were you thinking of, bringing her here? *She* could put us all in danger!'

'She's injured,' one of them muttered.

'I'm no danger to anyone!' Stella protested. 'I'm on my own. No one knows I'm here!'

'Shut up!' a blonde-haired girl snapped at her.

'Det!' Ket stepped forward. He patted Stella's arm and smiled again. 'It's OK.'

Det glared at him. 'It's not OK! It's far from OK!'

'She's probably been sent to spy on us. Maybe even by the Centre!' Abe agreed. 'We'll have to get rid of her.'

'What?' Ket stepped in front of Stella. 'But she rescued me yesterday! And she's injured. I'm sure Stella is no danger to us!'

'Yes, she's injured,' one of the twin boys repeated. 'We couldn't just leave her there.'

'She's a *Non-Lab*,' Abe snapped. 'Her own kind can care for her!'

'But they *don't*!' Tears sprang to Stella's eyes. 'They were going to take over my life for the next two years! Haven't some of you people escaped from the State Services?'

The young people surrounding her all looked bewildered.

The girls with braids spoke to Abe. 'Look, her foot needs attention. I propose we keep her here until we know a bit more about her.'

'OK. As a temporary measure. If she's got anyone following her we could use her as a hostage, I suppose,' Abe conceded. 'Put her in one of the stores and keep a careful eye on her. We'd better organise a stricter guard patrol and double the numbers on duty until we find out if we're safe or not.'

'I'll arrange a guard rota for the girl,' Det stood up.

Ket picked Stella up in his arms and followed Det to a small hollowed-out area at the end of a narrow tunnel. She was left with triplet boys to guard her. They all looked away uneasily when she tried to speak to them.

Shortly afterwards the girl with the braids appeared with Stella's rucksack and a roll of bandages.

'What's going to happen to me?' Stella asked as the other girl bent over her foot.

'Don't worry. Let's get your foot sorted first of all,' she smiled. 'I'm Sel, by the way.'

Over the next few days, Sel came to see Stella, re-bandaging her foot and helping her to exercise. Sometimes Ket would join them. They avoided any personal conversations with her and refused to answer any questions about their community, although Sel was very interested in finding out about the life Stella was running away from.

After about a week, Stella was awakened late one night by the sound of voices. She sat up as several young people were led past her. They were all dressed in white and looked around in surprise, questioning some of the others who were leading them. Sel was among them.

'We're OK now. We're safe here. Once Abe is back we'll explain everything to you.'

Ket hurried up to Sel. 'It's OK. Abe got away. He's hurt his arm, but it doesn't look serious. One of the guards was badly injured. They must have changed the rota!'

Stella asked Sel about the night's events the next day, but as usual she was tight-lipped about everything.

'You told me you were going to be cared for by the State. I did some research on State Services for young people and it sounds like a really good idea. Young people without stable families are cared for and educated by the State until they are sixteen and then live in supervised houses while they continue studying or training for work until they are eighteen and officially adults.'

Stella shook her head. 'It *sounds* like a good idea, I suppose. But the institutes where the young people are raised are pretty grim, and everybody really looks down on the State kids. Most people begrudge taxpayers' money being used on caring for them and educating them.'

'Mmm, the State Services could be our answer,'

Sel murmured. 'I must talk to Abe.'

'What do you mean?' Stella asked, but the other girl merely smiled.

'It's a big chance for us, Abe!' Sel said that evening as she sat with Abe, Ket and Det. 'Five of us can set ourselves up in a supervised house in Castlewell and enrol on a course at the local college. Valerie has agreed to take on the role as our State-appointed supervisor. She's researching all she needs to know this evening. I can easily produce all the documents we need. We'll be living freely among the Non-Labs as their equals. We'll actually be much safer there than hiding out here in the Caves...'

'No! Your idea is *totally* out of the question!' Abe snapped. 'What a crazy idea! Live amongst *Non-Labs*?'

'Sel's right,' Ket said. 'Just give it a chance –'

'No! No way!' Abe cut him off roughly. 'You would not only be putting yourselves in danger, but if – *when* – you were discovered, you'd be putting *all* the Labs in danger.'

'Every time we arrange a raid on the Centre we put everyone's life in danger!' Sel said. 'Look how close we came to getting caught this time! We were lucky you didn't kill one of the guards!'

Abe sneered, 'He was just a Non-Lab! Anyway, we got away, didn't we?'

'But Sel's right – the raids are getting more difficult. If we set up a home as State-cared-for youths, we could blend in. Stella could show us how to behave like Non-Labs,' Ket offered.

'No!' Det looked horrified. 'Abe's right! It's impossible. Think of the risks of living amongst Non-Labs!'

'Well, I'm all for giving it a try. Let's put it to the vote tonight, shall we?' Sel said, her face a stubborn mask.

Stella was able to walk around on her injured foot again and was making her way back from the wash area the following evening. Her guards were more relaxed with her now and had gone on ahead to what she considered her area. She stopped as Ket appeared with a plate of food for her. He placed his hand on her arm, glancing at the two Labs ahead of them.

'Be ready to leave in about an hour,' he whispered.

She waited with a trembling sense of excitement until Ket reappeared. He signalled her to be silent.

'Quick. We don't have much time!' He hoisted her rucksack onto his back and grabbing her hand, led her down the tunnel to where Sel was standing. She had a leather bag the size and shape of a thick book strapped across her chest.

'It's OK!' she whispered. She hurried on ahead, padding softly on the loose earth.

They travelled for an hour, weaving through different tunnels, some wide, some narrow and low, before Stella felt a fresh breeze on her face. Soon afterwards they emerged into the evening light. Stella took a deep breath and leaned against a tree trunk.

‘No!’ Ket pulled her arm. ‘We don’t have time to rest!’

They continued cautiously along a narrow track through the woodland. There was no light, except for that given by the moon. Suddenly Sel signalled them to stop. There was the sound of voices just ahead of them.

Sel turned to Ket. ‘Jed and Lon!’ She walked towards their voices. ‘Here!’

The twin blond boys appeared.

‘Abe has discovered you’ve gone,’ Jed told them.

‘He’s surrounding the forest now!’ Lon added.

‘We’re supposed to be searching the area from here to the river,’ Jed continued.

‘He doesn’t know we’re going with you,’ Lon said.

‘Where are we going?’ Stella asked.

‘We’ll explain later. We must move quickly now!’ Ket told her.

Stella pulled herself up, trying to hide a grimace as her ankle throbbed painfully.

Lon looked at her. ‘Come on!’ he said and pulled her onto his back piggy-back style.

‘You’ll delay us otherwise,’ his brother explained.

They travelled for many miles at speed, with Stella running or being carried by one of the blond twins. After a few hours they reached the river bank.

Ket was judging the best place to cross, when Sel signalled them to be silent. They had just hidden themselves behind some low branches when they heard voices and two policemen appeared on the pathway near them.

'I don't think they'll find that girl. Not alive anyway,' one was saying.

'No. It's been over a week now,' his partner agreed.

Their voices became fainter as they moved on. Sel peeped through the branches and then quickly withdrew her head and signalled for silence again. The five of them stood holding their breath as girl triplets appeared.

'Lon and Jed are covering this area, too. They would have found them by now if they were here,' one of them said.

'Maybe Sel was serious. Maybe they really *are* going to live in a town,' another said.

'Abe's right, it would be impossible to live safely amongst Non-Labs,' said the third. Suddenly the first girl signalled them to stop. She tilted her head.

Stella was sure they could hear her heart pumping. The others stood as still as statues.

'Policemen!' the second girl whispered.

'They're probably searching for the girl, too,' said the third one.

'Let's see if they have any news,' said the first, creeping forward.

Stella could just make out the shapes of the girls as they disappeared down the pathway the policemen had taken.

Shortly afterwards the girls returned.

'No news of her,' the first said.

'At least it proves that she wasn't a spy,' said the second.

'We're convinced, but it would take more than an overheard conversation to satisfy Abe!' the third girl said.

'Yeah!' the first nodded. 'He just *hates* all Non-Labs!'

Stella and the others stood for several more minutes before Sel signalled that it was all clear. They began on their journey again.

Ket had gone on ahead to find a good place to cross the river. Stella shuddered with apprehension as they made their way down to the fast-flowing water where he stood.

'Lon, Jed – guide Stella. I will stay close to Sel,' he instructed them.

Ket started to wade across the river, feeling his way carefully with his feet. Sel walked behind him, holding her leather bag high above her head. Lon followed, with Stella holding his hand tightly. Jed had his hand on her back as she gingerly stepped forwards.

All seemed to be going well, until halfway across the river Ket disappeared from view. Lon let go of Stella and grabbed Sel to steady her. Ket's head reappeared and he signalled the group to move further to the left. Without Lon's reassuring grasp, Stella felt panic rise inside her. She gave a cry and disappeared under the water, thrashing her arms and legs wildly. Her clothes were dragging her down and her lungs felt as if they would burst. 'This is it,' she thought, as she knew she could hold her breath no longer. Suddenly she found herself pushed to the surface of the water and gratefully took a huge gulp of air. Jed gave her another hard push onto the river bank where Ket and Lon hauled her to her feet. She pulled a long strand of waterweed out of her hair and looked around at them all, muddy and wet. Only Sel had managed to keep the top half of herself and her bag dry. Suddenly she threw back her head and laughed out loud. The others looked at her with open mouths at first, and then slowly began to smile.

Cold, hungry, and soaking, they travelled on for most of the next day until by sunset they had reached the tumbledown remains of a farmhouse. After checking there was no one around, they made a fire and opened some tins of food.

Stella was suffering most from the cold and Ket had found an old, grubby blanket in the farmhouse which she gratefully pulled around her as she tried to warm herself by the fire.

Sel had taken a laptop from the leather bag as soon as they arrived there and had started work on it. She reappeared as they began to eat.

'I've obtained new IDs for us all,' Sel explained as she spooned soup into her mouth. She hardly seemed to realise that she was eating. She nodded at Stella. 'You can collect it from the post office in Castlewell tomorrow morning in your new name.' She held out a phone bill with the name Ruby Devon and an address in Nottingham. 'You must get used to your new name quickly.'

Stella nodded then looked down at her clothes. 'But I can't go like this.'

'Of course not,' Sel agreed. She looked at the twins, 'You'll need to go into the town tonight for new outfits for all of us. And Stella – Ruby – will need to change her hair colour. Anything different to her natural colour. And bring women's cosmetics. We don't want anyone recognising her. We'll need money. I've a card set up for that.'

She stood up and beckoned to the twins. 'Come on. I've located a FineMart on the outskirts of town. There's an ATM there I can use.'

She turned to Ket as they prepared to leave, 'Clean yourselves up. You'll have to look decent. We've an interview with a landlord tomorrow, too. We'll be going with Valerie Sutton, the Non-Lab from the Centre. I have her ID here, too. She is going to be posing as our Social Officer installing us as State-cared-for students just out of Brightstart House in Nottingham, ready to begin our final two years' Independence Training. She has picked up details of the local college courses we can apply for.'

'State-cared-for students?' Stella looked aghast.

'It's a great disguise! And what alternative do we have?' Sel shrugged.

Stella watched the three of them disappear down the hill.

'Wow! Sel's really organised!' She shook her head. 'Have you fallen out with Abe and the others because of me?'

Ket stood up straight and shook his head. 'Not

exactly. You've forced us to do something we have been discussing for some time now.'

She waited for him to continue.

'Sel and I and some of the others consider Abe's way of thinking a bit too … extreme. We want to help our own kind, but we don't think he has the best solution.'

Stella shook her head. 'Who exactly are you? I never got any answers to my questions.'

Ket gave a gesture to take in the scene around them. 'Tomorrow, when we are in more suitable surroundings, we'll tell you more about us. I think it's time you knew the whole story.'

They both continued to clear up and then had makeshift showers using plastic containers and cold water.

Sel, Lon, and Jed appeared shortly afterwards. Each had a suitcase. Lon wanted to unpack them immediately, but Sel said they must all be reasonably clean before getting changed. She beckoned Stella to sit by the kitchen sink, once the boys had washed. She produced a box and applied a dye solution.

'We must wait for thirty minutes for the colour to take,' she told her. 'Go and sit outside while I clean myself up.'

Stella sat outside and soon forgot how cold she was as the boys put on a fashion show for her. Soon she was laughing as they dressed in different outfits, fussing over jackets and belts like children with new toys. Often they asked her advice about different ensembles, although she could hardly see the colours in the fading light.

'Come, Stella. We must rinse your hair again,' said Sel from the doorway. 'We must all get some sleep now. Ket, we can do first guard duty, Lon and Jed can take over from us in two hours.'

All immediately obeyed her. Stella sat and shivered while Sel poured cold water over her head and gave a sigh of relief when she was handed a towel and was able to rub her hair dry and some life back into her frozen scalp.

Soon she too was fast asleep on the hard kitchen floor, unaware of the changing rota of guards during the rest of the night.

She was woken by Lon gently shaking her shoulder. 'Wake up. We must get ready.'

Rubbing her eyes, Stella got up and looked around. The others had dressed themselves in their new clothes. Sel was packing all their belongings into the suitcase.

Jed gave a pile of clothes to her. 'Give me those clothes. We must not leave anything behind us. For Labs or Non-Labs to find.'

'You don't think Abe knows we are here, do you?' Jed asked. Lon also looked disturbed.

'No. Not yet. If we cover our tracks and merge fully into our new identities, we should be safe for the moment,' she replied. 'But we cannot underestimate him!'

'We chose well!' Jed gave Stella a nod of approval as she smoothed the purple jumper down over tight black jeans. She pulled on a soft brown leather jacket and wrapped a sequin-covered scarf around her neck.

'I've never worn such lovely clothes!' she said. 'What is my hair like? What colour is it?'

'Red!' Johnny told her.

'Like a ruby!' Leon added, grinning.

She gave a gasp as Lon held a broken mirror up in front of her. Her hair was bright red and uncombed it stood in spikes from her head. She gave a laugh, 'That doesn't look like me at all!'

'It's not meant to look like Stella. It's Ruby, remember. Put on some make-up, too, so you look older,' Sel told her. 'Well chosen, boys.'

'Yes, thank you, Lon and Jed,' the new Ruby told them.

'Leon and John,' Sel said. 'And Keith!' She pointed to Ket. 'And I am now, or will be when you have collected our IDs, Celia.'

'I want to be called Johnny,' Jed stated, glaring at his brother who was grinning smugly.

'John, Johnny – what's the difference?' the new Celia asked him.

'Two syllables! I don't want to be one syllable! Like all the Labs! Why did you give the others two syllables?' he pouted.

'What does it matter?' Celia shook her head.

'Hey, I'm one syllable, too!' Keith said, 'I like Keith! It has a good sound!'

'Ce-li-a! Three syllables! And La-e-on!' cried the new Leon.

'No, that's Le-on,' said Ruby.

'Ha!' Johnny pointed at him, '*Two* syllables! You can't cheat!'

'Well, at least I'm a *real* two-syllabler!' he retorted.

'Next time we get new identities, I want four syllables, or even five syllables,' Johnny complained.

'I hope we don't need new identities after these!' Celia said, putting the last suitcase on the table. 'Go and check everywhere, one last time.'

When Celia was satisfied they had completely eradicated any traces of their stay, the five of them set off.

'Later today you must go to the Post Office on Main Street, over there, Ruby. Once we have our IDs we can meet Valerie and get ready for our appointment with the landlord of the house we'll be renting. We must impress him. The house is perfect in size and location. But first we must go to the railway station.It is on the far side of town.'

'Why are we going to the railway station?' Johnny ventured. Leon looked expectantly at Celia.

'We must seem to have arrived in town by the normal means. Not just suddenly appeared. We don't want to arouse any suspicions,' Keith answered for her.

As they neared the entrance to Castlewell station Celia stopped them once again.

'We'll wait here, out of sight, until the train arrives. Then we can join the other passengers as they make their way into town.'

They waited silently behind some trees.

'OK, here we go,' Celia announced as a train pulled in and people began to get off. 'Follow the crowd. Look natural.'

Keith started to walk forward, his shoulders stiff, his eyes fixed firmly on the ground. Ruby linked her arm through his and smiled at him.

'That was quite a trip! I'm glad the rain held off. I wonder what our new home will be like?' She turned to Leon. 'Hey, easy with that suitcase! You nearly tripped me up!'

She gave him a smile to let him know she wasn't serious.

Finally, with small talk mainly from Ruby, they reached the centre of town.

'We'll go to a café while you collect two parcels from the Post Office, Ruby,' Celia told her.

Ruby glanced at Celia's face. She could see she was trying hard to hide her anxiety.

'It might be better if I come with you and order some food, then I'll know where to find you,' she offered as Celia visibly relaxed.

After installing them in a corner booth with bacon rolls, tea, and coffee, Ruby left them and made her way to the Post Office. She rummaged in her new handbag and pulled out an email receipt. Handing it to the old man at the counter, she smiled brightly.

He looked down at it and went into a room at the back of the building, emerging a moment later with two small brown parcels.

'Oh, great! I'm so glad they arrived on time! Sometimes it takes weeks for things to get through, doesn't it?' she said.

'I'll need some ID before you sign for these, miss,' the man told her putting the parcel on the counter.

'Of course,' Ruby began to rummage in her bag again, 'Oh dear! It looks like my card is in my suitcase! Well, I'll have to go back and get it! Oh, I've got this. Any use?'

She held out the phone bill with her new name on it.

'I'll trust you, lass. You've got an honest face,' the man replied after looking at the bill and pushing the parcels towards her. 'So what are you doing in this area? I don't think I've seen you here before.'

'No, I've just arrived. I've moved here with some friends,' she smiled at him, 'It seems like a lovely place. Beautiful scenery!'

'Yes, the countryside is beautiful. And it's easy to get to the bigger towns from here, too, for a bit of nightlife.'

At the tinkle of the doorbell, he looked behind her, 'Morning, Mrs Jarvis. Your books have arrived.'

Ruby slipped out as he handed the woman a large parcel.

She hurried back to the café and joined the others in the booth.

'Any coffee left?' she asked, handing the parcels to Celia.

'Could we have some more? And some more bacon rolls?' asked Johnny.

'We were a bit too … you know … about asking

for anything else,' Leon added.

Ruby smiled and went back to the counter to order extra food and drinks.

As she sat down again, Celia gave her three plastic cards to each of them. 'Ket – Keith- I thought we could get away with being seventeen. Then we only have ten months before you're an adult and eleven months before I'm one which will be a great help for us all. I didn't think the boys or Ruby would get away with it, so they're all sixteen.'

'ID, bank card, and Self-Drive car licence,' Ruby said, looking at her cards. 'I never actually passed my manual driving test. I failed it twice!'

'You can learn. It can't be too difficult. Many Non-Labs do it,' Celia said. 'We'll all have to learn if it's a school subject. And it's an essential skill to have anyway.'

Ruby slipped the cards inside her bag as the waitress came with their order. Soon, she was biting into the most delicious bacon roll she had ever eaten. The plates were soon emptied again when Celia glanced at the clock on the wall and announced it was time for their next appointment.

'Ah! One very important thing before we go.' She opened the second smaller parcel and peeled off a small plastic film. Glancing around to make sure there was no one nearby, she pushed up her sleeve to reveal a small tattooed code near her wrist. She pressed the plastic film over the tattoo. The code was completely covered and the plastic strip became almost invisible. Each of the boys was given a similar strip and carried out the same operation.

'Hey! Pretty good. Where did you get them from, Celia?' Keith asked her.

'A theatrical agency. I found it on the internet,' she explained.

'Along with false IDs and driving licences!' Ruby smiled, 'How do you find these things?'

'You have to know where to look,' Celia said simply.

'It's a bit itchy,' Johnny complained, rubbing his wrist.

'But better than being spotted!' Leon told him.

Celia's mobile phone rang as they left the café.

'Hi, Valerie. Yes, the ID arrived OK and the documents to show we're State-cared-for minors from Nottingham. Did your ID come through?'

'Yes. The email arrived yesterday. I spoke to a friend of mine who works in State Services and I picked up a few tips from her – without letting her know why I was so interested, of course. I don't think we'll have any trouble with your new landlord. He keeps it quiet, but he was actually State-raised too, so he has a soft spot for similar kids.'

Later that day, Keith had to keep on nudging Leon and Johnny as they were shown around the house by their prospective landlord.

'Hot water!' Leon whispered excitedly, turning on the tap.

'Look at this!' Johnny could hardly contain himself, bouncing on the sofa.

Ruby, Celia and Valerie were nodding as Mr Robinson, their prospective landlord, pointed out features and told them the ground rules for his tenants.

'I'll need two months in advance and a guarantee from your department, Mrs Sutton,' he said.

Valerie held out an official-looking document that Celia had created.

'Hmm. Seems OK. From Nottingham?' the man asked her.

'Yes, that's right. Do you know Nottingham yourself?' she replied, hiding her relief when he told her he had never been there.

'How long are you thinking of staying here? I do contracts for six months, initially, but we can extend it after that time if we're all happy with things.'

Valerie glanced at Celia. 'That'll be fine, Mr Robinson.'

'Well, things seem in order. When do you want to move in?' he asked.

'The sooner the better,' Valerie smiled at him. 'We've all come prepared with overnight bags, as we planned on looking around a few places over the next few days. But this place is perfect! I can arrange to have the rest of their things sent on from Nottingham later in the week!'

'I'll draw up the contract and see you here in an hour. If you have the deposit ready it's yours today,' he smiled back at them.

Later that day Leon and Johnny ran from room to room, excitedly pointing out the marvellous features, like hot radiators, carpets, comfortable chairs, and, best of all, soft beds! Neither of them could stay for long in one place.

'Come on, boys!' Keith pointed out, 'You've been in a house before! Remember the farmhouse where Miranda first took us?'

'That was so long ago,' Leon shook his head. 'And it wasn't like this!'

'No,' Johnny added, 'We get our own bedrooms here. There were lots of us in the bedroom in the farmhouse.'

'We need to sit down and discuss your college courses,' Valerie said. 'I've arranged an appointment for us all with the admissions officer at Castleford Advanced Training College Friday afternoon. They offer a variety of courses, starting each month. I'm sure there will be something you can do for the next two years until you're officially independent.' She gave out a handful of prospectuses.

Johnny looked at Leon, 'We could take a foundation course in Sports Science.'

'And join some of the sports teams, too,' Leon added. 'They have football, basketball, and swimming clubs!'

'And use of a gym!' Johnny beamed.

Celia looked up. 'I'll enrol on a computer course, though they appear to be of a very basic level.'

'The Media course looks interesting,' Keith said.

Ruby looked flustered as she flipped through the booklet, 'I was never that good at school…'

Valerie squeezed her hand, 'Don't worry, love.

Your main job is helping the others to adjust to what we consider normal life, so we'll enrol you on a part-time course to start with. There are plenty of practical courses that won't be too demanding. Later you can think about the career you want to follow.'

'Mmm, I could take a look at the Foundation Hospitality…' she said.

'That looks like a good choice! Can you all read through the prospectus carefully before our college appointment? Now let's sort things out for today,' Valerie stood up and handed Celia a pencil and pad. 'We'll start in the kitchen.

'You'll need food,' she said, opening the cupboards in the kitchen. 'Pasta, vegetables, the basics.'

'And soap and things,' Ruby added. 'Here, give me a separate sheet, I can do that list.' She sat down at the kitchen table and began writing.

'We'll all go to the supermarket now, while I'm here with the car,' Valerie continued.

'We don't have to wait until tonight and break in?' Leon sounded amazed.

'No. We have money and bank accounts – even if they're fraudulently set up,' Keith grinned at Celia.

'Yes. We're honorary Non-Labs now!' she added.

CHAPTER THREE

Ruby felt happier than she had in a long time as they sat down to the first meal in their new home that evening. As she looked at the faces around her, she felt a sense of belonging.

A tempting aroma filled the air as Leon appeared holding a large casserole and placed it in the centre of the table. Johnny appeared a few minutes later and put a large bowl of pasta beside it.

'That smells appetising,' Keith commented.

'Mmm, spaghetti Bolognese! It's absolutely delicious! Where did you learn to cook?" Ruby asked.

'We sometimes took cookery books as well as food and other stuff when we went to the supermarkets and shops in the night,' Leon explained.

'Ones with colourful pictures,' Johnny added.

'We weren't really able to make them in the cave kitchens!' Leon grinned at his brother. 'They weren't as well-equipped as this one! We've really enjoyed making this!'

'I was amazed at how you were able to cook really good food in the caves,' Ruby commented.

‘Where did you get it from?’

‘We had a team that went into the supermarkets at night when we needed things. Their security was usually pretty flimsy, so it wasn’t too hard to bypass,’ Celia said.

‘Celia can bypass anything!’ Leon said admiringly. ‘She’s a techno-wizard!’

‘We could cook quite a variety of stuff on the fires,’ Celia said. ‘We made sure we ate a healthy selection of food. Abe insisted. He also insisted on regular daily exercise to keep us as healthy as the day we were awakened. We shall continue to do so, starting from tomorrow morning!’

‘Don’t wake me up too early!’ Valerie groaned.

Keith pushed his empty plate away, ‘Tell us a bit about your background, Ruby.’

‘Yes, we must get to know each other better. So, first of all you must tell us about yourself – as Stella,’ Celia turned to her.

Ruby took a deep breath and explained how she had been raised by her grandmother after her dad had left them and her mother had died soon after that. She showed them the photos of her family.

‘There are no pictures of your father,’ Keith said.

‘No. And I don’t remember what he looked like. He left when I was still very young,’

‘Why did he do that?’ asked Leon.

‘I don’t know,’ Ruby shrugged, ‘Mum and Gran never really talked about him much.’

‘And you were still at school until recently?’ Celia sat forward eagerly. ‘So you were at school for how many years?'

Ruby totted up the years, 'Mmm, about ten years! I wasn't a very good student, though. I didn't really pay as much attention as I should have.'

'You didn't want to learn?' Celia looked surprised.

'Well, I suppose it may seem that way, but it wasn't really quite like that, either. I wasn't all that interested in the things they were teaching me.'

Celia shook her head sadly. 'What a great waste!'

'When your grandmother died wasn't there any other family member to take you in?' asked Keith.

'Gran's niece, Margery, but she didn't want me. So I would have to be cared for by the State until I'm eighteen. And now I've joined you, I will be, in theory, anyway!'

'Well, I hope our new life is better than living hidden in the caves,' Keith said.

Leon and Johnny nodded in agreement.

Ruby looked around the table. 'Now tell me about yourselves.'

Valerie shook her head. 'Another story that started with good intentions that went remarkably wrong! I was there at the beginning with Miranda. You tell Ruby, Keith.'

All eyes turned to him as he peeled the plastic strip off the code on his arm and rubbed it. He showed her a tattooed code: KET 87269.

'This is what we are. The mark of an SP – a Spare Part! Though we prefer to call ourselves Labs – that is people created in a laboratory, as opposed to your kind, Non-Labs.'

'Spare Parts?' Ruby frowned.

'Yes,' Leon whispered. 'We are Spare Parts for Non-Labs. Wealthy ones and their children.'

Ruby felt a shudder go down her spine. Celia nodded at Keith to continue.

'You are aware of the Medical Centre, in the open land near Hambleton?' he continued. 'Well, what is visible, even if you get through the security guard around the compound, reveals only a tiny part of the activities that go on there.

'The visible building houses the administration offices and ten research laboratories. This is what the visitors and subscribers see. What they are not made aware of is that there are several underground levels where the main work is carried out.

'The original idea for this centre was admirable. Dr Miranda Cheung was involved in this. The staff researched and carried out cloning procedures to produce cells that could be used when a person was injured. To help them repair and stimulate regrowth of damaged organs and tissue. Her vision was primarily to help innocent people caught up in wars, especially children. She established a committee to raise funds to finance the organisation. However, over the years, many of those on the committee became greedy, and began to attract new subscribers who were willing to pay whatever price requested for a supply of body parts and organs to replace damaged ones. For example, the US president's son. Have you noticed how often he has been injured in the dangerous sports he's so fond of? And how he always makes a miraculous recovery?'

Ruby nodded her head. 'My grandmother and I were talking about him last month. He was seriously injured in a racing car but managed to survive and made a remarkably quick recovery.'

'Yes. Simon survived because he had a new brain ready to be transplanted. That was the end of his third Lab. There is a new one near maturity for him now.'

'But … if he has a new brain, how does he remember all the things he knew before?' Ruby asked.

'If the injured brain is not too damaged, they are able to download some of the knowledge and memories from it into the new brain before it is transplanted,' Celia explained. 'If it is extensively damaged, the Non-Lab must relearn all the previous knowledge, except what is already programmed into the Lab – the basic skills a Non-Lab will have acquired by the age of sixteen. All Labs were originally programmed to have their mother tongue as their first language; but Abe decided it would be best if all Labs had English as their first language and their mother tongue as their second. So all freed Labs can easily communicate with each other.'

'And does the president know all of this?' Ruby was astonished.

'Subscribers are told that stem cell research makes it possible for tissue, organs, even the brain, to repair itself. They choose to accept this with very little proof. It suits them. They pay enormous amounts of money and feel they are getting their money's worth.'

'How is this place run? How do they get away with it?' Ruby asked. 'And how come you all escaped?'

'So many questions!' Celia gave a slight smile. 'We'll try to answer them all.'

Her voice took on a disembodied tone, as if she was recounting medical facts that were nothing to do with her:

'Embryos are cloned from tissue from the subscriber and/or their offspring, whichever is requested. Subscribers can also pay extra for several clones to be produced, as the president did. That's why there are many sets of twins and triplets. These embryos are kept at a certain temperature, in certain conditions for two years in what is called the Nursery Ward, a room on the first floor underground. By this time they have matured to the level of a five-year-old Non-Lab – a human child. Then they are move to the Childhood and Adolescence Ward. They remain there for five years where they are conditioned and programmed to reach early adulthood within this time, about sixteen in Non-Lab years. All through their formative years their bodies are chemically and electrically stimulated to promote the ultimate organ and muscle development. As well as the basic knowledge, their brains are given the talents requested by the subscriber. Such as music, art, law, politics, science, and sport. Finally they are stored in the Mature Ward. That is, if they are not required before then. The best years for harvesting tissue and organs is when the Lab has reached the Non-Lab equivalent of sixteen to thirty years, so they are suspended in this period for as long as possible in the Mature Ward.'

Her voice suddenly took on a softer tone.

'Keith – Ket – was the first one to be awakened, by accident. The temperature regulator on his capsule in the Mature Ward was faulty and he became conscious.' She looked across at Keith, who took up the story.

'The first thing I remember about this world is a pair of eyes looking down at me. And as I moved my arms and legs, which must have been for the first time, she smiled at me, so I imitated her and I smiled back. It was Miranda! Dr Miranda Cheung.

'She was so surprised to find I could respond to her. She helped me out of my capsule and let me walk up and down the ward. Past all those rows and rows of capsules! She couldn't believe I could talk to her. And I could eat like her. Over the next few weeks she told me that she had often felt uneasy about how the research was developing. She felt the whole project was quickly spinning out of her control. They were no longer working towards the dream of helping war-torn countries. It was all about making money. Only the rich were benefiting. She wanted to do something about it, but knew she would meet serious opposition from the other committee members; they would not be willing to give up their huge profits.

'A newly matured Lab was put in my capsule that afternoon, and I went back to her farmhouse with her that evening. Miranda spoke to her seniors about the possibility of a Lab waking up and being able to survive, but no one was willing to listen. In fact several of them became quite hostile. That's why we kept our existence a secret. Over the next few weeks we managed to smuggle two more out, including Abe. His twin was due to be smuggled out to join him, but on the same day he was taken away for a brain transplant.' He looked down at his hands.

'Once they use the brain, the Lab is discarded,' Leon said softly.

'Discarded?' Ruby asked.

'Any useable organs are sold to outside medical agencies. The rest is used for medical or cosmetic research, then disposed of,' Johnny continued.

Ruby put her hand to her mouth. 'Oh my God! Poor Abe!'

'We continued to smuggle out Labs slowly. Abe was very frustrated about how slowly we were working. Miranda said we couldn't go any faster without alerting the others. She told him she had arranged a meeting with the government Head of Social and Medical Welfare who was involved with the setting up of the Centre. It seemed that things would finally happen. He promised her he'd call for a thorough investigation and that she would head the team, but shortly before that happened Miranda was killed in a hit and run accident. The driver of the car was never discovered. Another Non-Lab worker who supported Miranda suddenly backed down after his eldest daughter was seriously injured in a skiing holiday a few days after Miranda's death.'

There was silence for a moment, then Keith continued, 'Abe took over the rescue plan. He moved us out of the farmhouse and up into the caves in the hills. As well as Valerie, we have another Non-Lab supporter in the Centre and two Labs working there, unknown to the other workers there, so we have some access to information about what is happening there. Over the past year we have been able to free groups of about ten to twenty mature Labs at a time. Every few months our Lab contact at the centre helps Abe and Sel to sneak into the Centre and set the timer so that a group of mature Labs wake up at a set time when we know there would be less staff on duty, usually at night. Sel is also able to fix the security videos so that they replay earlier events of the evening and we aren't spotted taking the Labs off the premises. There are about ninety Labs in the caves now. Abe's plan is to release as many Labs as he can, and build up an army to overcome the staff at the Centre.'

'Didn't the people at the Centre notice a large group of mature Labs have gone missing each time?' Ruby asked.

'Of course they did, but after each rescue operation we leak information to other similar medical centres hinting that a Russian medical company, Solstov Innovations, has acquired new valuable information on advanced stem cell research from a western company and will sell them to the highest bidder. The Centre gets to hear these rumours and blames Solstov, who always deny any involvement,' Keith said.

'No one really took Miranda seriously when she hinted that maybe the Labs were able to live independently. She never let them know that there were actual Labs like Abe already free as she was worried about what might happen to them,' Celia added.

Ruby shook her head. 'Why don't all you free Labs just make public what is happening at the Centre?'

Keith sighed. 'We had thought of that, but we are afraid of what might happen to the developing Labs. The Centre management might just turn everything off, or worse, to cover their tracks. We'd be risking the lives of hundreds of Labs. It would be too dangerous.'

'Without someone in a powerful position on our side, we are helpless,' Celia added.

'The committee members are too powerful, too rich,' Keith nodded in agreement. 'We've since discovered that the government Head of Social and Medical Welfare is himself one of the bigger shareholders.'

'The subscribers themselves are in positions of power all over the world, government leaders, on the boards of huge company conglomerates. We can't stand against them,' Celia continued. 'They can silence us so easily. They have so many of us Labs in the Centre at their mercy, especially those in their developing stages.'

'Yes, what are Labs worth? We have no identities or possessions, except for what we steal. We don't even have names, just codes,' Keith looked down at his arm. 'The only strength we have is in the growing number of freed Labs.'

'You said you had an alternative plan to Abe's. What is it?' Ruby asked.

'We don't think his idea of raising an army against the people who run the Centre is a good idea. We thought about setting Labs up with false papers, as we have now, in different towns and cities around the country,' Celia said. 'The main problem was that a newly mature Lab is equivalent to a sixteen-year-old Non-Lab, so they cannot live independently. Not many of them could pass for a young Non-Lab adult, especially as they are not used to living in normal Non-Lab society. We couldn't risk them standing out and maybe being questioned by the authorities. However, when you told us about the State supervised houses for sixteen-year-olds, we had the answer to our problem! We can all live as students or in some kind of trainee work for two years, or one in some cases if a Lab can get away with looking seventeen, then we will be independent adult members of society!'

'Many of the Labs are from donors from different countries, so we decided we could create IDs for them as overseas students. As long as they have the paperwork and an official adult to supervise them, we can set them up in similar houses, too,' Valerie continued. 'In fact, I'm going to be pretty busy in this new role!'

'At our last meeting, Abe objected to any of us leaving the safety of the caves. He said we'd be in constant danger of being discovered. It would lead to all the Labs being put at risk. He wouldn't even consider it!' Keith added.

'So, how many Labs are willing to set up home with their new IDs?' Ruby asked.

Celia and Keith looked at each other.

'No other Labs supported us, actually,' Keith said. 'They're all afraid of speaking out against Abe. But, once they see how we are surviving in the Non-Lab world, I'm sure we will be able to persuade more to join us!'

'We're going to have to make a success of this and get Abe himself on our side!' Celia added.

'Well, I'll do anything I can to help you settle into the … Non-Lab world!' said Ruby enthusiastically.

'Spoken like a true Lab!' Keith smiled, 'We're honorary Non-Labs and you're an honorary Lab!'

They sat up late that night talking about their plans and how life could be in the future.

'Well, I'd better be getting off now,' Valerie said finally. 'I'll be back on Friday for your college appointment. You've a few days to get used to life here. The sooner you start to live as Non-Labs, the better. You mustn't do anything that will arouse people's suspicions. This is where they'll depend on your advice, Ruby. '

'I'm happy to help!' she assured them. Looking at the boys' worried expressions, she added, 'Really, being a Non-Lab isn't that hard!'

As she closed her bedroom door that night, Ruby heard her name called. Leon stood outside the room with his brother, 'Johnny and I are a bit nervous. We're glad you're with us in this strange new world, Ruby.'

'I'll try and make it less strange for you, boys!' Ruby reassured them. She felt a glow of happiness spread though her as she slipped into bed.

'This is great!' Johnny said as they walked down towards the town centre the next morning. 'We can walk openly in daylight!'

'And we have a real house!' Leon added.

Ruby smiled. It seemed strange to hear them talk of things she took so easily for granted, though after the last few weeks, she did appreciate the home she had now.

Leon suddenly sighed, his happy expression evaporating.

'What is it?' Ruby asked him.

'All the other Labs. They don't have any of this,' Johnny spoke for him as his brother nodded.

'Well that's why it's so important you learn to act as Non-Labs as quickly as possible. Then you can show other Labs how easy it is, and help them start their free lives in their own homes,' Ruby told them. She stopped outside a bookshop. 'I'm going to get a map of the area in here. Why don't you two practise your Non-Lab skills and each buy yourself a book. Watch and listen to me, then choose your own books, ok?'

The twins looked at each other, took a deep breath and nodded.

'Good morning,' Ruby said to the young girl behind the counter. 'I'm looking for a street map of the town. A detailed one, please.'

'Maps over there,' the girl pointed to the side of the shop.

As she took a map off the shelf and glanced through it she heard Johnny clear his throat and approach the counter.

'Good morning,' he said to the girl. 'I'm looking for a book of boys' names. Names with many syllables.'

There was a pause. Ruby glanced up at the girl, who was smiling, 'Long names for boys? Let's see what we have over here,' she said as she led him to another shelf.

Johnny looked across at Ruby and gave her a happy smile.

Leon stood in the centre of the shop looking down at the floor, his brow furrowed in concentration.

'Can I help you at all?' the girl asked him.

'Ummm, yes. I'd like a book about sport,' he said hesitantly.

'Any sport in particular? Come and have a look through these.' The assistant led him to a shelf. 'There's plenty to choose from!'

Leon too, glanced over at Ruby with a triumphant smile as he followed her.

'You did very well today!' Ruby told them as they made their way home again. 'Three shops, and you told that old gentleman the time, Leon! And you dealt with those giggling girls in the park by the river very well, Johnny!'

'Why did they keep laughing?' Johnny asked.

Ruby shrugged. 'I suppose they thought you were two good-looking lads!'

Leon and Johnny looked at each other with bemused expressions.

As they reached their front door, Keith opened it.

'Hi,' he said. He looked at the bags they were carrying, 'I see you've been shopping.'

Johnny hurried into the lounge and pulled his book out of the bag.

'Look!' he said. 'Next time we change IDs, I'll have the longest name! Ab-sol-om, that's only three syllables. Ah! De-me-tri-us, four syllables!'

Celia rolled her eyes and flicked through Leon's book, 'This will be very useful on your college course! Well done for thinking of it, Leon.'

'Yes, I thought it would!' he nodded, giving his brother a smug look, but Johnny was frowning over the pronunciation of another name.

Ruby pulled out the street map book. 'I thought this would come in useful.'

'Good. We're going to need a Self-Drive car, so I've ordered one which will be delivered tomorrow morning. It's in your name, Ruby,' Celia said. 'We'll take it out of town and practise manual driving. I can easily override the Self-Drive function once we're somewhere quiet.'

She noticed Ruby's worried expression.

'It can't be *that* hard! Most Non-Labs can at least operate a Self-Drive! You probably won't even need the manual skills, but it would raise suspicion if the Self-Drive *did* break down and you had no idea about the manual operation. If we're to win Abe over, we must make sure we don't leave *any* room for suspicion,' Celia continued. 'I've downloaded a series of simulated driving lessons, used by many driving schools. You can practise a few and you should be ready to drive by tomorrow.'

'But …' Ruby began.

'It's not that difficult. Keith and I have already completed the first set. You can practise this evening.'

Celia clicked a button and pushed the laptop towards her. 'We can't waste time, Ruby. Concentrate!'

For the next few hours, Ruby tried out different simulated trips and studied the image of a manual dashboard.

Celia sat down beside her making encouraging noises. 'See. It isn't that hard, is it? After our test drive tomorrow, we'll all be ready to drive!'

As soon as they had finished eating that evening, Celia set up the laptop to project the simulated drives onto the lounge wall. Ruby, who had offered to do the washing up, could hear the whoops of delight as

Johnny and Leon quickly worked their way up through the different levels of lessons. She took a deep breath as she put the last plate away and went back to join the others.

Celia was testing Keith on road signs when the doorbell sounded. Everyone froze as Ruby went to open it. Celia switched off the laptop when Mr Robinson, their landlord, was led in by Ruby. He put a large plastic container on the table.

'Mr Robinson has brought us some homemade cakes,' Ruby told them.

'Just called round to make sure everything is OK,' the old man said. 'My wife made you some cakes to welcome you to your new home. Mmm, that's a fancy-looking computer!' He pointed at the laptop.

'Isn't it! One of the new American models. The boys were playing one of those racing games,' Ruby told him.

'Oh, don't let me disturb you!' Mr Robinson said.

'Not at all!' she continued, 'I want to watch *Champions* and these would be lovely with a cup of tea! Can I get you one, Mr Robinson?'

'Well, if it's not too much trouble.' Mr Robinson settled himself down in a nearby chair. '*Champions*? It's on in five minutes. I haven't seen it for a few weeks now. My wife likes the dancing competition!'

Celia flicked the television on. 'Which programme do I select?'

'Channel 3,' Ruby told her, returning with a tray of teacups. She placed it on the table, 'There you are, Mr Robinson. Leon, give this to Keith, will you?' she handed him a cup of tea and then opened the container of cakes.

'Wow! Such cakes!' Leon's eyes were wide as he reached inside the box, his sleeve slowly slipping up his arm.

Ruby playfully slapped his hand away. 'Leon, you'd better wash your hands first and fix your sleeves, hmmm?'

Leon and Johnny exchanged looks of horror as he pulled his shirt over the tattooed code and both quickly went to the kitchen. Ruby turned to chat to their landlord as Keith and Celia joined them.

'So, do you think Bill Blazer will win again? "Bill Blazer Blazes to Victory!" Some people say the show's rigged, that's why he always wins!' Ruby continued.

Mr Robinson sipped his tea. 'That's why my wife doesn't want to watch it anymore! I don't think it could be fixed, myself. It's filmed live!'

'That's what I say!' Ruby exclaimed. 'How can he work out which game will come up next? It's chosen randomly. He can't spend all week practising all of them, can he?'

Soon all eyes were on the television. At first, only Ruby and Mr Robinson made comments and sounds of encouragement for their favourite team, but after ten minutes Leon and Johnny were just as involved in supporting the opposing teams.

The cakes and tea had long been finished when Mr Robinson stood up to go.

'Well, I'm glad to see you're all settled in so well.

Anything you need, just call by our house at the end of the road there,' he said as Ruby showed him out.

Celia sat up as Ruby came back into the lounge.

'We have to be more vigilant!' she said. 'If it wasn't for Ruby's quick thinking, he could have seen our codes! We must keep a plastic strip ready at all times.'

The others nodded.

Celia looked across at Ruby with admiration in her eyes, 'Ruby, you can talk for so long on trivia, which Non-Labs seem to do so much. It kept him distracted! Well done!'

'We call it small talk, just a way of being friendly.' Ruby told her.

'Don't forget, Celia, Ruby *is* a Non-Lab! She can do things we're only learning to do!' Keith pointed out.

'I do forget that sometimes, Ruby.' Celia gave her a smile again.

Later that night, at Celia's insistence, they all went for a run on the hillside behind the house. Celia, Johnny, and Leon quickly disappeared into the darkness. Keith stayed beside Ruby.

'OK?' he asked.

Ruby nodded, not having enough breath to make a reply.

After a while Keith suggested they turn back. They sat in the back garden waiting for the others to return.

'It is sometimes difficult for you, isn't it?' he said.

She nodded, 'You're all so fit, so clever, so ...

everything I'm not!'

'We are created this way in the laboratory. I suppose you have been created the way you are, more by nature,' he looked at her. 'I like the way you are created, Ruby.'

She was glad he could not see her blush in the darkness.

'Do Labs have feelings … relationships … within their community?' she asked him.

'We all feel for every Lab. Each one of us is an important member of our community,' he replied. 'That's why it is so important we free all Labs from the Centre as soon as possible.'

He stared into the distance, his mind far away. At the sound of the others returning, he gave her a quick smile, stood up, and walked towards them.

The next morning they stood around a second hand Self-Drive car. Ruby's hand shook as she signed the papers that made it officially hers.

'I know, getting your first car is so exciting, isn't it?' the man smiled at her. 'Even if it isn't brand new!'

'So it's all taxed and insured and ready to drive, then?' she asked him.

'Yes, for you and your named drivers. It cost quite a bit, but as your friend said, you'll all be using it to save money on public transport, so it's worth it.'

He nodded at Celia, who stood exchanging technical details with one of the men from the garage.

Soon after that the men left.

‘We’ll go to the old airstrip north of the town in Self-Drive. Once we’re there we can all do a manual practice,’ Celia said.

They all got into the car. Celia narrowed her eyes and looked at the controls, ‘Slightly different to the simulator, but most are pretty obvious.’ She switched on the engine and the car slipped smoothly forward.

Leon and Johnny were chattering and laughing like excited children. Keith, in the front seat beside Celia, was carefully observing all her actions and occasionally asking questions, nodding his head thoughtfully as Celia replied. Only Ruby seemed nervous.

Once on the deserted strip they all took turns with the Self-Drive application. Then the twins began to argue over who should be first to try out the manual controls. Celia selected Johnny, getting Leon to sit beside him while she sat behind, leaning over to remind or give any advice they needed. After ten minutes the boys swapped seats. Next it was Keith’s turn to take the wheel. Ruby sat on an old bench at the side of the strip, trying hard to remember the facts she had learnt on the simulated drives on the laptop the previous evening, but it was like being back at school. Her mind had gone blank.

Finally, she sat in the driver’s seat.

‘Go when you’re ready, Ruby. Just remember all the things you did on the laptop last night,’ Celia smiled at her.

After several false starts, Ruby managed to get the car started without stalling it. She could feel Celia stiffen as she crunched gears and drove along the beach at erratic speeds.

'Don't change gear yet! Wait until you hear the tone change!' she told Ruby. 'Steer to the left! You are going to hit that rock! Slow down!'

Finally, the car shuddered to a halt.

'I can't do this!' Ruby cried.

'Of course you can! Anybody can …!' Celia began sharply.

Keith appeared at the side of the car and opened the passenger door.

'Celia, go for a run with the twins,' he suggested in such a way that she climbed silently out of the car.

He sat beside Ruby, watching as the other three disappeared in the distance. With an exaggerated sigh, he turned to her and smiled.

'Now, try again without all the pressure. I don't think you'll be ready to drive a manual today, but you should be able to manage the basics.'

'But … Celia thinks I will be able to drive as well as she can,' Ruby said.

'Don't worry. Between us we'll always have a driver until you feel confident in yourself. Don't let Celia intimidate you!' he smiled.

By the time the others returned, Ruby was able to drive the car fairly smoothly. She still struggled with braking and gear changes, but it didn't feel such an impossible challenge anymore.

'A good morning's work! Now most of us can be relied on as drivers when required!' Celia commented as Keith drove them home.

'But that doesn't mean we'll waste our time driving around pointlessly,' she continued as Johnny and Leon looked at her innocently. 'This car is not a toy! It's a useful tool in Non-Lab life!'

'Sometimes living like a Non-Lab is *so* good! I can't wait to get a manual car in two years' time!' Leon whispered to his brother who nodded in agreement.

Ruby looked down at her plate and moved her food around without much appetite at lunch later that day, while the twins chattered excitedly.

'Don't worry, Ruby. You will soon master this new skill,' Keith told her with a smile.

'Not as quickly as you Labs can. Many Non-Labs take lessons for months before they pass their test and are free to drive on the road,' she said.

'Months? To learn such basic skills?' Celia sounded incredulous.

'Don't forget, Celia, Labs are *programmed* to be good at something! Non-Labs have to learn from scratch!' Keith reminded her.

'That's true. But we are also good at learning. Non-Labs do not seem to be quick at acquiring new skills,' Celia replied.

'Who chooses the skills for each Lab?' Ruby asked them.

'Our subscribers select them,' Johnny told her.

'They generally choose the things they are particularly good at,' Leon added.

'Do you all know who your subscribers are?'

Ruby continued.

'I looked at the Centre records,' Celia told her. 'The actual names are not listed, but Johnny and Leon's subscriber is a famous…'

'Let her guess!' Johnny shouted. He looked at Ruby smiling.

'Mmm …' She looked at the twins. 'A golfer? No. Tennis player, swimmer. Ah! A footballer!'

'How did you guess?' Johnny asked.

'You're very active, so it had to be a sportsperson!'

'Yes – at least, he used to be active. He was in his sixties when he had us created. He had almost killed himself with alcohol and drugs. And he had fallen out with any remaining friends and family he had left. He planned on renewing most parts of himself until he would be able to make a miraculous comeback to the football scene!' Johnny told her.

'And impress everyone!' Leon added. 'But, unfortunately for him – though not for us – he died before they were able to carry out an operation to replace his heart and lungs.'

'What about you, Keith?' Ruby asked. 'I can't think what you subscriber could be.'

'My subscriber's an actor. She had me created for her son. She's hoping he'll become interested in the theatre, too.'

'Ah, that's why you chose the Sound and Vision course at the college,' Ruby nodded.

'And what about Celia?' Johnny asked.

'Someone really clever! Very organised,

knowledgeable … a scientist? No? Someone who works with computers?' Ruby suggested.

'Yes. He's American. Often called on for his skills in combating computer hackers. I was created for his daughter but she died in a car crash when she was a young child, so I was to be discarded. Abe kept me safe until I was mature, and then I was awakened and taken to the Caves.'

Suddenly she pushed her plate away, 'Anyway, enough guessing games. There's work to be done. We'd better make sure we know what we're going to say at the college interview on Friday. I've produced educational levels for us all at standard passes. Most students have reached that level by sixteen.'

Ruby felt just as nervous as the others as they were shown into the office of the College Principal later that week. Valerie gave each of them a reassuring smile as they sat down.

Mrs Walker looked through the papers Valerie had handed her. 'Mmm, Mrs Sutton, so these five State-supervised youngsters have settled into their new accommodation and are all ready to start college now?'

'That's right. They're all very pleased that your college provides suitable courses for all of them as they really wanted to stay together.'

'I see their educational levels are all standard. Celia and Keith both decide to change courses, did they?' Mrs Walker asked.

'Yes, they were on an art course, but both felt it wasn't for them,' Valerie explained.

'I hope they won't be chopping and changing all the time!' the principal frowned. 'Do you think they'll be able to cope with the courses here?'

'We both feel we've made the right decisions this time,' Keith smiled at her confidently as Celia nodded in agreement.

'And I hope you've all read and agreed to the code of conduct we expect of all our students,' Mrs Williams said sternly, looking around their faces.

'Yes, they have. These youngsters are very hard working and very keen on starting their Independent training,' Valerie smiled.

Mrs Walker paused for a moment. 'We have young people from a variety of different backgrounds, and most go on to worthwhile careers. All it takes is a bit of determination and a lot of hard work!'

'These youngsters will show you that they have what it takes, Mrs Walker!' Valerie said.

After some more questions for the would-be students, Mrs Walker stood up and shook their hands. 'I'll get some of the students to show you around and let you see where you'll be working, then we'll see you all here on Monday!'

'So we start on Monday!' Leon repeated as they reached the house.

'Yeah! Did you see the astro pitch?' Johnny said.

'And the size of the gym?' Leon added.

'There was some interesting equipment in the Media wing,' Keith said.

'Are you OK, Celia?' asked Ruby. 'Was the IT

suite OK?'

'It looked great. I was just a bit, you know, worried about …' she began.

'Working with Non-Labs,' Keith added quietly as she nodded.

'Don't forget, *I'm* a Non-Lab and I'm harmless!' Ruby pointed out.

'Yeah, but you're *our* Non-Lab,' Johnny said.

'And you know all our secrets already,' Leon added.

CHAPTER FOUR

Despite their initial fears, they all enjoyed their first week at college. The coaches in the Sports department were impressed with the high skill levels of Leon and Johnny and their good humour soon made them popular with the other students. Celia played down her skills and kept a low profile in her department, spending her lunchtimes with Ruby and Keith. Keith quickly settled into his course and was surprised at how much he enjoyed it.

'So things are going really well, aren't they?' Ruby remarked as they all sat down together after their evening meal at the end of the third week.

'They certainly are!' Leon replied.

'We've been chosen to play in the first team on Sunday!' Johnny added.

'Yes, I'm really enjoying this course,' Keith nodded.

'Yes, it's going pretty well. So I think it's time we got in touch with Abe,' Celia said. 'To show him it *is* going well and to convince him that it's time more Labs were free to live as we do.'

'We need to have a firm plan if we are to persuade him to agree to it,' Keith said. 'Who do you think the next group should be? And where can they study?'

'Ruby could stay at each new home at first to help them settle in, as she is doing with us,' Johnny suggested.

'How would you get IDs for the overseas students?' Ruby asked.

'I've done some research,' Celia explained. 'Gifted scholars can apply for academy and university places from the age of sixteen if they have a nominated adult to be responsible for them. And there's another scheme that allows sixteen-year-olds to come to the UK to study English for periods of up to a year – again with a responsible adult. Valerie can help us out again at first but she'll need someone to help her if we're talking of setting up all the Labs in the caves. It'll probably be quite easy to hack into the records of most European government offices for ID and national insurance numbers, but I'm only fluent in Italian, Spanish, French, and Japanese. I have very limited knowledge of Eastern European languages!'

'Det has Russian as her second language. And she's fluent is several other Eastern European languages,' Johnny pointed out.

Celia's eyes narrowed. 'So we'll have to convince Det and Abe to see things our way! I'll email Det and arrange a meeting with her and Abe. Here? Or at the Caves?'

'Here! On our own territory,' Leon suggested.

'Yes! It's scary enough standing up to Abe!' his brother added.

Ruby cleared the table as the others gathered

around Celia's laptop.

She filled the dishwasher and stood looking out of the window. A shiver went down her spine as she thought of the impending visit. Neither Abe nor Det had been at all friendly towards her, the Non-Lab. She doubted that their attitude would be different this time.

Keith entered the room and picked up a tea towel.

'You don't have to be afraid of Abe, Ruby. You know that we'll all stand beside you, don't you?'

She nodded, 'Yes. But I don't think he'll like having me around. Or Det.'

'They'll have to realise that Labs need Non-Labs to survive in this Non-Lab world!' he said. 'Anyway, *we* all like having you around.'

The door was flung open and Johnny appeared.

'Hey! Abe and Det will be here tomorrow, as soon as it gets dark!' he cried.

Abe made it quite clear what he thought of their new life from the moment he arrived the next evening.

'Well, you certainly seem to be happy, living the easy life in the Non-Lab world,' he remarked as he entered the house and looked around. He slumped back against the wall, refusing to sit down with the others.

'It's the standard all people have a right to, Non-Labs and Labs,' Celia said simply.

'I don't care about Non-Labs,' Abe cast a glance at Ruby. 'But I do care about my people.'

Keith nodded. 'We all want the same thing, Abe.

A better life for the Labs! That is why we asked you to come tonight.'

Ruby smiled quietly to herself as she watched Det run her hands over the smooth material of the sofa. She had spotted her earlier on in Celia's bedroom, stroking her face with Celia's soft dressing gown, then closing her eyes in rapture as she lay down on the bed. She had jumped guiltily as Abe had called her name from downstairs. Abe may enjoy his Spartan life, Ruby thought, but it wouldn't take much to lure Det towards a less arduous lifestyle. She brought her mind back to the present conversation. Celia was explaining the plans they had of setting up similar homes around the UK for all the freed Labs eventually.

'How many freed Labs do you have in the Caves now?' she asked him.

'Ninety-four,' he replied. 'Soon we'll need more space. We were thinking of starting a new colony in caves further north.'

'A lot of hard work and time was spent getting the Caves to their present standard,' Keith began. 'It would take a long time to make another one.'

'And they are still pretty basic,' Celia added.

Abe bristled. 'The Caves are a place of safety to many of our people! And don't forget, they were your home, your shelter, not so long ago!'

'Abe, when Miranda died, you took us from danger in the farmhouse and led us to safety in the Caves!' Keith said. 'We will never forget that!'

All the others nodded in agreement.

‘We’re not here to quarrel. We’re here to plan the closing of the Centre and freedom for all Labs just as you are!’ Celia added fervently.

‘So, tell me, if we follow your plans how can we guarantee the safety of our people?’ Abe was sceptical.

‘Any day, the Caves could be discovered. There is no guarantee for safety of the Labs there.’ Celia countered. ‘If we are living openly in Non-Lab society, blending in with everyone else, we have a much better chance of surviving. That is what we have been doing, successfully, for the past three weeks. It was a bit nerve-wracking at first, but we’ve had our Non-Lab teacher!’’

‘Yes, Ruby has helped us blend in, making sure we don’t give ourselves away. She’s a great teacher,’ Keith added, smiling.

‘I don’t want a Non-Lab teaching me anything!’ Abe sneered. ‘How do you know you can trust her?’

Ruby felt her face flush, ‘They know they can trust me because we’re friends! They do as much for me as I do for them!’

‘Yes, Ruby is one of us now!’ Johnny sat up straight.

‘We’d trust her with our lives!’ Leon added.

‘Your plan to build up an army of Labs to take over the centre will take too long to put in place and isn’t necessarily going to succeed,’ Keith said. ‘If we have more Labs living in Non-Lab society, they’ll be in a position to make contact with people in the Non-Lab world who could have some influence in closing down the Centre. We might even be able to get some of our own kind into stronger positions by getting some of our students involved in politics.'

Heated discussions went on long into the night. Finally, Abe agreed to put forward Celia's proposal to the other Labs in the Caves that week.

'I'll join you for that meeting,' Celia said. 'I'd like to explain to them how we are getting on here in the Non-Lab world. I planned to come and help out with the next rescue operation, anyway. Have you organised it, Det?'

She nodded, 'We've everything set up for the seventh, but we need your help to disable the CCTV for the night.'

Celia frowned. 'It's getting more difficult to get around their security systems each time.'

'We have no alternative!' Abe said sharply.

'I know,' she sighed.

'We'll be there,' Keith nodded.

CHAPTER FIVE

'The guards have left this section,' Mark's voice came softly through the transmitter in Det's ear. She nodded at Abel who signalled to the others as he pushed open the door to the Mature Ward. Quietly they worked their way along the capsules, reassuring the disorientated youngsters as they helped them to their feet.

'Quickly!' Abe softly urged them.

Suddenly Det appeared at the doorway, 'Mark said they have two extra guards in this wing. They weren't written in the log, they're on high security orders. They're on their way to the ward now!'

Celia frowned. 'They've never had four guards on before!'

After a few seconds, Abe grabbed Keith's arm, 'We'll deal with them! Just get everyone out safely.' The two of them slipped out of the door.

There was a subdued air in the Caves that night. Abe and Keith had returned half an hour after the others. Keith's shirt was torn and he had the beginning of a black eye. Abe's hands were bruised.

'We were extremely lucky to get out tonight,' Celia said. 'It wasn't lack of planning on our part, we had everything in place as usual – false CCTV footage showing, decoy scents for the guard dogs and we moved everyone even quicker than last time! But they nearly caught us out with their extra guards. I'm worried about how long we have before they discover us here in the Caves. We have shown that we can live safely amongst Non-Labs, I think we are safer out there.'

The others watched Abe silently. Slowly, he nodded. 'Perhaps you are right. Wherever we live we are in danger until we get the Centre closed down!'

A week later Celia and Keith returned with Det and Abe to Castlewell. Celia explained what had happened on the last rescue mission. 'We're not going to be able to get many more Labs out of the Centre easily. We *must* plan a way of shutting down the Centre as soon as possible,' she told the others. 'Keith and I did manage to convince quite a few of the Labs to leave the Caves and we've plans to set up two new homes – first one in Manchester then later one in London.'

'There's a college reading week coming up, so we thought we'd use that time for you, Ruby, and the boys to help the Labs settle into their Manchester home for a few days. Valerie will be with them initially as their supervisor to enrol them at the music academy there,' Keith explained.

'I will need Det to work with me to input data into the Eastern European government offices' websites,' Celia added. 'So she's going to move in here and enrol on the same computer course as myself. Valerie is setting that up.'

Det looked pleased with the plan.

'As Abe is going to be working with us and at the Caves, he'll need some Non-Lab ID, too,' Celia continued.

'You'll get some of these!' Leon said, pulling out his different ID cards.

'This is the best one!' Johnny said excitedly, holding out his driving licence for Det to see. 'Only Self-Drive until you're eighteen, but you have to learn how to drive manually too. It's great fun! I can't wait to get a manual licence when I'm eighteen.'

'How did you get these?' Det asked Celia.

'You just have to know where to look on the internet,' she gave her a wink.

'Do you all have driving licences?' Abe asked, taking the licence from Johnny.

'Yes. Nearly all Non-Labs drive. It's a very useful skill,' Leon said.

'How did you all learn so quickly?' he asked.

'I downloaded a series of simulated lessons used by many driving schools. We practised on those, then we just needed an hour or so of practical experience.'

'And then you all could drive?' Det looked surprised.

'Yes. Except for Ruby. She is a slow learner, I'm afraid,' Celia said.

Keith noticed Ruby's embarrassment. 'Don't be so harsh, Celia! It is more difficult for Non-Labs to learn new skills. And Ruby has many other good qualities!'

Ruby's head was buzzing as she climbed into her bed that night. In the next room she could hear Celia and Det talking in low voices. They were to share the room, with Det on a guest bed. Abe had also agreed to stay for at least one more day as Celia had arranged for new IDs for both of them, due to arrive at the local post office in a day or two. Abe was to be registered as seventeen, the same as Keith.

Det had been quite happy with the new name of Bernadette.

'It's quite common for a Non-Lab with the name Bernadette to be called Dette,' Ruby had explained. Johnny couldn't believe Det would want to settle for a one-syllable name and pulled out his book of boys' names to show Abe.

Abe said he had no wish to be called by a Non-Lab name.

'You must!' Celia had insisted. 'We must fit into the Non-Lab world, for our own safety and that of all the other Labs!'

Ruby had suggested Abel, as the full name closest to his original one, and he had pulled up his sleeve to reveal his code, *ABE 32498.*

'I don't have a *name.* I have a *code* printed on my arm! I am a *Lab*!' he had spat.

'I have some special plastic things to cover that up. So you don't get spotted, *Abel*!' Celia had said bluntly.

Ruby shuddered as she thought of him sleeping on

the sofa downstairs.

The house was quiet when she woke up the following morning. She pulled on her dressing gown and padded down the stairs. Gently pushing open the lounge door, she could make out the sleeping figure of Abel on the sofa. He lay on his back with his arms flung above his head. His body was lean and well-muscled, his hands and arms were rough and scarred, but his face looked so young as he slept. Ruby realised that for all his bravado, he was only a boy, not much older than she was herself.

She quietly made her way to the kitchen, made herself a cup of coffee and walked over to the open French windows, looking out at the hillside that stretched beyond their garden. A flock of birds wheeled in the blue sky. The sun beat down, warming her face. Everything looked so calm and peaceful. She decided she would go for a long walk over the hillside later that day and relax before she began the next part of her life as Non-Lab instructor. She smiled to herself as she thought back to her earlier life at school. She had had no idea about how things were going to work out then. In fact, her future seemed pretty uncertain now.

She was so lost in her own thoughts that she wasn't aware of Abel's presence until he stood beside her.

'It's a beautiful view, isn't it?' she commented.

'Labs don't get to see much daylight. Except in this house!' he answered sharply. His expression was hard; there was no sign of the young boy she had seen as he slept. His lips curled in a sneer. 'So, you're to be our new instructor in Non-Lab life, are you?'

She sighed. 'I just want to do anything I can to help.'

He clicked his tongue, 'I've never felt I needed help from a Non-Lab.'

She went back into the kitchen and made a second coffee for herself and handed one to Abel, who took it from her ungraciously.

'Say "Thank you for the coffee!"' Ruby told him firmly. 'Your first lesson on living in the Non-Lab world! Good manners!'

They both stood glaring at each other. Finally a look of amusement flickered across Abel's eyes.

'Thank you for the coffee, Ruby,' he said.

'You're welcome!' she retorted, turning and leaving the room.

Later that day, Abel was dismissive of the new clothes and items Dette had bought with Celia.

'If we are to merge in with Non-Labs, we have to look the part!' Celia told him sharply.

'Where does the money come from?' he asked her.

'It's paid monthly from funds from the Centre,' Celia replied. 'I transfer various amounts from several accounts under different expense headings. Then it's filtered through several other accounts before it reaches the individual accounts I set up. So there's no way it can be traced to us.'

'Won't they begin to notice money going missing

as you set up more and more accounts, Celia?' Keith looked worried.

'I can easily cover up to five million per year. I would be nervous about going over that, though,' she replied. 'And I have a separate portfolio for our shares. They're making a good profit!'

'Have you been studying the stocks and shares, too?' Dette asked her.

'Not really. I don't take any risks. I just hack into the companies that look promising,' Celia admitted.

Dette looked at her admiringly. 'I have so much to learn from you, Celia! We must make out a budget for the new homes we are to set up. Abe – Abel – come and look at our plan for the students to go to Manchester Academy, to study music. Valerie said the music academy is keen on taking in talented students from abroad as well as from the UK. Celia and I were thinking of the twins, Min and Jay, and Saf. We thought the boys Url and Pel could live happily with them. All their subscribers highlighted music as one of their programmed skills and they are all exceptionally talented. We will set up the second group as soon as Ruby feels they've settled in. That will be in London, in two separate houses, close to each other so they can communicate easily. And Ruby can go and see them too,' Celia continued. 'We've chosen Zaf, Oll, Peg, and Joe for the first house, and Ben, Dil, Lok, Hal, Cal, and Fay in the second house. They will enrol as State-cared-for students on an introductory course in European Government and Politics, with plans to continue to degree level once they reach eighteen.'

'That's fourteen Labs at once!' Ruby looked pleased.

'Yet we've scores of freed Labs and we will still be making plans to release more from the Mature Ward, so that doesn't sound so good, does it?' Abel said, the sneer returning to his face as he looked at her. 'And don't forget, the Nursery Ward is being replenished daily!'

'We're going to find it even more difficult to free Labs from the Mature Ward,' Celia exchanged a look with Abel. 'The quicker we find a way to close the whole Centre down the better!'

'And surely the Labs are in a stronger position to do that living in the Non-Lab world?' Ruby said. 'By getting involved in campaigns for human rights and things like that.'

'We aren't even considered human!' Abel pointed out.

'So maybe that's where we start,' Keith said. 'Then we'll be ready when the time comes.'

'For the moment, we need to sort out the new houses,' Dette said before Abel could reply.

After discussing the details of her role in the plan, Ruby set out for a walk in the surrounding countryside. Since she had joined the Lab household, she had become much fitter and she soon found herself on a hillside overlooking the town. She sat down and idly picked a handful of daisies and started to string them together into a chain, as she used to when she was a child. She looked up to see Abel walking towards her. As he reached her, she gave a wary smile.

'Johnny told me you had headed up this way,' he said, sitting down beside her. 'I need to talk to you.'

His eyes scanned her face. 'I know the others trust you completely…' he began.

Ruby bit her lip as she carried on stringing the daisies together carefully. 'I know you find it very difficult to accept that a Non-Lab can be a friend to your own kind.'

Abel plucked a blade of grass and chewed it. 'If you were ever in a situation where you had to choose to save a Lab or a Non-Lab, what would you do? I know that I would *always* choose my own kind. Would you betray us, the Labs, to protect your own kind, the Non-Labs?'

Ruby looked thoughtful. Eventually she sighed. 'I can't think of a situation that would make me betray the people I have come to see as my family – Keith, Celia, Johnny and Leon. I feel very strongly about the other Labs and the way they are treated at the Centre. All the Labs should be free to live equally alongside us Non-Labs. I want to help you all to get there.'

Abel gave a mirthless laugh and stood up. 'What a speech! But I wonder if you'll be so convincing when things get tough!'

Keith appeared suddenly. He helped Ruby to her feet and put his arm around her protectively. '*We* are all convinced, Abel! You trust Valerie and Mark, why can't you learn to trust other Non-Labs?'

'Valerie and Mark were friends of Miranda. They have proven their loyalty!' He held Ruby's eyes with a cold stare and jabbed a finger at her. 'If you *ever* put any Lab in danger, you will have me to answer to!' He turned and strode off down the hill.

Keith felt Ruby tremble. 'Don't worry. He'll come round.'

Ruby sighed. She wasn't so convinced.

CHAPTER SIX

'My God! How can this have happened *again*? What's wrong with the security in this place?' John Baxman slammed his fist down on the table. 'I believed after what has happened in the past that we'd have sufficient security in place! That's the fifth time in the last year that SPs have been stolen under our very noses!' He slammed his fist down again. 'I thought you said security had been tightened! Someone's head will roll for this!'

'It was, sir, it was! We've increased security since the last incident. I had several new guards on patrol last night –' the nervous, white-faced senior security officer spluttered.

'Oh, yes – the two men who were knocked out! Some protection they offered!' Baxman scoffed. 'They said they were set upon by two men – but gave no clear description of either of them! No use whatsoever.'

'Our new guards are no lightweights, but they said the men who set upon them were extremely strong…'

'Probably some steroid-pumped Russians! I'm sure Solstov is behind these break-ins!' Baxman muttered. 'How can they move ten SPs from under our noses?'

'We've checked the CCTV footage. There's no sign of a break-in or of any vehicles on the road outside. The SPs just seem to have vanished! I don't know how they could have got past us again…' the security chief continued.

'And yet they have!' Baxman's eyes narrowed. 'They must be getting help from an insider. Call a full security meeting for this morning. I want everyone in this compound questioned – from the bottom right up to the top level! And make sure those two guards don't breathe a word of the break in to anyone. Understand? We can't have *any* bad publicity at this point.'

'I fully understand, sir!' The security officer almost ran from the room.

There was a light tap and the door opened again. Gilshaw came in.

'We have a crisis, John,' he said.

'Tell me about it!' Baxman answered shortly.

'A medical crisis,' Gilshaw continued. 'We're scheduled to perform a kidney transplant this afternoon…'

'The theatres haven't been affected, have they?' Baxman frowned.

'No, but the SP we need for the transplant … isn't there anymore,' the surgeon replied.

'Oh. Who's the subscriber?' the other man asked.

Gilshaw named a well-known Japanese businesswoman. 'It's her only daughter.'

'She's one of the major shareholders. Can't you

use another SP?' Baxman suggested. 'There must be another one that would be compatible.'

'There is a danger of rejection, I'm afraid.'

Baxman looked him in the eye. 'This operation *has* to go ahead and it *has* to be successful. I don't care what you do, but you're the surgeonand we can't afford any setbacks at this point. Within the next month we're hoping to sign a deal worth billions with the US company and we can't afford any rumours or bad publicity *whatsoever* that might get in the way of this deal!'

Gilshaw took a slow breath and nodded. 'I'll see what we can do.'

'And you'll *do* it, Gilshaw!' Baxman held his gaze.

CHAPTER SEVEN

'Well, Simon, you're looking in great shape! Have you completely recovered from your last accident?' the television presenter said to the young man sitting beside him.

'Yes! Right back to normal again!' the young man grinned. 'Thanks to modern medical developments!'

'So, are you planning on slowing down a little now?' the presenter continued.

'Not if I have anything to do with it! Although my mom and dad aren't too keen on me going back to motor racing, unfortunately!' Simon shrugged.

'And you say you're planning a longer trip to England soon, to look around colleges in central London?'

'I'm really keen on studying in London. The city looks great. And the social life! But don't tell my dad I said that!' he laughed.

Celia got up and turned off the television.

'Another discard?'

Keith nodded. 'Yes.'

CHAPTER EIGHT

Though Ruby was feeling more confident about using the Self-Drive car, she had decided to take the train on her first visit to the newly set-up house in Manchester. The twins were accompanying her and were very excited travelling by train.

'Johnny, sit down!' Ruby whispered to him. 'Don't touch those switches!'

He sat down as Leon arrived with cans of soft drinks and several bags of crisps. He pulled out bags of sweets from his jacket pocket as he joined them. Both boys eagerly tucked into them.

'Celia would go crazy if she saw you now!' Ruby said.

'She can't see us, though!' Leon grinned, tossing a sweet up and catching it in his mouth. Two teenage girls nearby looked around at him and giggled. Johnny gave them a wink.

'Johnny! We're on serious business today!' Ruby reminded him.

He leaned forward. 'Don't worry, Ruby. We know. They'll need all our help getting used to their new life.'

Leon also put on a serious expression, despite the

bulge of toffee in his cheek.

When they arrived at the house, Valerie opened the door and ushered them inside. Min, Jay, and Saf stood just inside. Ruby recognised them as the three girls she had met on the hillside on the night she had first run away

'Jed!' One of the girls exclaimed as all three hugged Johnny, then Leon. A tall blond boy appeared followed by a shorter, dark-haired boy.

'Let's go into the lounge,' Valerie suggested.

They sat down, the girls looking nervous.

'I'm Ruby,' she introduced herself, 'I was Stella last time we met! And you must always call the boys Leon and Johnny now. And you are …?' she turned to the first girl.

'Jay. I mean Jade!' she replied.

'And I'm Miyu, originally Min,' her twin said.

'I am Saf, now Sakura,' the third said.

All spoke perfect English with a trace of a Far Eastern accent.

Ruby turned to the boys.

Leon pointed to the tall blond boy. 'What is your name now, Url?'

'Yuri,' he replied. He sat very straight with a serious expression on his face.

'And you, Pel?' Johnny asked him.

'Pellier! Easy to remember!' the French boy smiled.

'It's lovely to meet you all!' Ruby said.

'They all enrolled at the music academy today,' Valerie continued. 'They passed their auditions with flying colours. The panel were very impressed to see such talent.'

'It was so good to play such wonderful instruments!' Sakura said as the other girls smiled and nodded.

Pellier grinned. 'Yes, the academy has some great instruments. And we got the chance to buy our own main instrument today, as well!'

'Celia managed to present their purchases as a State grant, so each one now has a decent first instrument,' Valerie explained. She stood up, 'I must get going now. Good luck with your new life here! Ruby and the boys will be here to help you settle in over the next few days.'

Ruby smiled as she re-entered the lounge after seeing Valerie to her car.

'It's a bit tricky at first, living like a Non-Lab!' Johnny was saying.

'But you soon get used to it!' his brother added.

'Have you any questions to start with?' Ruby asked.

The three girls looked at each other, Sakura cleared her throat, 'Our main concern is mixing with Non-Labs and remaining inconspicuous.'

'Well, you're dressed appropriately, so now you just have to get used to mixing with Non-Labs. Why don't we all go for a walk now? And you can start to get your bearings,' Ruby suggested.

Soon they were all walking around the town centre,the eyes of the girl twins widening as they saw the tall buildings..

'Girls! Relax!' Johnny sidled up to them. 'Don't act as if you've never seen a building before!'

The two girls nodded as Johnny continued to advise them in a low voice.

Ruby smiled to herself, thinking of the first few trips into town she had made with the twins and their barely contained excitement.

Leon was showing Sakura, the young Japanese girl, a map of the town centre. She studied it earnestly.

'You don't look too worried, Pellier,' Ruby said to the French boy.

'No. It must come from my subscriber!' He smiled at Ruby, 'I am looking forward to studying music. To be quite honest, life was often boring in the Caves. Except for the times when Abe had us training!'

'Won't it be good when all Labs can live a free life; doing the things they enjoy doing?' Ruby said.

'Do you think that day will ever dawn?' Pellier asked her with a wry expression.

She looked at him, 'Was your subscriber by any chance a philosopher?'

'No. He is an officer in the French army. I was created from his son's cells,' he replied.

'How do you feel about … being created in that way?' Ruby asked him.

'How do you feel about being created in the way you were?' he shrugged again. 'I'm here. I don't really think about it.'

Ruby gave a smile and looked ahead to where the

twins and the three girls were standing. They joined them.

'Jade was saying she'd like to try out a new instrument. There's a music shop here,' Leon told them.

Pellier's eyes lit up, but then he looked down. 'Celia has already bought us each an instrument and a piano for the house.' He kicked at a stone.

'Well, we could just have a look; you may need a second instrument. You could say you have them on loan if anyone asks how you could afford them,' Ruby told him.The smile returned to his face.

They spent an enjoyable hour looking through the instruments and trying out several of them. The shop assistants were obviously delighted to have such talented musicians in their shop. The girls and Yuri tried out several stringed instruments. Pellier disappeared into the wind section and was soon torn between a saxophone and a bassoon. Ruby drifted in and out of the two rooms, until she realised that an impromptu performance by the three girls had drawn quite a crowd. She nodded at them to select their instruments and soon after that ushered them out of the shop. So much for being inconspicuous!

They walked back to the house with all the new students happily smiling and chatting to each other. They would probably fit in quite easily, Ruby thought. Musicians and arty types were allowed to be a bit different without arousing suspicion.

Each evening the house rang out with music, sometimes the students performed together, sometimes individually. During the next few days, Ruby and the twins took them to the supermarket, on buses and trains, and walked around to get to know the town. She was pleased to see the girls becoming more confident. She was glad they had Pellier with them. His laid-back character never caused him to feel unsure of himself.

At the end of the week, Ruby felt she and the twins could return to their own house. On the last evening the twins cooked a special meal.

'I am so full!' Leon said spreading himself out on the sofa afterwards.

'It was good!' Pellier agreed, pressing the television remote as he sat down beside him.

'Well done to the chefs! I'll get us some coffee,' Ruby said, carrying a pile of plates out to the kitchen.

She returned ten minutes later to find the others watching the television with wide eyes.

'Why is he pulling her clothes off?' Yuri asked as the couple on the screen exchanged passionate kisses and stumbled towards the bedroom.

Ruby gave a short laugh. 'It's pretty obvious, isn't it?'

Seven blank faces turned towards her.

'Oh, no!' she shook her head. 'You really don't know, do you?'

'Could you explain, please?' Pellier asked her.

'Well, they're going to …' she glanced at the screen where the woman was now pulling the man down onto the bed beside her, 'They're going to … have sex!'

Leon frowned. 'Is that when they mate?'

'Yes,' Ruby could feel her face burning. 'Well … not always. Sometimes people do it for fun. Like those people!'

The girls exchanged looks, as if doubting that what was happening on the screen could be fun.

'Didn't you talk about this at all in the Caves? At least about mating?' Ruby asked them.

'We did not think of mating. The Nursery Ward is full of developing young,' Yuri told her.

Ruby steeled herself, 'Well, now you are in the Non-Lab world, especially at parties and other social gatherings at university, you are going to need to know something, or quite a lot actually, about … sex. And protecting yourself.'

'You mean it can turn violent?' Sakura whispered. The other girls' hands flew to their mouths.

'No … well, hopefully not,' Ruby cast her mind back to the sex education lessons she had had at school over the past few years. She took a deep breath and began to explain the basics.

The next morning Ruby hugged each of them in turn as they stood beside the train to take her and the twins' home.

'You must telephone immediately if you need any help or advice. Anything at all,' she told them.

'We will,' the girls said.

'This new life promises to be most interesting,' Yuri gave them a slight nod.

Ruby turned to Pellier, 'You will all look after

each other, OK?'

He gave her a solemn nod, 'Labs always stand together!'

CHAPTER NINE

He had woken up in the night again, calling out. She had rushed in to see him sitting upright in bed, his eyes staring unseeing ahead.

'It's OK, it's OK, my love,' she had comforted him. 'It's just a dream! You're OK now!'

'It was the same thing, but I see a bit more each time, Mom!' he said turning to her.

'Do you want to talk about it, honey?' she asked gently.

'I'm in the orange room, I can hear the humming noise, all like last time. But this time … I opened the lid …' he said slowly.

'What lid?' she asked him. But he shook his head.

'I don't know!'

She handed him a clean pair of pyjamas. 'Take a quick shower and get changed while I change the sheets. You're covered in sweat, Simon! Perhaps we should make an appointment to see Dr Flynn again tomorrow?'

'No, I'll be fine, Mom,' he said later, climbing back into bed.

She pushed his hair back and kissed his forehead. 'I think you've being overdoing it lately, Simon.

You've never really given yourself time to get over your last accident!'

'I'm fine,' he had repeated sleepily.

CHAPTER TEN

Back at home, Ruby spoke to Celia about the time it took to settle the Labs into their new home.

'It took us a few days longer than we had planned, but we wanted to be sure that they were confident to deal with life on their own. I was thinking, once the students settle in, couldn't some of them help out with the new houses?' she suggested.

'Yes, that may be an option,' Celia nodded.

'Celia, can I ask you something?' Ruby ventured. 'The twins are certainly popular with the girls, aren't they? Can Labs have relationships, you know, close ones …?'

Celia looked at her questioningly.

'Can Labs … have sex?' she said bluntly.

'Oh, that.' Celia looked thoughtful. 'At the Centre they are able to take sperm and egg samples for further research. So, I assume Labs can.'

'And what about Labs having … close relationships, with Non-Labs?' Ruby continued.

'We have no knowledge of this at all. I suppose we will need to explore this scenario at some point,' Celia agreed.

Ruby sighed. 'I think we need to think about it

now! Labs are going to be meeting people on a social level in the Non-Lab world!'

She told Celia about her last evening in Manchester and her efforts to give them the basics in sex education.

'Thank you, Ruby. We should have thought about this before. I will speak to Abel to make sure all Labs are prepared before they move into their own homes,' she told her.

Two days later, Ruby and the twins set off for London to visit the two new homes set up there.

'At the first house we will meet Zaf, Peg, Joe, and Oll; officially known now as Sophie, Megan, Joseph, and Oliver,' Ruby told the twins.

'I remember Zaf, Peg, and Joe! The two girls were from the same subscriber!' Leon said.

'They joined us in the Caves at the same time. Oll was at the farmhouse with us,' Johnny added. 'Who's at the other house?'

'Ben and Dil – twins, Lok and Hal – also twins, and Fay and Cal,' Ruby read from the notes Celia had given her. 'Ben, Dylan, Lucy, Helen, Fiona, and Carla. They're all going to be studying politics and philosophy or languages at a sixth form college. I hope they settle in as well as the others did.'

Johnny and Leon grinned at each other.

'From our meetings at the Caves, they will have no trouble settling in!' Johnny said. 'They are like Abel about the Labs. What was the word Keith used?'

He turned to Leon.

'First-firstent?' his brow creased.

'Fervent?' Ruby suggested.

'That's it!' his face lit up.

Ruby found both sets of students much more confident and adventurous than the group of musicians in Manchester. They quickly settled in to their new lives. Within a week they had all joined several different organisations supporting different political parties and charities.

'We need to work to make Non-Labs aware of the unfairness of inequality amongst all people,' Sophie told them one evening.

'By putting ourselves in positions to have a voice for other disadvantaged groups; we hope eventually to build a network to support the freedom of our own people,' Megan added.

'We are enjoying our new-found freedom and are eager to free all Labs!' Lucy said.

'Yes!' her sister leaned forward. 'We hope to do so much!'

'I'm sure they would be able to help other Labs set up houses in London,' Ruby told Celia when she and the twins had returned to Castlewell a few days later. 'They're already very confident.'

'I will speak to Abel about this when he comes tomorrow. We're planning on setting up two new homes in the north of London. They could help establish the newly freed Labs,' Celia said.

Abel arrived the following morning as Ruby came down for breakfast. He glanced at the clock.

'Ruby just came back from London last night. She

deserves a rest,' Keith told him.

'Lon and Jed have already gone out to exercise. They didn't waste time lying in bed!' he commented. 'Maybe they understand the urgency of our situation!'

'If I had got up an hour earlier it wouldn't make things happen any faster, would it?' Ruby snapped at him.

Dette and Celia looked at her in surprise. Keith turned away to hide the smile on his lips.

Abel pushed back his chair and went out of the door as Ruby sat down at the table. She quickly finished her breakfast and went to get dressed. She was furious with herself for letting Abel rile her, yet she was secretly pleased she had annoyed him in return.

'Just because I'm a Non-Lab!' she hissed under her breath. 'I can do *nothing* right in his eyes!'

As she came back down the stairs there was a knock on the front door. She opened it to see two young girls standing there, holding tennis racquets.

'Hi, are Johnny and Leon here? We have got the right house, haven't we?' one of them asked.

'Yes. You do have the right house, but they're out at the moment. Oh, here they come, now,' Ruby replied as the twins jogged around the corner.

'Johnny!' the second girl waved at the boys, 'We've taken up your challenge! We're just off to play tennis at the park! Want to join us?'

The boys looked hesitant as Celia appeared beside Ruby.

'Why not, boys? It's Saturday, you haven't got any classes today!' Ruby smiled. 'Come in, girls. They'll need a shower before they join you.' She waved her hand in front of her nose, grinning. 'Come into the kitchen and have a coffee while you wait.'

Celia gave a brief hello and then disappeared upstairs. Abel glared at Ruby before leaving the house.

The three girls chatted happily in the kitchen. Ruby learnt that they belonged to most of the sports clubs the boys had joined. She smiled to herself, wondering if that was a coincidence.

She gave the girls the prepared version of their background growing up together in Nottingham and moving to Castlewell to study.

'This area is so much nicer than where we were living. It was really industrial. And the college is great,' she told them. 'Which course are you taking?'

'I'm taking French and Jane is on her second year of Tourism,' the first girl, Sara, told her. 'I've seen you in the canteen, with the two other girls who live here.'

'Yes,' Jane nodded. 'They seem nice, though a bit shy.'

'Who's shy?' Johnny asked striding into the kitchen, followed by his brother.

'Not you two, that's for sure!' Jane laughed.

'Come on, then!' Leon said. 'Let's beat you at tennis like we did at squash!'

'Don't be so sure!' Sara cried as they left the house. 'Jane has a wicked backhand!'

Ruby was putting the cups in the dishwasher when Dette and Celia came in.

'Do you think it's wise to have Non-Labs in our home?' Celia said.

Abel appeared in the doorway his arms folded across his chest. 'She's right. How can we feel safe? I certainly don't want them coming round when I am here. I don't enjoy the company of Non-Labs!'

'The more we blend in with the community, the safer we will be,' Ruby said in a level voice. 'Isn't it the plan for Labs to live amongst Non-Labs freely one day? How do you feel about it, Dette?'

Dette frowned. 'You know, these past few weeks, since we have started our college course with Non-Labs, I've begun to realise that there is not much difference between Non-Labs and ourselves.'

'Except many of *us* are not free!' Celia added.

'Yet!' Ruby said.

'Not much difference between Labs and Non-Labs?' Abel gave a snort of derision, then turning on his heels he left the room.

Over the next few weeks Johnny and Leon often invited other students back to the house and visited other homes. Celia and Dette were more reticent about inviting people, but were finding it easier to settle in at college through talking to the twins' new friends.

One evening Jane and Sara arrived with a boy a few years older than them.

'This is Isaac, my brother,' Jane explained. 'He's not a student anymore, he's out there in the big working world!'

Isaac explained he was a trainee reporter on the local newspaper.

'Today Castlewell, tomorrow London!' Jane quipped.

'Well, we all have to start somewhere, don't we?' he retorted good-naturedly.

'Castlewell's not exactly teeming with big news stories, is it?' Sara laughed.

'You never know what dark secrets are hidden behind closed doors!' Isaac gave a mock frown.

Dette let the cup she was holding clatter to the floor.

'Oh, there goes another one!' Ruby laughed. 'I thought I was the only butterfingers round here! You lot had better get off to the squash court or you'll be late!'

CHAPTER ELEVEN

He sat at the window and pulled the duvet around him. Outside, far below, he could see a man walking along the dark road. He wondered who he was and why he was out so late. Perhaps he was going home after being out with some friends. Perhaps he was a shift worker. Perhaps he was troubled in his sleep, too and was taking a walk to clear his mind.

His strange dreams were becoming more and more frequent lately. He went over the last one again in his head now he felt calmer.

He'd pushed open the lid and climbed out. The room seemed vast. It was lit by a dim orange glow. Something whirred gently in the background. He remembered the floor had felt cold on his bare feet. He'd walked, slowly at first, as if each step was something new for him. He looked around him and saw…

That's when he had woken up. He sighed. Every dream showed him a little more. And he knew there was still more to see.

CHAPTER TWELVE

The next morning Celia and Dette gave Ruby details of the next group of Labs to be settled in two houses in a London suburb later that week.

'Ben and the others will take care of two more new houses in their area. Valerie has enrolled them on a short course in office management and English,' Dette explained.

'We want you and Keith to visit all the Labs in London and make sure everything is OK,' Celia said.

Ruby and Keith found the Labs in all the houses had settled in to their new lives. The students in Ben's and Sophie's houses were still very politically active.

'We are arranging a petition to be presented to the Prime Minister on the inequalities in education around the country,' Sophie told her.

'Without access to a decent standard of education, too many young people can't escape poverty!' Megan added.

'You mustn't get mixed up in anything that may lead to you becoming involved with the police,' Keith warned them. 'It's great to have ideals, but the safety of the Labs comes first!'

Ben nodded. 'Don't worry. Yes, we're all aware of our restrictions at the moment. Our own people must come first.'

Keith decided to stay an extra day in London to view possible future properties and suggested that Ruby took some of the others go and see the sights.

Lucy and Helen eagerly agreed and persuaded Ben and Dylan to join them. Sophie, Megan, and Joseph decided to come too.

'We can start at the Tower of London,' Helen said, spreading out a visitor's map of the city.

'Then go on to the London Dungeon!' Ben and Dylan suggested eagerly.

'No! I think I'd prefer to visit Madame Tussaud's,' Megan said. Her brother and sister nodded.

'Well, we could start at the Tower of London, then we can split into two groups,' Ruby said. 'Then in a few weeks' time you could take some of the newcomers around yourselves. None of them wanted to join us today.'

'London is a busy place after the Caves!' Lucy said.

Ruby felt as excited as the Labs as they walked around the Tower. She had never visited London in her old life. She was wandering around admiring the huge suits of armour when she heard a familiar voice.

'Ruby, what are you doing here?' Isaac was standing beside her.

'I'm visiting a few friends down here and we're doing a bit of sightseeing.' she smiled. 'And you?'

'I'm staying with my uncle for a few days. He persuaded me to look after a friend of his today as he's busy. So we're doing the sights, too!'

At that moment Sophie, Megan, and Joseph appeared, followed by Ben and Dylan.

'Are you ready to go now, Ruby? Ben and Dylan are impatient to get to the Dungeons!' Megan laughed. 'Oh, hello,' she added, turning to Isaac.

Ruby noticed Isaac's expression as they were joined by Helen and Lucy.

'What's this? A twins convention? And triplets, too?' He looked bemused.

'Something like that!' Ruby decided not to try to explain. 'Well, goodbye, enjoy your day!'

She mulled over it for the rest of the day and told Keith of her meeting as they drove back home that evening.

'Twins and triplets are not so strange, are they?' he asked her.

'Not really, but it does seem strange that we should be involved with so many,' she replied. 'How can I explain the situation?'

'What did he say? A convention? Tell him he was right!' Keith suggested.

Ruby wasn't convinced.

She felt ill at ease when she bumped into him in the main street near his newspaper office.

'Oh, hi, Isaac,' she said brightly.

'Hi. I haven't seen much of you lately,' he said.

'I've been pretty busy,' she replied.

'How come you know so many twins, and triplets,

too?' he said.

Ruby looked away. 'Multiple births aren't as rare as you'd think these days, with IVF treatments. Did your uncle's friend enjoy the London sights?'

'And I looked up your old Nottingham address. Funny thing, it doesn't actually exist!' Isaac continued, ignoring her question. 'Where do you all come from?'

'What is this?' Ruby knitted her eyebrows, 'The Spanish Inquisition?'

She started to walk past him, but he caught her arm.

'Where are you all from?' he repeated, his face near hers. 'What have you got to hide?'

She drew back. 'I don't know what you're talking about, Isaac! You're getting a bit carried away with your big news story ideas!'

She shook his hand off her arm and walked away. As soon as she had turned a corner she leaned back against the wall and took a deep breath. She must go home and speak to the others immediately.

'Things could become dangerous if he continues to investigate our lives,' Celia pointed out.

'God knows what Abel would do to him if he thinks he might be a threat to us!' Dette said vehemently.

Keith took a deep breath. 'Isaac does not know much about us yet, and we'll have to make sure we don't give him any more information.'

'Yes, we must all remain calm. Give him nothing to fuel his ideas,' Celia agreed.

Over the next few weeks Isaac found Ruby's household polite, but very distant from him. He was never able to talk to one person without several more joining them. He felt increasingly frustrated. There was something mysterious about that household. And he had to find out about it.

He spent the next few weeks secretly surveying the house, until one day his patience was rewarded.

First the twins left for college with Dette and Celia. Half an hour later, Keith drove off. And finally he gave a sigh of relief as Ruby stepped out, locking the door behind her, and walked off in the direction of the supermarket. Crossing the road, he silently slipped around the back of the house.

His hand shook as he tried the back door of their house. Locked, as he had expected it to be. He glanced around but could see no windows left open. He reached inside his pocket and pulled out a bunch of skeleton keys. A friend of his at university had shown him how to break into his own flat when he had accidentally locked himself out and he had used this method on one or two occasions since. He had never thought he would use it for illegal purposes, but he told himself that this was justified.

He took a deep breath as he felt the lock give and the door open. He stepped inside and pushed it closed behind him.

'Hello?' he called and satisfied the house was empty began a quick search.

There seemed to be nothing of interest in the kitchen. The lounge had two laptops, but he knew it would take him too long to work out passwords to gain access to any useful information, so he headed upstairs. He made a quick search of each room and was finally rewarded when he reached into the pocket of a jacket hanging in Ruby's wardrobe.

It was a list of names and addresses. 'Zaf – Sophie, Peg – Megan, Ben – Benjamin, Dil – Dylan …' his eyes narrowed, the girl with Ruby in London had referred to Ben, and Dylan. There were two London addresses underneath. He let himself silently out of the house.

He spent the next three days in London visiting the addresses from the scrap of paper and found that the people he had seen with Ruby were living there. From the neighbours he learnt that they were quiet students who were pleasant enough but who mainly kept themselves to themselves.

He followed Ben and Dylan to two political meetings and also followed them one evening to the house where Sophie lived. They seemed to be living a very similar life to many other students in London. On his last day in London he decided to follow the girls. They left university at lunch time and headed in a different direction on the tube than they normally did. They arrived at a house and were let in by a young girl. Isaac was unsure what to do, but soon the door opened and Megan and Sophie emerged, with two more girls, twins again! Isaac followed them along the road to a small park. They sat on a bench near a duck pond. Isaac sat on a bench nearby and opened a newspaper.

'It is so different after the Caves,' one girl was saying.

'It is at first, but you get used to it, Lily!' Sophie told her.

'Our course finishes next week and then we have to start looking for work! It's worrying!' the girl shook her head.

'Yes,' a second girl said. 'We must fit in fully with Non-Labs! What happens if we can't?'

'Milly and I could put all the Labs in danger!' the first girl looked near to tears.

'Have you spoken to Ruby or Celia?' Megan asked them.

They shook their heads, 'We feel as if we've failed them. Their plan was working so well until we left the Caves!'

'You mustn't feel like this!' Helen told them, 'If you're not ready for the workplace, you don't have to start just yet! Valerie will arrange things. Phone Celia.'

Lucy stood up, 'You're right. We must phone them immediately!'

Isaac watched as the girls walked out of the park and headed back home. Then he opened a notebook and jotted a few sentences down. He gave a satisfied sigh and stood up. Time to return to Castlewell.

It was nearly a week before he spotted Ruby alone in the supermarket. He hurried after her.

'Hi, Ruby! Been busy lately?' he said with a grin.

'Just the usual,' she leaned past him and started to fill a bag with apples.

‘Aren’t you going to ask me what I’ve been up to?’ he continued.

Ruby shrugged, ‘It looks as if you’re dying to tell me. Have you found a good story?’

‘I have!’ he stood in front of her. ‘Have you heard from Megan? Her friends, Lily and Milly – also twins, as it happens – are worried about working with the Non-Labs.’

Ruby froze for a moment. She knew they had phoned Celia the previous week.

‘I’m afraid I don’t know what you’re talking about, Isaac,’ she said.

‘I think you do, Ruby! It would make a good news story, wouldn’t it?’ he said evenly, watching her face closely.

He pulled the piece of paper he had taken from her jacket from his own pocket. ‘This is just the start!’

‘Where did you get that?’ Ruby asked him angrily, making a grab for the paper. He moved it out of her reach.

She pushed her trolley to one side and headed out of the shop with Isaac hurrying after her.

‘Wait!’ he called.

‘Why don’t you just go away? Your cheap newspaper story may end up costing people’s lives!’ she hissed at him.

‘I don’t want to hurt anyone. But I do want answers,’ he said.

She stopped, looking flustered.

‘OK,’ she nodded. ‘Come to the house tomorrow

evening, at nine o'clock. But you must *not* breathe a word of this to anyone, you must *promise*!'

He nodded his head solemnly, 'Then you will give me some answers?'

'It's not up to me!' she cried, hurrying away from him.

Keith sprang up as Ruby burst into the house a short while later.

'Ruby! What is it?' he asked.

'We must talk! All of us! Now!' she whispered.

Soon they were all sitting in the lounge. Ruby sat white faced. She took a deep breath and blurted out, 'Isaac knows something about us! I'm not sure how much!'

'What does he know? How did he find out?' several people said at once.

'Start from the beginning, Ruby,' Keith patted her arm, 'Calm yourself.'

'Somehow Isaac got hold of a bit of paper. I'd written down the names and addresses of Megan and Ben and the people in their houses. I'd taken the details from Celia,' Ruby could not meet the eyes of the others around her. 'I really don't know how he got hold of it! I did mean to destroy it as soon as I got home!'

There was a deathly silence.

'OK. We must get Isaac to come around here and find out what he does actually know,' Keith said.

'I told him to come here at nine o'clock tomorrow evening,' Ruby told them.

'What if he has already prepared a newspaper

story about us?' Dette cried. 'Maybe we should get him round here right now!'

'Wait!' Celia urged her. 'Ruby was right to give us some time to think about this, before we see him.'

'Let's discuss a plan of action before he joins us tomorrow,' Keith said. 'And we'd better ask Abel to come immediately.'

By midnight Abel had joined them. He turned a scornful eye upon Ruby, who, though pale-faced already, seemed to blanch even further.

'So we'll have to get rid of Isaac. He will have to meet with an unfortunate accident!' he said as he strode into the room.

'No!' Ruby cried out. 'No! You can't harm him!'

'You have left us no choice,' Abel swung around to face her.

'No, Abel,' Keith said. 'Ruby is right, we can't hurt him. We can't do away with every Non-Lab that becomes aware of our background.'

'Not every Non-Lab,' Abel countered. 'But any Non-Lab that puts us in danger before we have established ourselves in a secure position.'

'Keith and I have given the matter some thought. We need something to bargain with,' Celia ventured. All eyes were turned hopefully to her.

'What do you mean?' Johnny asked her.

'If Isaac has important information about us, how can we be in a position to bargain with him?' Leon looked puzzled.

'What does Isaac want?' Celia continued.

Ruby looked at her and nodded slowly, 'A big

news story to get him noticed in the media world.'

'And you have given it to him!' Abel said as Ruby cringed again.

'No she hasn't, not yet! I see what you are getting at, Celia!' Dette began to smile, 'I think it might just work!'

Keith nodded, 'It's a risk, but it gives us some hope!'

'It may even work in our favour!' Celia commented.

'I don't really understand …' Johnny began as his twin shook his head, too.

'Isaac wants a big news story. If we persuade him to wait, he will have the biggest news story ever!' Celia explained.

'So, we'll take *another* Non-Lab into our confidence? And one who is an unknown factor to all of us? That's insane!' Abel stood up, clenching his fists.

'He's already in a position to put us all in danger!' Celia insisted. 'We need to have him on our side now!'

'How can we trust *any* Non-Lab?' Abel snarled, staring at Ruby. He stormed out of the door.

Dette stood up and followed him, 'I'll go and talk to him. I'll see if I can persuade him to consider your idea.'

Abel's face was still sullen as they sat with Isaac in their midst the following evening.

'First tell us what you *do* know, and we'll fill in the details,' Keith spoke quietly to Isaac.

'Well, I suppose I don't know that much really, but I've a gut feeling that things aren't what they seem with you people,' Isaac looked less sure of himself surrounded by them all than he had with Ruby on her own.

'So …?' Celia prompted him.

'I know you are in contact with groups of students around the country. Many of them are twins, like you boys. I know these students are going under false names. And I know some of them are nervous, afraid of another group called the "Non-Labs" …' He looked up as Johnny stifled a giggle. Celia silenced him with a glare.

'And, I know you didn't go to Sherwood State school,' he finished.

'So you don't really know that much at all, do you?' Abel sneered.

'I have addresses and enough to start an interesting newspaper story on the increase in twins and triplets among the student population. This is worth further investigation!' Isaac turned to him, his face flushed.

'Who'd be interested in this?' Keith asked quietly.

'My uncle – he's a reporter for *The Times* – some of his friends, some of my own colleagues,' Isaac continued doggedly.

'How could you find out more, if we don't cooperate?' Abel asked him.

'I'd gain public interest by writing an article about twins and triplets. I'd start by interviewing some of these students!' he took the paper from his pocket. In a flash, Abel had removed it from his hand. Isaac looked at him. 'I do have copies, you know! I left some stuff with a friend, for security, before I came here today!'

There was silence for a moment.

'Isaac,' Keith broke the silence, 'your interference at the wrong time may cause the loss of lives, *hundreds* of lives! You will have to wait for your big story until the end of our plan.'

'I *knew* there was more to this! I can wait! I *swear* I wouldn't print anything that may endanger lives!' Isaac looked at him eagerly.

Keith looked around the room. The others nodded, except for Abel who turned away with a grunt.

For the next hour Isaac listened with widening eyes, occasionally asking a question, as Celia and the others explained the situation and their plan to free the Labs.

At one point Isaac turned and smiled at Johnny, 'That's why you laughed when I said a group called the "Non-Labs"! I'm one of them!' Johnny grinned back and nodded.

Finally there was silence.

'Wow! *What* a story!' Isaac gave a soft whistle. 'Surely we could break in, like you've done before, and free the rest of the Labs?' he said, leaning forward excitedly.

'We could free the Mature Labs, yes. But what about the developing Labs in the Nursery Ward? There are over two hundred of them at the moment,' Abel pointed out.

'Couldn't you free those, too?' Isaac asked him.

'We've never tried arresting the development of the Labs in the Nursery Ward. They are on an accelerated growth programme. We don't know what the results would be if we stopped their development before maturity. They're not like Non-Lab children,' Dette told him.

'Look, if I got my uncle who's with *The Times* to publish this story, we could get everything out in the open! Get the Centre closed down straight away!' Isaac suggested.

'No!' Abel shook his head vehemently. 'If the story came out, who knows what would happen to the Labs in the Centre, especially the vulnerable ones who are still developing! We need someone important to go in and take control completely with some of us beside them.'

'This story must not be made public yet!' Celia warned Isaac.

'Hmmm … I can see that! Look, I still want to help you. I'm sure I could be useful in some way, you know,' he said.

Abel grunted. 'Our Non-Lab friend, Ruby, *helped* us by supplying you with crucial names and addresses!'

Ruby blushed and looked down.

'No, she didn't!' Isaac reached inside his pocket and pulled out the skeleton keys. 'As we're all being honest, I have to admit I looked around your house one day when you were all out.'

He gave Ruby an apologetic smile. 'Sorry!' He spread his hands. 'Hey, it's a skill that you may find useful! And I also have useful contacts in the press, through my uncle.'

Keith nodded slowly. 'Yes, you may indeed prove a useful ally, Isaac.'

Abel glared at him again. 'But if you *ever* do, or *think* about doing, something that will put any Lab in danger, you will regret it!'

Isaac stood to face him. 'I'm on your side! It's in my interest to keep this story under wraps until the correct time, the same as it is for you.' He paused. 'Hey, maybe we could even be friends?' He held out a tentative hand. Throwing him a derisive look, Abel turned away.

The following day Ruby found Isaac beside her in the supermarket again.

'Shopping again?' he asked her.

'I didn't get anything the other day, don't you remember?' she smiled.

'I'm glad we're friends again.'

She nodded as she reached for a box of cereal from the top shelf.

'Here, let me,' Isaac said, passing one to her. 'See? I'm useful already!'

Ruby smiled again. 'You'd be even more helpful if you let me get on with my shopping.'

She continued to the next aisle, with Isaac beside her.

'So, any developments?' he asked.

‘Nothing new since we saw you yesterday!’ she said.

‘Are you going to be setting up new homes soon?’ he continued. ‘Maybe I can help?’

‘Celia organises these things, it’s really not up to me,’ Ruby said.

‘I’d like to be involved as much as possible! Then when the Centre is exposed, I will be able to tell the real story from the inside!’ Isaac told her.

‘I’ll speak to Celia,’ Ruby promised him.

He approached her again the next day when he called around with Sara and Jane.

‘Have you seen this?’ he asked, unfolding a national newspaper. He showed her the story on a political rally to be held in London the following day. A group calling themselves “Forever England” were to march through the city centre to protest against the number of immigrants allowed into the UK. ‘Are any of your group involved?’

She got up and signalled him to follow her to the garden. ‘Ben and some of the others are holding a counter-meeting at the university.’

Isaac frowned. ‘That could be an explosive situation! Isn’t it dangerous for them to take part in it?’

‘Yes!’ Ruby nodded, ‘Abel has tried to persuade them not to attend, but Ben and Megan insist they must stand up for what they believe in or they might as well be still living in the Caves!’

Isaac looked thoughtful. ‘I’ll get in touch with a friend of mine who works for a London paper. He might have some details about this march.'

'That would be helpful, Isaac,' Ruby said. 'Abel must be very worried or he wouldn't be planning on going to London himself.'

'Tell him maybe I can be of use if I go with you to London,' Isaac told her.

But Abel was adamant that Isaac did not accompany them to London when Ruby suggested it later that evening.

'We don't need his help! We can take care of our own!'

'He has friends in London. He's going to find out what they know about this demonstration,' Ruby told him.

'He is not travelling with us. He can stay with his friends,' Abel said, and turned away.

Ruby phoned Isaac to tell him.

'I know you are trying to be helpful, Isaac. Abel finds it difficult to trust Non-Labs,' she said. 'It will be a while before he accepts your help. He's still not happy to have me around but Celia insisted I go with him to London as I could be useful.'

'Well, I'm going to go to London and cover the story anyway. I'll phone you if I hear anything,' Isaac sounded disappointed.

The following day Ruby, Abel, Ben, and the other Lab students from London were in front of the university where a large podium had been set up.

Several of the students had made speeches about the right of people all over the world to be allowed to travel freely.

Ben was speaking about the lack of equality between the different countries and how many people like himself would like to see opportunities and resources shared out more equally.

'We don't need to divide the world into places you *can* go into and places you are *barred* from! We need to *open* the boundaries between countries!'

Ruby stood near Abel, watching him speak.

'He obviously feels very strongly about this,' she whispered to Abel.

The Lab's face was set. 'I am not happy about him bringing such attention to himself and the others!'

Just then Ruby's phone began to ring; it was Isaac. She moved to a quieter place so she could hear him.

'Ruby! Things aren't looking good! My friend has heard that the Forever England group have hired some hecklers to join the university demonstration. They'll be here soon! You'd better get your people out quickly!' Isaac told her. 'The police are to be sent in. There's bound to be some arrests!'

'Ben's on the podium speaking at the moment! The others are near him. I can't see Abel. He was here a moment ago! Where are you, Isaac?' Ruby felt her heart racing.

'Calm down, Ruby. We'll be all right. I'm near the podium. I'll speak to Ben as soon as he gets down and get him to get the others together. I'll get them out on this side. You find Abel and both of you get as far away from here as soon as you can, OK?'

As soon as Isaac had rung off, Ruby began to look around for Abel. She finally spotted him near the entrance to the university and pushed her way through the crowds to join him.

'Abel! We've got to get out of here quickly! There's going to be a disturbance! The police are on their way; people will be arrested!' she blurted out.

'We must get Ben and the others,' he cried, turning towards the podium.

Ruby caught his arm. 'Isaac has them, look!'

Ben was speaking to the other Labs and all were following Isaac at a swift pace.

Ruby and Abel were near the entrance of the university when suddenly there was shouting. Several people were pushing their way through the crowds towards the podium. There was the sound of someone screaming. People began to try to leave the square, but a cordon of mounted police blocked them.

Ruby looked with frightened eyes at Abel. He grabbed her hand. 'We can't get out that way! Come on.'

He ran into the building, pulling her behind him. At the end of the corridor someone shouted at them to stop. They ran down another corridor, trying door handles, but they were all locked. Finally Abel found one that opened and pulling Ruby in behind him, closed the door. They stood closely together in the dark, Ruby trying to breathe quietly. She knew they were in a storage cupboard from the smell of polish. The handle of a floor polisher pushed painfully into her back. The sound of running footsteps outside made her heart pound. She gripped Abel's jacket tightly.

'They couldn't have gone any further this way!' a voice said.

'All the rooms are locked,' another answered him.

'Try the caretaker's cupboard. He doesn't always remember to lock it,' the first voice said.

Abel held tightly to the door handle, his face pinched as the person outside tried to move it.

'No. It's locked,' the voice finally said. 'Let's try the cloakrooms. They may be hiding in there.'

'Better be quick before they have time to double back!' the second man answered.

Ruby and Abel listened to the sound of their feet moving away.

As Ruby gave a sigh of relief, Abel pulled her closer to him. She could feel his heart beating against her. Then slowly he lifted her chin and kissed her gently on the lips. She gave a gasp of surprise.

He quickly released her.

'Sorry! I…' He stopped speaking as they heard voices outside the cupboard again.

'Beats me how they did it! But they've somehow got out.'

'Better get back to the desk,' the second voice replied, 'before more of them get in!'

They stood in silence for several more minutes before Abel opened the door and beckoned her to follow him.

It was getting dark when they finally arrived at

Ben and the other students' house. Isaac was seated in the lounge talking to Megan when they entered. He stood up smiling.

'We've been watching the news! We were so relieved to finally hear from you. What happened?'

'We tried to get through the university building, but ended up stuck in a broom cupboard and eventually had to make our escape through a window in the ladies' toilets!' Ruby giggled. The events of the day had left her feeling light-headed.

'I told you I might be of use to you!' Isaac beamed at Abel, who gave him a wry smile.

'Thank you for your quick actions today, Isaac. You did indeed prove to be extremely useful. It seems I was wrong – not *all* Non-Labs are bad news!' Abel flushed slightly as he caught Ruby's eye.

'We phoned Celia, so they wouldn't be worried about us when they see the news tonight,' Ben said.

Abel looked at him, 'I think you must keep a lower profile until the Labs are in a stronger position to speak out, Ben.'

He looked at Megan and they both nodded.

'It's true. Our arrest could endanger many others. But I hope it's not to be too long before we are in a position to speak out, Abel.'

'We are freeing as many Labs as we can, but it's a slow process and there are not enough of us to bring about the closure of the Centre without putting any Labs in danger. If only we could formulate a plan to accomplish that, we'd all be free tomorrow!' he sighed.

They had been talking for several hours when Abel's phone rang. He went to the hallway to answer it. His face was solemn when he rejoined them.

'It looks as if we're going to have to make a move quicker than we planned. Fil, one of the Labs working undercover at the Centre,just phoned the house. He has heard rumours that the Centre is to be taken over by an American company, and they're planning on setting up similar sites in several countries around the world! We'd better head back, Ruby.'

As they drove along the motorway, Ruby watched Abel staring stonily ahead. He hardly seemed to be the same person who had held her close and kissed her in the darkness.

CHAPTER THIRTEEN

He walked past rows and rows of capsules, each with a slumbering occupant. He put his hand to his forehead, suddenly feeling incredibly tired. It became difficult to put one foot in front of the other. He steadied himself on the nearest capsule and rested his head against it. On the other side of the smoky glass a girl slept, unaware of his presence. He closed his eyes and slid gently down to the floor.

This time he woke up feeling calm. He knew what he had to do. Somehow, he had to find the sleeping girl!

CHAPTER FOURTEEN

'We can only sit around here while the Labs at the Centre are in danger!' Ben paced around the room.

Megan nodded. 'I also feel helpless. What can we do? If Abel cannot find a solution, who can?'

'Whoever it is, they'll have to find one quickly!' Joseph said.

'We should try and get some sleep now,' Oliver said, getting to his feet. 'Tomorrow we could phone the Manchester Labs and see if they have any ideas.'

It was late, so the students from the second house stayed the night. The following morning they were up early and set off home across London. As they emerged from the tube in the city centre, Joseph stopped at a kiosk to buy a newspaper.

'Phew! Look at that!' he said nodding at the front-page headlines and photos from the university demonstration. 'I'm glad we got out in time!'

Sophie had noticed a young man nearby. From his accent she realised he was American. He was with two other young men, while close by were two burly, older men. Bodyguards, so he was obviously someone important. He had glanced across at her, then suddenly stopped talking to his friends and stared at her. He turned and said something to his friends then made his way towards her.

'I know you, don't I?' he asked. He nodded at all four of them. 'I do know you, don't I?'

The bodyguards appeared beside him.

'I think we'd better go, Simon. Your father will be expecting you!' one of them said.

'Just give me a minute,' he said, his eyes fixed on Sophie's face. 'I know you all, from somewhere, don't I?'

Sophie shook her head, 'No, I don't think so.'

'We haven't been here that long,' Joseph said.

'And we've never been to America,' Megan added.

The young man was wiping sweat from his face; he had turned pale. 'If only I could remember where I know you from.'

'Come on, Simon,' one of the bodyguards looked anxiously at him, guiding him towards a black limousine which drew up beside them. 'You don't look too good. Better get back to the hotel.'

Simon continued to stare at them as he let himself be seated in the car.

Sophie turned to Megan and gave a shudder. 'That was eerie!'

Oliver looked at them. 'You know who that was, don't you?' They all looked at him. 'If I'm not mistaken, that was Simon Armstrong, the son of the US president. He's on an unofficial visit to England, before he starts studying here next year.'

'Oh, yes. I read about that,' Megan said.

‘He has also made many trips to England to visit the Centre.’ Oliver added softly.

Sophie gasped. ‘And he thinks he knows us!’

‘We must phone Celia as soon as we get home.’

‘This is amazing! How could he have any recollection of his time in the Centre before the operation?’ Johnny said after Celia had told her of Sophie’s phone call.

‘Perhaps his machine was faulty and he began to wake up, as I did,’ Keith ventured.

‘There could be other donors around the world who also have similar memories,’ Dette said.

‘We haven’t heard of any up to now,’ Celia said. ‘The American takeover bid needs our attention right now! On Monday they are holding talks to set a date,’ she shook her head.

‘We’re in increasing danger every day! We *must* find a way to bring about the closure of the Centre as soon as possible!’ Keith’s face was grave. ‘How many Labs are free now, Abel?’

‘Just over a hundred,’ he replied.

‘If only the Non-Labs running the Centre could understand how Labs feel!’ Leon said.

‘Instead of seeing us as just spare parts! ’ his brother added.’

‘We need someone important who will listen to us!’ Leon continued.

‘Someone with as much weight behind them as the people running the Centre!’ Johnny said.

‘Maybe that’s it!’ Ruby ventured.

Everyone looked at her expectantly.

'It's probably a stupid idea...'

'Go on, Ruby,' Keith prompted her.

'If the son of the president of the United States has memories of being at the Centre, maybe *he* can help us,' she suggested.

'Ruby may have found a solution,' Celia breathed. 'How can we persuade the president's son to help us?'

There was silence for several minutes which was broken by a sudden cry from Isaac.

'I've got it! I'm sure it could work!' he shouted.

'You'd better go and join the others, Ruby,' Isaac said glancing at his watch. 'Are they all here?'

'Yes. Sakura, Jade, and Miyu just arrived a few minutes ago,' she said. 'I do hope it all works out!'

'It will!' he replied confidently. 'Just make sure everyone follows the plan.'

Ruby had just disappeared through the door when Simon appeared flanked by his two bodyguards. The older men positioned themselves by the bar as Isaac stood up and approached Simon with his hand out.

'Thanks so much for agreeing to be interviewed, Simon!' he shook his hand warmly. 'You don't know what this means to me! It'll really help my standing with the paper!'

'And low-key, as you promised me, hey?' Simon gave him a smile.

'You bet! Beer?' Isaac asked him.

'A Bud, please. Sorry! I know I'm in England!'

He gave a rueful shrug.

Soon the two young men were sitting talking. Led by Isaac's questions, Simon chatted easily about his life in the US and his plans for studying in England A young man approached their table.

'Hi, Isaac. Didn't know you were up in town this weekend!' he said.

'Quick visit only, Ben! Maybe I'll catch up with you next time!' he replied.

Simon looked around and blinked rapidly as he saw Ben retreating.

'I think I've met him before,' he murmured.

'Well, you were telling me about American football! Not at all like the game we play here, is it?' Isaac continued.

'What? Eh, no …' Simon's attention was diverted again as twin girls waved across at Isaac before sitting down at a table on the far side of the bar. 'Their faces are familiar, too!'

'Have you visited many other places outside London?' Isaac asked him.

'Yeah, a few places; I went to …' Simon, his eyes on the doorway, had suddenly turned pale.

Isaac looked concerned. 'Hey, are you OK?'

'It's *her*!' he whispered, as Sakura, Jade, and Miyu came in. Sakura looked at them and smiled. Isaac beckoned them over. They were followed by one of Simon's bodyguards.

'You OK, son?' one of them said, glancing around the table. 'Your mom said if you're not looking too good …'

Simon took a deep breath and nodded his head, 'I'm fine, just great, Geoff. Catching up with some old pals here!'

With a second glance around the table, Geoff left them to join his partner at the bar.

'I saw you, sleeping … in that glass box!' Simon whispered to Sakura.

She nodded and put her hand over his.

Simon gave a gasp. 'You're not going to tell me I imagined it? You saw me, too?'

'I didn't see you. I was not awakened then. But we think we know what happened,' she replied.

The other girls exchanged glances and nodded.

'Where did I see you? When?' Simon asked them. 'And the others?'

'We must take you to where it happened,' Sakura told him.

'It's not a place many … people … know about,' Miyu added.

'It'll have to be a secret. No one else can know just yet,' Isaac said. 'Not even them.' He gestured towards the bodyguards.

Sakura looked into his eyes, 'Are you willing to put your trust in us, Simon?'

'I *do* trust you. I feel I know many of you,' he gave a short laugh. 'You know, I've been thinking I've been going nuts these past few months!'

'No, you're not, but this story may be difficult for you to accept,' Sakura squeezed his hand gently. 'You were in England on several occasions before you came to study in London, weren't you?'

'Yes, but I wasn't really aware of much of my surroundings! I was in a hospital in a medical centre somewhere north of London,' he shrugged. 'So I met all you guys then, did I?'

'We think it is best to go to the Centre to enable us to establish exactly what happened. And to tell you all the things you need to know,' Sakura told him.

The following week Simon set out for the Centre with Sakura, Isaac, and Celia who was driving.

'Tell us about your dreams, Simon, in as much detail as you can,' Celia told him.

Simon slowly recounted his dreams, telling her that, unlike the other occasions, he had felt calm when he woke from his last dream.

'I knew I had to find the sleeping girl. And I did!'

'With a little help!' Isaac pointed out.

'We heard how you had reacted to meeting the students in London,' Celia told him.

'You did?' Simon looked around him. 'Do you all know each other?'

They nodded.

'And it's all connected to the Centre?' he asked.

'You must know about the background to the Centre, Simon. This may be difficult for you ...' Celia began.

'I know about it. My dad had some stem cells cloned from my tissue which they use to repair me when I get injured,' he said.

'There's more to it than that, Simon,' Sakura told him.

‘They don’t stop at stem cells; they produce human clones and keep them as spare parts for the humans they are created for. Sometimes more than one copy, like twins or triplets of the donor,’ she told him.

Simon gave a disbelieving laugh, ‘What, you mean they create whole body copies of the donors and just pick out the bits they need?’

He shook his head as they all nodded.

‘That’s correct,’ Celia told him.

‘But why don’t these new people just walk out?’ he continued.

‘They are kept sleeping,’ Sakura said.

‘In those capsules …’ Simon whispered as she nodded again. ‘You mean you’re one of those …?’

She caught Celia’s eye in the mirror and watched her nod. Turning her wrist upwards she gently pulled the plastic strip off to reveal her tattooed code – SAF 24912.

‘Yes, Simon, I am a Lab,’ she told him. She gestured around the car, ‘Apart from Isaac, we are all Labs.’

‘Labs?’ Simon repeated.

‘Labs – people created in a laboratory, unlike Non-Labs, myself and you, created under normal conditions,’ Isaac explained. ‘We decided it might make things a bit easier for you if I came with you today, one of your own kind.’ He took a deep breath. ‘Actually, I’m a bit nervous myself. This is my first visit to the Centre, too.’

Simon sat back in his seat, a stunned expression

on his face.

A short while later the car turned off the road and headed along a narrow lane. Suddenly it swung onto a dirt track and soon afterwards drew to a halt. Celia and Sakura climbed out and signalled the two men to follow them. They stood outside a small wooden door almost hidden behind a covering of ivy. Celia spoke on her mobile phone and the door opened to reveal Abel. They entered and the door was closed swiftly behind them.

'Has he been informed?' Abel gestured towards Simon.

'Of the basics only,' Celia replied. 'It's probably better if he visits the Mature Ward before he is given any further information.'

Sakura held out her hand to Simon, hesitantly.

'Are you ready, Simon? Would you like to look around the room from your dreams?'

He nodded without looking at her.

Abel walked to a large frosted glass door and entered a code into a keypad. The door slid back to let them enter.

The orange glow and gentle humming seemed very familiar to Simon.

Sakura started to walk slowly towards the far side of the room.

'No, wait!' Simon whispered. 'Let me show you where I saw you!'

He looked around, his brow furrowed in concentration.

'Now, I was … here? … No, one row back! Yes!'

he walked towards a capsule.

'I got out of here and walked up this far. Then I turned to the right. I walked back one, two, three rows.'

He pointed to a capsule, 'You were there!'

Sakura smiled and nodded slowly. She looked around.

'I remember being awoken, and taking my first steps! It felt so strange, yet somehow familiar …'

Simon nodded. 'I felt that way exactly!'

'Yes, a Lab brain is programmed to have the physical skills of a young adult; although it was a new experience, you felt you had done it before,' Celia explained.

Simon walked around looking down at the sleeping faces. He stopped in front of a capsule and gazed at its occupant.

'There was a different person sleeping here when I was here,' he whispered. Celia looked away.

'We must leave now!' Abel told them. 'A new shift begins in ten minutes and all wards will be inspected.'

Soon they were all in the car heading away from the building.

'Where are we going?' Simon asked. 'I don't think I'm ready to return to my London flat and friends just yet.'

'If you agree, we would like to take you to our house. It's quite nearby,' Celia glanced at his face. 'I live there with four other Labs and a Non-Lab. We could discuss this matter.'

‘Do you agree to this, Simon?’ Sakura asked him.

He nodded. For the rest of the journey he remained silent, gazing out of the window.

Soon they drew up outside the house and got out. Ruby opened the front door and smiled at Simon gently.

‘Come in. I’m Ruby, a Non-Lab, like you. We have plenty of coffee and sandwiches ready! You’ve had quite an ordeal, Simon!’

After introducing the twins and Dette they all sat down in the lounge.

‘I think I know what happened,’ Simon began nervously. ‘I know I went to the Centre on three occasions, when I was injured in serious accidents over the past few years. I suppose that on the last occasion I must have somehow wandered into the room where the Labs were sleeping. Somehow I got myself into one of those capsules and…’

He looked disappointed as Celia shook her head. ‘It couldn’t have happened like that, Simon. First of all, you were too severely injured to get out of bed. And secondly, all the rooms containing Labs are under tight security.’

Simon looked puzzled.

‘I’m afraid you’ve lost me! At the Centre, in the … Mature Ward … you told me I *had* been there. Now you are telling me I can’t have been there!’

Everyone was silent for a moment, then Celia gave a cough and began to speak.

‘This may be difficult for you to understand. And it may also come as something rather shocking. But, what seems to have happened is –'

'No!' Simon interrupted. Suddenly his hands shook so much he slopped coffee on to the table as he put the cup down. He put his hands to his eyes. 'I know what you are going to tell me!'

Sakura put her hand on his shoulder. There was a long silence.

'Simon …' she began.

He took a deep breath and sat up.

'No, let me say it, and you can tell me if there's anything … different. The … person in my dream, who woke up, walked around, saw you … he was the Lab. The one who slept in a capsule in there.

'He fell asleep on the floor; it must have been the anesthetic. He was being prepared for the operation, wasn't he? *I have his brain, don't I?*'

Celia sighed and nodded. 'Yes, Simon. The staff must have been lax. They must have set the dials incorrectly, which allowed him to wake up. There is no record of this. They must have covered up their mistake.'

Simon was looking down at his hands, 'I have had three serious operations over the past few years. How much of me is … Lab?'

'We could check through your records. But are you sure …?'

He looked up at her. 'I want to know everything!'

Celia beckoned him to sit next to her. She turned to her computer screen and brought up his details.

He gazed at the screen and gave a harsh laugh, 'Heart and lungs, kidney, left hand, both feet, pelvic bone. And I've got through two brains!'

He turned to the others. 'I'm almost a Lab myself! How many others are like me?'

'We have no report of any other donor experiencing such memories, so far,' Abel told him.

'Oh God! This is awful!' he cried. 'All those … people … just created so their body parts can be used for … people like me!'

He looked around the room, 'This can't go on! We must stop it! Get this place closed down! Right now!'

Keith nodded, 'We were hoping you would support us when you learnt of the true work of the Centre.'

'And that you would help us to achieve this,' Sakura added.

'I will, God help me, I will!' Simon said fervently. 'Tell me how I can help!'

A week later Simon sat with his parents in the family lounge in the White House.

'Do we have to talk about this right now, Simon?' his mother asked him. 'Your father has only just come home after a gruelling two months! Can't it wait?'

'No, Mom. I'm afraid this can't wait!' he replied. 'I've got some news for you. Some rather shocking news!'

He told them of his trip to the Centre and how he had recognised the room where he, or rather, his Lab, had been. His mother was sobbing quietly and his father was grim faced as he drew to the end of his account.

'So you see, Mom,' he gave a short laugh and spread his arms, 'not all of me is what you gave birth to twenty-one years ago!'

His father shook his head. 'So you have memories that belong to this … other character?' he said slowly.

'The only vivid ones are the ones from inside the Centre, just before the operation. But I find that I can do things, or I know things, that I should have no knowledge of. For example …' he walked over to the piano and played the start of a popular song. 'My Lab was given pretty good musical knowledge during his development, but I only had about half a dozen piano lessons when I was nine, didn't I? Also, I discovered that I know a lot about European history; things I definitely didn't study at school. I thought it was a bit strange, but I assumed I'd picked up some facts from the TV or something.'

'This girl …?' his mother began.

'Sakura? Yes, she is also a Lab,' he told her. 'All the people I met are, except for two Non-Labs, humans that is. But the Labs living free lives at the moment are not revealing their true identities yet. They will decide when they are ready to do so.'

'And you went to the Centre, alone, with these strange people?' his mother clutched his arm. 'My God, what were you thinking of?'

'Mom! You are missing the point entirely! They are cloned humans created as spare parts for wealthy people! People like us!' Simon cried.

'Look, son,' his father began, 'if this is true –'

'There is no *if*, Dad! It is true! I *saw* them! Sleeping in capsules. Rooms full of them!' Simon interrupted. He looked at his father. 'It is essential that you get involved, Dad. And not just here in the US, but all the countries who have subscribed to the Centre. The Centre must be closed down immediately, and the Labs set free!'

'Why don't these … Labs … just walk free?' his mother asked. 'Why does your father, or you, for that matter, have to get involved?'

Simon recounted the background Abel, Celia, and the others had told him.

'So we need to approach this problem carefully so no one is put in danger, including the developing Labs.'

The President sat silently, fingertips placed together. Finally he looked up.

'I need to make some phone calls. And book a flight to London as soon as possible,' he looked at Simon. 'Get in touch with the leaders of these … Labs. I'll need them to accompany me.'

'And me, of course!' Simon said.

'No, son. I don't want you going back to the Centre. I'll take it from here,' his father said.

CHAPTER FIFTEEN

'We're always pleased to see you here, Mr Armstrong,' Sir Philip said as he shook his hand. 'I'm delighted it's not to arrange medical treatment for your son this time! He's been quite a popular patient here over the years! This time you want a guided tour of the Centre? Though let me assure you, when the planned takeover goes ahead, it will not affect any of our present subscribers.'

He turned to Abel and Celia, 'And we have here …?'

'My… mmm … advisors. They both have an informed knowledge of the Centre's background, Sir Philip,' President Armstrong told him. He noticed the puzzled frown as the other man eyed the teenagers. 'Yes, they are young, but as you will find out shortly, they're pretty well informed.'

'Ah! Well, let me introduce our management team: John Baxman, Tony Vittori, Peter McClaren, and Penelope Chiswick,' Sir Philip continued. 'I know you wanted the Head of Social and Medical Department here, too, but unfortunately he had an important prior engagement that he could not cancel at the last minute.'

'Could I just ask you all, are you fully aware of the nature of the work of the Centre?' the president said.

'Of course!' Penelope said. 'The medical advances we have made in stem cell research mean we are able to treat injuries and illnesses previously deemed fatal.'

Mr Armstrong nodded, 'That's part of the Centre's manifesto, yes. But at what price?'

'Oh, you haven't been listening to the gossip about how we should consider the feelings of the cells we use, are you?' Baxman sighed in exasperation. 'Our meeting with the American company, Medicfrontier, is taking place in three days! We just don't have time for this now!'

'I'm afraid the takeover is not going to go ahead, Mr Baxman,' the president said softly.

'But ...? What ...? You can't be serious! It's a multi-billion-dollar deal! We've been talking about this for months now! Don't be taken in by those "hug a cell" crackpot ideas! We're not going to throw this chance away, I won't let that happen!' Baxman spluttered.

'Calm down, John. I think we had better let the president explain himself, before we decide if the takeover will go ahead or not,' Tony said tersely. He looked at Mr Armstrong.

'Dr Miranda Cheung, the founder of this Centre, was a strong supporter of the good work done here initially. But we do know that before her tragic death she had raised issues with the moral ethics of creating near-human products to be used in the experiments carried out here.'

'How do *you* know what Dr Cheung was concerned about?' Sir Philip asked him.

The president turned to Abel, who cleared his throat. 'Some of us were closely involved with Dr Cheung. She was about to demonstrate that these, as you put it, "near-human products" are capable of living independently away from the Centre.'

'You mean the research items in the capsules in the Mature Ward?' Peter asked.

'Yes, that's what they are! Items. Spare parts. Not human beings!' John Baxman spat out.

Penelope shifted uncomfortably. 'But we were always told that they were nothing more than a complicated bundle of cells. Designed in human form …'

'Exactly!' Baxman fixed his eyes on Mr Armstrong. 'How can you possibly be taken in by these … fictional flights of fancy?'

Abel pulled up his sleeve.

'Welcome to my world,' he said softly, peeling off the plastic strip to reveal the code on his inner wrist.

'You are a … a …? Oh my God!' Peter struggled to his feet, knocking the chair over backwards as he did so.

The others sat open-mouthed.

'Pull yourself together, Peter!' Baxman muttered.

'Yes, I am one of the "spare parts" you create here in the Centre. There are many of us who have been freed over the years.'

'There were rumours of some of the mature SPs going missing. Something to do with a Russian company trying to find out more about our work...' Peter began.

'All rumours, nothing else!' Baxman gave a harsh laugh. 'We hear dozens of those stories! And this is another story! Well done! You certainly got some of us going for a minute. Neat tattoo there!'

'This is not a story that is going to go away! You cannot silence my kind anymore!' Abel's voice was rising.

'Let's all remain calm. Shall we take a tour of the Mature Ward? One of the Labs has been readied for awakening,' Celia looked around the table and then held Abel's gaze. His shoulders were trembling.

'How the devil did you get into the Wards?' Baxman glowered. 'There are serious breaches of security here, Sir Philip!'

The team made their way to the ward silently apart from occasional mutterings from Baxman.

Penelope and Peter moved closer together as they entered the ward dimly lit with an orange light. There was only the gentle background hum of machinery as they stopped in front of one of the capsules where a man in a white coat stood waiting.

'Stand back, please. We don't usually have so many people around when we awaken a Lab,' he told them. He nodded to Celia who turned a dial on the display at the top of the capsule. He waited a moment until the occupant began to stir, then he gently raised the lid.

'Time to wake up!' Celia whispered softly as a young woman uncurled herself and stepped out of the capsule. She wore the simple white uniform that emphasised her strong slender arms and legs. She pushed her long black hair away from her face and looked around her. Celia took her hand and smiled, 'Ready for a little walk, Gen?'

The woman nodded and looked around bemused. 'I am Gen?'

'Yes,' Celia showed her the code tattooed on her wrist. She pushed up her sleeve to reveal her own wrist, 'And I am Sel.'

There was a stunned silence as the two walked away slowly around the ward, Gen occasionally stopping to ask Celia a question.

The president was the first to speak. 'Perhaps we had better adjourn to the committee room?'

'I was just about to say that myself,' Sir Philip nodded.

Peter gestured vaguely around the room, 'But … all these capsules … are they all capable of … coming to life?'

'They are *already* alive,' Abel pointed out. He looked at the faces of the others; Penelope was clinging to Peter's arm; Tony was looking confused. Only John Baxman was staring stonily ahead.

Back in the committee room, there was a long silence. Celia gave out cups of coffee to each of the other people, as they did not seem capable of doing this simple task themselves.

'How can this have been happening? How did things go so far?' Peter shook his head.

'But, don't forget – we are saving lives! Enabling injured and disabled people to have a better standard of life! Let's not forget the Centre's good work!' Baxman pointed out. 'Look at your own son, Mr President – he would not have survived his last three accidents without the Centre's intervention!'

'Yes, for those who could afford it, we have done a great deal of good work,' Sir Philip agreed.

'And at what price to the Labs?' Abel added.

'Labs?' Tony asked.

'You called us "SPs", or Spare Parts, a term we found unpalatable,' Abel said with a frown. 'We renamed ourselves Labs – those created in your laboratory – as opposed to your kind, Non-Labs – those created by normal human reproduction.'

'Where do we go from here?' Penelope shook her head, still feeling dazed.

'Well, obviously the American deal cannot go through,' Tony said.

'That's right. The Centre will be closed, immediately!' the president said.

'Well if it must, we better do it with least amount of publicity. Make the best of the situation!' Baxman looked at Sir Philip. 'We'll need to get our lawyers on to it immediately.'

'What about all the … Labs … in the Centre?' Penelope asked.

'Turn off all the equipment before anything else

wakes up, I say!' Baxman had just put his coffee cup down on the table when Abel flew across the room and landed a punch squarely on his nose.

Simon was back at the Labs' house that evening. All were watching the television.

'I thought the Centre would be on the news tonight,' Leon commented.

'Just a brief account of the American deal falling through, but no mention of why,' Johnny said.

'I can't get through to my father!' Simon looked at his phone, frustrated.

'It's a complicated situation. Celia has just phoned,' Keith told them, coming into the room. 'They've only just left the meeting. The lawyers and the government are already involved. And one of the committee members has somehow ended up in hospital with a broken nose!'

'Abel's doing, I suppose!' Johnny said as Leon shrugged.

'Celia said there are many difficulties ahead. The first one is finding a place for the Labs still in the Centre to live,' Keith continued.

'What other problems are there? Why hasn't the story been made public yet? Why aren't the Labs free?' Simon asked him.

'Celia didn't have time to go into everything on the phone. She'll fill us in on the details later,' he paused. 'She's going to stay at the Centre for the moment. Both she and Abel feel it would be in our best interests, and those of all previously freed Labs, to continue under our present IDs until the future of the Labs is clear.'

It wasn't until the following week that Celia and Abel visited the house, late one evening.

Dette hugged them both. 'We've been so worried about you!' she cried.

Abel smiled and patted her arm. His face looked pale and drawn. 'We knew things would take time, but there are so many issues that we hadn't thought of.'

They settled themselves down in the lounge.

'Well?' Keith looked at Abel.

'Where do we start?' Celia shook her head. 'The first problem we had was that the Labs are considered minors as we are awakened at the human age of sixteen – that is documented on the Centre medical records – so Valerie has agreed to be our official guardian, along with the lawyer appointed for us, Declan O'Brien. Our demands have to go through them.'

Abel sighed. 'We have insisted that accommodation for the Labs still in capsules at the Centre is completed as soon as possible; so a compound of prefabricated housing is being erected in the grounds.' He looked at Celia. 'We've insisted on good standards of accommodation and facilities for the Labs who'll live there initially. Mark and Valerie have arranged a team of Labs and Non-Labs to care for the Labs in the Nursery Ward until they reach maturity, and then they too will be freed.'

‘What about those in the Caves?’ Keith asked him.

‘They will join the newly freed Labs in the Compound. It’s better that you and all the Labs already living outside do not reveal your true identities at the moment. There are so many legal issues to be dealt with. We now have several lawyers involved – and the government, too, of course!’

‘Why hasn’t the whole story been made public yet?’ Johnny asked him.

‘As one of the committee members said, “we have opened a huge can of worms!” O’Brien has prioritised establishing us as a race. That’ll give us a much stronger standing. The lawyers representing the subscribers have two main issues: whether they have any rights to ownership of the Labs they funded to be created, and also whether they are entitled to compensation and a refund of the fees they have already paid. The government is hoping to resolve some of these issues before making things public.’ Abel sighed, ‘Also as leader of the Labs, I’m to stand charges of breaking and entering, and kidnapping. Oh, and I am also personally accused of causing actual bodily harm to John Baxman. But the big question is, are we going to be accepted by society? Or be the freak show of the decade?’ Abel spread his hands

Leon let out a long whistle.

‘Is there anything we can do to help?’ Ruby asked him.

He gave her a brief smile, ‘All we can ask you,

Ruby and Simon, is to continue to support us Labs as you have done up till now! We're going to need all the Non-Lab friends we can get!'

Keith gave him a grin. 'Finally, Abel! You are beginning to appreciate the help our Non-Labs friends can give us!'

Abel shrugged.

A week later the story was finally released to the public. International television stations and newspapers were buzzing.

Celia read the article that appeared in a national newspaper:

DARK SECRETS OF THE CENTRE REVEALED!

Over the past week, the residents of Hambleton and other small towns near to the Advancement of Medical Technology Centre have watched as over a hundred prefabricated buildings were delivered to the site. Yesterday, the arrival of one hundred military personnel aroused further curiosity.

Two weeks ago the takeover bid of the Centre by the American company Medicfrontier was unexpectedly called off at the eleventh hour.

We are finally able to reveal the truth behind the scenes. A story that sounds more like science fiction than real life in this sleepy English town.'

The article went on to give details of the secret medical advancements that had been developed at the Centre. It also included comments by government officials.

Celia quickly read through the article in the *Times* and phoned Keith.

'So it's finally out in the open,' he said. 'Isaac just phoned to tell us that they're holding a press conference at ten o'clock at the Centre, to be shown live on BBC One. The Prime Minister, Sir Philip, and Abel will be answering questions.'

Keith, the twins, and Ruby were in front of the television at one o'clock.

The Prime Minister was asked how medical developments had got this far without any questions being asked.

'Well, the government was given to believe advanced stem cell research was taking place here. We were not informed at any stage that whole organs, never mind complete human-type bodies, had been created.'

'It beggars belief that this research continued to such a level!' a woman said. She turned to Sir Philip, 'Did no one raise any objections to the extent the research had progressed?'

'Dr Miranda Cheung did, two years ago!' Abel said.

'But, unfortunately, Dr Cheung died in a tragic accident before she was able to give us detailed information about her fears,' Sir Philip quickly countered. 'Now we have been made fully aware of the extent of the medical developments here, we are working together to deal with this situation as best we can. The government and Abel, as leader of the, erm, Labs, have our full cooperation.'

'The Labs?' a young reporter called out. Abel explained the origin of the term.

'How do you see life for the … Labs … in the future?' another reporter asked.

'We would like to integrate fully with the Non-Lab world,' Abel said. 'Live alongside you, as equals.'

'How many Labs are there?' another reporter asked.

'There are over five hundred at the Centre who will live in the new compound being built for them on the Centre's land. Not all have reached maturity yet, though, so they will be moved out gradually,' Abel told him.

'How will this all be funded?' a woman asked.

'Completely by the Centre,' Sir Philip answered.

'What makes Labs different from us humans? Have you got any special powers?' the same reporter asked.

Abel shook his head. 'No; though we are programmed to develop to a greater level of fitness and strength. We do need to follow a strict exercise regime to maintain this level once we leave the capsules, as your people do. Our intellectual development has also been programmed during our formative years.'

They spent the next hour answering questions

before Sir Philip stood up and signalled the end of the interview.

'What about the donors of the stem cells? What rights do they have?' a reporter called out.

'We are, at present, holding talks with the subscribers and their lawyers,' Sir Philip answered. 'Now I'm afraid I must close this conference. A government-appointed team is to make a tour of the new compound for the newly freed Labs. They will make their findings and observations public within a few days. Thank you, ladies and gentlemen!'

Keith switched off the television and looked around at the others.

'Abel was right. This is just the beginning of the story!'

'They weren't too critical of the Labs, were they?' Johnny said.

'Yes, they were more critical of the Centre staff,' his brother added.

'Isaac told me that several of the subscribers are arriving for talks with the Centre staff and the government officials tomorrow!' Ruby told them. 'His uncle said it's all hush-hush at the moment!'

'Abel is pushing our lawyers to establish the Labs as a race as soon as possible. Amnesty International has said we have a strong case,' Keith said. 'They think that our demands for equal rights with Non-Labs should be met.'

'Celia has arranged for me to work with the newly freed Labs on the Compound. They will need some help fitting in with Non-Lab life, just like you did,'

Ruby said. 'I'll still be going to college part-time but I'll have accommodation at the Centre; we don't want anyone connecting me with you yet.'

'We'll miss you, Ruby!' Johnny said.

'Yes,' Leon agreed. 'First we lose Celia and now you!'

'We'll be able to meet up some evenings and weekends!' Ruby told them.

'You'll be working *alongside* Abel!' Johnny pointed out.

'Yes, I'll need a break every now and again!' Ruby said, only half joking.

Meanwhile, at the Centre, Celia was searching through files on the computer. She clicked her tongue in frustration as she twice came up against 'Access Denied' screens. Her brow furrowed as she once again keyed in a password, and her face lit up as the screen changed to show a list of data. She pulled a memory stick out of her pocket and quickly copied some of the information onto it. As she heard voices nearing the room, she pulled the memory stick out and pushed it into her pocket, closing the programme in front of her. She had opened a different file as two people entered the office.

'Hi, Mark, Valerie,' she swung her chair round. 'I was just taking a look at the organisation of the Centre's data. The man from the MoD seemed to think that splitting the data into three sections, interdependent on each other, would be the best way to safeguard it from future misuse.'

'Leave that to them to sort out, Celia,' Valerie replied. 'You've enough to worry about for the moment organising the new compound.'

As the three of them sat and discussed arrangements for the next few days, Celia fingered the memory stick in her pocket.

CHAPTER SIXTEEN

'Is this *all* we are to expect?' he walked briskly, hands plunged into his pockets. She struggled to keep up with him.

'But Abel is asking for equal rights for us, the same as the Non-Labs!'

'And we are all to sit quietly, waiting to see if they are going to be gracious enough to grant us our rights! Grateful for any crumbs they toss our way. Existing as second-class citizens.' The youth stopped and stood looking angrily at the ground. Slowly he raised his head. 'No! That's not good enough for me! No substandard race is going to treat *me* like this!'

The girl, who was about his age, looked less sure of herself. 'What are you going to do about it?'

'I am going to show them who *is* superior!'

He started to walk again. She stood for a moment, then hurried to his side.

'How are you going to do that?'

He walked on in silence for a while, then stopped and faced her again.

'The Centre. It wasn't *all* bad, you know.'

'They were creating us Labs as spare parts for their own people!' she protested.

He nodded slowly. 'Yes, but they were able to create beings of a much higher standard than their own flawed species! Think of the Centre as the springboard for a future, perfect race! Don't you want to be part of the new world?'

CHAPTER SEVENTEEN

'Thank you for attending this meeting at such short notice,' Sir Philip nodded to the people sat around the large oval table in the Centre's conference rooms.

'Well, we are all greatly shocked by this news!' the oldest of the men said.

'Stunned!' echoed another to a chorus of murmurs.

'Surely we aren't the only subscribers?' asked one woman, looking around the table.

'No. There are too many to bring together for one meeting. This is the first meeting of subscribers and lawyers in the UK. Similar ones are being arranged in other countries that have subscribers involved with the Centre,' Sir Philip told them. 'Now, I'm sure you will have many questions for us.'

'I would like to speak on behalf of the subscribers that I have been asked to represent,' a silver-haired man stood up. 'First of all, why were my clients not informed of the true nature of the operations carried out at the Centre? They were all led to believe that your research enabled replacement organs for themselves and/or their children, but nothing more than that.'

John Baxman stood up. 'Before each operation, patients, or the patient's parents in the case of a minor, were given a brief outline of what their operation would involve. Until recently, the human cell … products … we used were simply seen as being just that, products of our research, an extension of a group of cells. When we were made aware of their unexpected advanced level of development, we immediately called a halt to all operations.'

'And suspended all stem cell development until further notice,' Sir Philip added.

There was a moment's silence and then the older male subscriber spoke up again.

'So, what we have now are clones of ourselves, or our children, walking freely around?'

'And these clones are campaigning for their own rights as citizens?' another man said.

'I believe they are actually campaigning to be recognised as a race,' the lawyer told them.

'A race that we have unwittingly paid millions of pounds to produce!' a woman added.

'God! Wouldn't it be creepy to suddenly come upon an exact copy of yourself walking along the street?' a younger woman shuddered.

'I think it would be really cool to meet *me*, face to face, in the flesh!' A British pop star stood up. 'Hey, we could perform together at my next concert! Me and my clone! Hey, yeah! Mirror images!' He began to play an imaginary guitar.

'We're not talking about some gimmicky trick!' Baxman said tersely.

The pop star threw up his hands. 'OK! I know – clones are for life, not just for Christmas!'

His wife sighed and pulled him back down into his seat. 'Can't you *ever* take anything seriously, Zorro?'

Everyone's attention was pulled back by the sob of a middle-aged woman.

'My husband and I paid millions of pounds to save our daughter, who is suffering from a rare, inoperable brain tumour. And now you are telling me we can't save her? But there will be an exact copy of her walking around when she … if she …?' She broke down in tears.

'Hey, come on, love. Let's not be too pessimistic here. I'm sure there will be something they can do.With the latest medical advancements …' Her husband tried to comfort her. 'They've only *suspended* stem cell research. The Centre owes us at least *some* help. After all, they did take our money!'

'Yes, that's another thing. What about the money we invested? Will we be refunded fully?' the older man asked.

'Hey! We invested because we all have money to spare!' Zorro pointed out. 'I, for one, would like to be involved in the future of the clones. Labs, they call themselves, don't they? We saw some of them on the TV the other week, didn't we, honey?'

'Yeah! You're right, Zorro, baby! They do need our help, we owe it to them! You're all heart under that tough veneer, baby boy!' His wife leaned forwards and kissed him loudly.

Several of the other people tutted impatiently.

'Well, I think Zorro is right about the Labs needing as much support as they can get,' the young woman said. 'We subscribers are innocent in all this. But so are the Labs!'

CHAPTER EIGHTEEN

Vincent Craig watched the photographs playing on his computer screen.

There she was, smiling up at the camera. Teeth white against shiny black skin; little pigtails sticking out at angles from her head. He remembered the outfit she was wearing, red shorts and a matching T-shirt with a picture of a puppy on the front. How she'd loved that outfit! They had always promised that one day, when she was bigger, she'd have her own real puppy.

He sighed deeply, for that day had never come. Even though they had spent a fortune on ensuring a long and happy life for Marissa, the car crash that had left him in a wheelchair had ended her short life. All the money they had spent on stem cell research at the Centre in England had been no use. She had died instantly on impact. She wouldn't have felt any pain, the doctors had told him and her mother. But they had lived with the pain every day. He had never been able to move on. Vanessa, Marissa's mother, had recovered from her injuries over the years. She had tried to make him think of the future, and had even suggested that they try for another baby, as they had planned when Marissa was alive. Her words had fallen on deaf ears. Finally, she had left him and was now married for the second time, with two boys. She'd kept in touch with him, occasionally phoning, and there was always a Christmas card and a birthday card from her.

He watched as several other pictures played across the screen, then paused another one. This one was of Vanessa and Marissa on her fourth birthday; her last one. He looked carefully at Vanessa. She was a good-looking woman, smooth dark skin, large oval brown eyes. Her hair was braided into narrow plaits, with beads threaded into the end of each one. He had always laughed when she groaned about the time it took to have it done at the hairdresser.

'So, why do you put yourself through it?' he had asked her.

'Men!' she had shook her head. 'You just don't understand, do you?'

Vincent hadn't been surprised to hear her voice on the phone a few weeks ago, when the news about the Centre in England had been made public.

'Just wondered if you were OK, Vince,' she had said. 'With the Centre in the news so much at the moment.'

'Do you think there's a possibility that Marissa's … cells … were not destroyed?' he had asked her.

'We did request that they were. And cancelled our subscription, when … when we lost Marissa,' she had replied. 'Why would they keep them?'

'I don't know. They seem to have done lots of

things you wouldn't expect them to.'

'I doubt it, Vince. I keep telling you, you must let yourself move on! Anyway, how are you keeping these days? What are your summer plans? You know you're always welcome to drop by here anytime you want to, if you're over visiting your sister,' she continued. 'Bill and the boys would love to meet you.'

'I'm pretty busy at the moment, Vanessa, I don't think I'll be going anywhere for the next few months.'

'You work too hard, Vince! Relax sometimes!' she had laughed.

Vincent looked at the picture of Marissa and her mother again, then shut down the computer and determinedly turned his mind back to his work.

CHAPTER NINETEEN

Two Months Later

Ruby stepped down from the bus at a stop near the Centre. She smiled as she turned off the main road and began to walk towards the main entrance. Though she loved working with the Labs, she had enjoyed spending the weekend with Keith, Dette, and the twins.

They had spent the afternoon watching the twins play in a friendly match with the local football team. They had been singled out when they had played for the college team a few weeks earlier. Now there were talks of them playing for Castlewell Rovers. Their college tutor was very excited.

'You boys have the makings of stars, and I mean big time!' he enthused. 'Though it's a great team, Castlewell Rovers isn't going to be able to hold you for long, not when the bigger clubs see what you can do!'

There was an air of great excitement when Celia had joined them on Saturday evening. Keith also had news to tell the others. He talked eagerly of an idea he had proposed.

'I have spoken to Jade, Sakura, and Miyu, and some other Labs gifted in music, with the idea of holding a concert to raise public awareness of the Labs,' Keith said. 'Simon is also eager to help and is going to contact talented Non-Labs to perform. Each musician will perform, without admitting to being Lab or Non-Lab. Hopefully we can promote the things we have in common rather than the differences between us.'

'That's a great idea, Keith!' Ruby said. 'Isaac could see if his uncle has contacts with celebrities who want to perform!'

'We have already started rehearsals at Manchester University. I worked with the university sound technician. He said I was a natural!' Keith smiled. 'And he asked me to work with him on the night!'

Keith had described the different equipment they had used and the various effects they were aiming for. Ruby hadn't understood much, but she was pleased to see him so animated. Another Lab working alongside a Non-Lab happily – there was hope for the future!

Ruby's good mood continued as she walked towards the entrance and noticed there were no reporters hanging around.

Suddenly, a group of teenage boys appeared from nowhere, walking along the road towards her.

'Told you there wouldn't be a way in!' one of them muttered.

'We could have found one! You give up too easily!' another muttered.

'Yeah! You're scared you're going to bump into one of them freaks!' the third jeered.

Ruby stopped in front of them. 'They're not freaks!' she said angrily.

'Yeah?' the second boy stepped up to her. 'And how would you know?'

'Maybe she's a freak herself!' The third boy's eyes narrowed.

The first boy grabbed her arm. 'Let's find out, shall we?'

Ruby swung her free arm and sent him flying backwards. 'Get your hands off me!'

Another of them grabbed her from behind, pinning her arms to her sides. She stamped hard on his foot.

The first boy, recovering his breath, put his face close to hers. 'That was a mistake!'

As he grabbed her hair, a shout was heard. Ruby breathed a sigh of relief as she recognised Abel's voice.

'Let her go, *now*!' he ordered.

'She's only one of them freaks! Why should you care?' the boy muttered, releasing his grip slowly.

'Let's go, Steve!' one of the others muttered.

By this time Abel stood in front of them.

'That's right, Steve! You'd better go! *She's* not one of *those freaks*,' he stood up tall and menacing. 'But *I* am!'

Two of the boys had started to back off. Steve slowly put his hands down and started to follow his friends.

'Watch your back!' he hissed at Ruby as he left.

Abel grabbed Steve's arm and pulled him around

to face him, 'No! *You* watch *your* back! If any harm comes to her, or to *any* of my friends, you'll have *me* to deal with!'

Steve winced and rubbed his arm as Abel released it. He scurried after his friends.

'Thank you!' Ruby said.

'That was foolish, Ruby,' Abel said. 'You're no match for three youths!'

'I know, but I just couldn't listen to them calling Labs freaks! I hate it!' she said stubbornly.

They both watched as a long back car with tinted windows drove past and turned into the Centre gates.

Abel nodded in the direction of the car, 'Another meeting with the Lab lawyers! Just when I think we have everything sorted, someone comes up with another impossible loophole and we seem to go back to square one again!'

Ruby squeezed his arm. 'I'm sure everything will work out in the end, Abel.'

He was silent. Ruby was suddenly aware of his eyes on her hand and quickly released his arm.

'I'd better get a move on!' she said and began to walk towards the Centre entrance. She stopped as Abel called her name.

'You're a loyal friend to the Labs. That's why you may find yourself in similar situations, targeted by Non-Lab thugs like those ones. You have to learn to defend yourself. I'll teach you. Starting tomorrow.'

Surprised, Ruby merely nodded before setting off for the first of many identical prefabs. The newly awakened Labs were happy with their living arrangements, quickly settling into their new surroundings and all eager to learn more. This one was the home of Jill, a lively girl with an American accent, and Beth, a gentle, quiet girl with a Scottish lilt to her voice.

After greeting her, Jill told her that they had been given a present by a well-known pop star. The three girls set out for the Hall, which was used as a study area at one end, equipped with computers and a dance and gym area at the other. As they entered, a girl was playing a baby grand piano while her twin performed elegant ballet steps nearby. A handwritten card was propped up on the piano:

> *To all our new friends, especially the musical ones! Play and enjoy! X*
> *Zorro*

Ruby read it and smiled to herself. She had heard of his positive attitude towards the Labs from Abel. She sat in the office describing some of the events of the day to Celia later that morning.

'Most of the houses are pretty much organised now. Some of the Labs have been talking about venturing beyond the Compound. I said we could discuss the different situations they might find themselves in – shopping, going to the cinema, sightseeing. But this time I won't be showing students with their true identities hidden around, will I?' She looked at Celia. 'I'm afraid of what the reaction to Labs in a Non-Lab world will be.'

'As we all are, Ruby! I think we have to see what the next few weeks will bring. Our lawyer has drawn up a convincing argument to put forward for the Labs at the court case tomorrow. Let's hope Abel manages to sit quietly in court,' Celia told her. 'He can still be so volatile!'

'He's had more self-control and a more positive outlook lately, Celia,' Ruby ventured. 'And I'm sure he'll listen to O'Brien's advice.'

Celia shrugged. 'I hope so.'

'Thank goodness the court case went well, Abel!' Dette hugged him the following evening.

'So, tell us what happened!' Johnny urged him as Leon nodded his head eagerly.

'O'Brien, our lawyer, presented our defence very well. He insisted that the Labs could not be charged with either breaking and entering or kidnapping as it was clear that what we were doing was rescuing our own kind from certain death. Wexford, the Centre's lawyer, refused to accept this and said we should have presented our claims through legal channels. O'Brien argued that as we had no legal standing we did not feel we were in a position to be taken seriously by officials. And the judge ruled in our favour!'

'Thank goodness!' said Ruby.

'What about your charge, Abel? Of ABH against Baxman?' Celia asked him.

'I'm to be tried for that at a separate hearing,' his face took on a sullen expression. 'O'Brien wants me to apologise to Baxman for my actions, but there is no way I'm apologising to him! Except to say I'm sorry I didn't hit him harder!'

Celia looked worried. 'Abel, don't forget you're standing for all the Labs when you stand up in court.'

He patted her shoulder. 'Don't worry, Celia. I understand that. I won't let the Labs down.'

She smiled. 'Let's hope we can move on now.'

'We still have a lot of work to do!' Abel reminded her. 'We must arrange a meeting as soon as possible to set out our demands of the Prime Minister. Dermot O'Brien is good, but he is not a Lab!'

Later that week, Abel introduced the lawyer to the others.

'Dermot O'Brien, this is Keith, Celia, and Dette – Labs – and Ruby – Non-Lab.'

O'Brien shook hands with each of them then sat down and opened his briefcase, 'Let's look at your demands first and prioritise them.'

'First of all, we want to be recognised as a race,' Abel said. 'This will put us in a stronger position to tackle any prejudice as we will be protected by law against racial discrimination. Secondly, we want to have dual nationality – British, as we were created here, and the nationality of our donor. If they meet these demands we will be able to claim our ordinary human rights.'

'The definition of "race" is not clear and is frequently disputed,' the lawyer told them, picking up a paper. 'Race can be classified by geographic origin, or people can be defined by their physical attributes. Neither of these is relevant to your case.'

'So we will need new criteria to classify Labs,' Keith pointed out. 'That may well help with the definition of "race".'

'Under the present law Labs do not qualify for British nationality as they do not have parents born in the UK. They do not have parents at all! I assume the same problems would arise with the dual nationality request,' Celia said.

'We need to have proposals to deal with these problems ready to present to the Prime Minister next week, or else we will be faced with an even longer delay,' the lawyer pointed out.

'There have already been enough delays!' Abel said.

'I suggest first of all we define a "Lab",' the lawyer said. 'Then consider how Labs can be classified as a "race". We must put forward a clear argument on why Labs are entitled to British nationality, and finally dual nationality.'

'Labs are new, so we will need some new ideas!' Dette remarked.

'I'll go and get some more coffee and sandwiches,' Ruby offered. 'I think this is going to be a long session!'

The following morning the Prime Minister picked up the sheaf of papers handed to him by O'Brien.

'*The Labs are to be recognised as a "race"*. This is under consideration at the moment, I assure you. Mr

O'Brien –'

'Yes, Abel has told me that this is so, but there seems to be some delay, due to the fact that the Labs are not actually defined as a particular group. We have made a suggestion, if you refer to the second sheet, Mr Cartwright …' the lawyer replied.

'A Lab is to be defined as a human who has been created under laboratory conditions through the process of cloning cells. A Lab must be able to exist independently after a period of maturing.' The Prime Minister nodded his head after reading and then turned back to the page.

'As a race, the Labs will have access to all rights of other human races and will have recourse to law if these rights are not upheld. The Labs will be expected to uphold all human responsibilities, and to respect the rights of all races, including other Labs, following the laws of their chosen domicile.

All Labs are to have automatic right to citizenship of the country where they are created.

All Labs with donors from a country other than the country of their creation will have the right to nationality of that country, in some cases holding dual nationality.'

Mr Cartwright looked up at O'Brien. 'I can see the reasoning behind these proposals. But of course, as you will be aware, we must consider each point carefully. The last point will involve discussions with other countries.'

'We are aware of this, Mr Cartwright, but I must

also point out that continued delays are having an adverse effect on the integration of Labs into British society – where they were unwittingly created,' O'Brien replied. 'If we could at least resolve the first issues, the Labs would feel more confident of their own standing – certainly in this country. As Simon Armstrong, the US president's son, pointed out only last week, we do not want a repeat of the apartheid situation in Africa or the bloody battles that had to be fought for African-Americans to gain equality before the Labs are awarded their rights.'

'Oh, no, no, of course not!' the Prime Minister answered quickly. 'I can assure you, and the president, that the situation of the Labs is a priority for the British government at the moment!'

He sighed and shook his head, holding out a document to O'Brien. 'I have to tell you that as well as considering the demands of the Labs, lawyers representing some of the subscribers have also made claims about their DNA being, as you yourself pointed out, unwittingly used, and their rights and responsibilities in this scenario. Especially towards Labs still in the Nursery Ward.'

O'Brien drew a deep breath. 'I don't think Abel or any of the other Labs are going to be happy with this. Some donors are claiming they should have parental rights over the younger Labs.' He looked at the older man. 'And how do we establish the ages of *any* of the Labs?'

Abel told Celia, Ruby, and Dette of the latest

developments that evening.

'The Labs must stay together, surely,' Dette said, 'Until they are mature enough to make a decision to join their donor families if both parties are willing. Isn't that what was initially decided?'

Celia sat up straight. 'I agree with you. We must stop these demands as quickly as possible.'

'How do we do that?' Ruby asked her.

'With threats! If they want to make claims to the Labs in the Nursery Wards we will make counter-claims against every donor!'

Abel smiled. 'I think you have something there, Celia. If all the Labs make claims on their donors, we could find many Labs will be heirs to great fortunes! And we all mature at a much greater speed than Non-Labs. Some siblings may feel pushed out of their rightful places! I'll phone O'Brien immediately.'

'What if I take a small group of Labs on a day trip to London?' Ruby said to Celia a couple of days later. 'Some of them are complaining about having to remain in the Compound all the time. We don't need to tell anyone who we are. I could ask Isaac to come with us. Then, maybe after a few trips, he could write an article for the *Times*,' she continued. 'Demonstrate how we can all integrate easily.'

'That's a good idea, Ruby. It would be an excellent way to introduce the Labs to the Non-Lab world. If you have Isaac with you, you should be OK,' Celia agreed.

A few days after that, four of the Labs from the

Compound set off with Ruby for the local railway station.

'Isaac will meet us at the tube station in London,' Ruby told them.

Geoff and Peter, twins with an English subscriber, were anxious to visit the Science Museum.

'We can all take a look round there first, then Beth and Jill can choose the next place to visit,' Ruby suggested.

One of the Centre guards had walked with them until they were near the station, then turned back. They were just about to enter the station when Ruby groaned. Leaning against the station entrance were Steve and his friends. A mean grin spread across his face when he saw her.

'Look who it is! Little Miss Do-Gooder and her freak show! Without her hard-nut freaky friend!' He pulled himself upright, barring their way.

'Just ignore them!' Ruby whispered, trying to keep her voice even.

One of Steve's friends was staring at Beth. She blushed and looked down.

'Hey, come on, Steve! Let them past,' he said.

Steve swung around to him, 'Did you hear that, Callum? Frank's a freak fancier!'

'Come on, they're just like us. Leave them alone!' Frank repeated.

'Like us? Let's take a look, shall we?' Steve stepped forward, putting his hand out towards Beth.

'Lay off, Steve!' Frank pulled Beth back out of reach and stood in front of her.

Ruby held up her mobile phone. 'My friend's just a phone call away! He's waiting for us on the platform at this moment!'

'You're lying!' Steve said, but he sounded unsure.

Callum looked nervously about as Ruby raised her eyebrows and started to punch in numbers. He backed off, holding up his hands. 'I'm out of here, Steve!'

Steve swore and started to follow him. Frank stayed where he was.

'I'm sorry about that,' he said with an apologetic smile to Beth.

'No. You were very kind,' she replied softly.

Ruby told Isaac of the incident as the others looked around the Science Museum later that morning.

'Mmm. I'm afraid it is going to happen. There have been several threats made to MPs who support the Labs,' he grimaced. 'There was a fierce debate on the television the other night for and against the Labs being equal to normal humans!'

'What can we do?' Ruby sighed.

'We can only try to make as much good publicity for the Labs as we can. Keith and his friends' idea for a concert will, hopefully, help. They've got Zorro's backing! He says he can't wait to go on stage with his Lab! They've got a few other big names interested. Several Labs are keen to take part, too. Some of their subscribers are talented musicians.'

'All we need is a famous musician or film star to

adopt a Lab, and we're home and dry!' Ruby quipped.

'Hey! Come on! Let's just enjoy today! Where's next on the agenda?' Isaac said.

They visited the Tower of London and all marvelled at the view from the London Eye. Geoff and his brother found the waxworks at Madame Tussaud's rather disturbing.

'Why would they want to make wax clones of people?' he asked Ruby. 'Can they *do* anything?'

'Or are they for medical purposes?' his brother added.

'No, you just look at them,' Ruby told them.

The two boys exchanged puzzled looks.

It was late when they stood waiting for the train to take them back to Hambleton.

'Are you sure you don't want me to come with you?' Isaac asked Ruby for the second time.

'No, but thanks, Isaac. Abel is going to meet us at the station,' she replied. 'You've been a great help today!'

'I've taken notes, and some great photos!' he replied. 'Let me know when you plan your next trip, won't you? I'll get a good article from this!'

Ruby climbed onto the train behind the others and turned to give him a smile. 'Thanks, Isaac.'

Abel was waiting for them at the station and listened to their excited chatter as they walked back to the Compound.

Ruby noticed a solitary figure walking towards

them on the opposite side of the road who paused and looked across at them. It was Frank. Beth also noticed and gave him a smile as he caught her eye.

Abel and Ruby watched the others head back to their house.

'Today has been such an experience!' Jill said with a sigh.

'It has indeed,' Geoff agreed.

'I hope it's not too long before we can be fully integrated into the outside world,' Pete said.

'I hope so, too!' Ruby nodded.

The next morning Ruby was up early to join Abel for her self-defence lessons. He had been instructing her for a few weeks now and she felt she was getting better. Whenever she could, she practised the latest moves he taught her; partly so she would be able to defend herself if attacked and partly to avoid his silent displeasure if she made any mistakes.

Soon they were going through the steps she had been taught over the past few weeks.

'Quite good, Ruby. I can see you have been practising,' Abel commented.

Ruby blushed with pleasure. 'I practise every morning!'

'Well, let's see if you can defend yourself now!' he said, walking around to face her. He suddenly grabbed her throat and she stepped back, startled.

He released her. 'It's no good learning the moves if you can't apply them, Ruby!' He shook his head.

'But I wasn't ready!' Ruby protested.

'If someone attacks you, you won't always be ready.'

'Try again! A different move!' she insisted.

Abel made a few attempts to catch her out, but each time she was able to break his hold.

'You are certainly improving, Ruby!' he conceded. Then suddenly he moved behind her and pinned her arms to her sides.

'What would you do in this case?' he whispered in her ear.

Ruby felt his warm breath on her neck. She relaxed and hung her head. As he began to release her she swung around and knocked him off balance with two quick moves. He stumbled and fell backwards, pulling her down on top of him.

She looked into his eyes, laughing, 'You didn't see that one coming, oh great teacher!'

'No!' he agreed. 'You fooled me there! I thought you'd given in to me!'

The laughter died on their lips as they looked into each other's eyes.

'Abel!'

They heard Celia's voice moments before she turned the corner. They both sprang to their feet.

'Oh, here you are,' Celia smiled. 'Keith has just been on the phone. They have a date set for the concert. Tickets have been on sale for only an hour and they have already nearly sold out!'

'Oh, that's really good news!' Ruby said. 'I hope they have reserved tickets for us! I'd better go and check how many Labs would like to attend, too.'

'We have reserved tickets for Labs and Non-Labs here at the Centre and Compound,' Celia assured her. She turned to Abel as Ruby left them.

'What progress is she making at self-defence? It still amazes me how slowly Non-Labs acquire new skills!'

'She's making good progress, Celia. She shows determination. She has excellent qualities for a Non-Lab,' he said quietly.

'All praise and no complaints today, Abel? Are you in a good mood to hear about the concert?' Celia said. 'There are so many well-known Non-Labs involved! Simon has got several American performers to participate, and Keith has arranged with Zorro for some of us to attend the backstage party afterwards. This could do so much for our cause!'

As they reached the office, she pulled a piece of paper from her pocket. 'Oh, I nearly forgot! O'Brien asked you to ring him this morning. I hope he's finally got the Prime Minister to agree to our terms!'

'Or it could be about the ABH charge,' Abel groaned. 'I'm still not prepared to apologise to Baxman!'

Later that day, as she was walking on the road towards the Centre, Ruby was dismayed to see a familiar figure heading towards her. She stopped and pulled her phone out of her pocket.

'I can have help here in a minute!'

Frank held up his hands.

'Please! I didn't mean to scare you. I just wanted to talk to you! Just for a moment.'

He stood in front of her and thrust his hands deep into his pockets.

'OK, I'm listening,' she said.

'Look, I'm sorry about my mates. Well … and me, to start with. But, now … I mean … I don't think you're freaks. The Labs, I mean,' he stammered.

'I'm glad to hear that. Frank, isn't it?' She gave him a tentative smile.

'Yeah,' he continued. 'Well, I just wanted you to know. And your friends … the Labs, I mean. I think they're all just regular guys, like us. I won't let anyone say anything against them! I stick up for them now, you know. Anything I can do to help you people, just let me know, OK?'

'Oh, thanks, Frank,' Ruby said. 'We certainly need all the support we can get!'

'Well, you can count on me!' he nodded, walking away from her. 'And your friends, the ones you were with the other day, let them know, won't you?'

'I will, Frank.' Ruby smiled warmly.

CHAPTER TWENTY

Simon's mother had come to London to accompany him to the concert. He joined her for breakfast at her hotel.

'It's a pity your father can't join us, but the talks in the Middle East are continuing longer than they planned,' she said. Her brow furrowed. 'You're still looking so pale, Simon. Are you working too hard or is it just this dreary English weather getting to you?'

'I'm fine, Mom!' he smiled. 'Don't fuss! It's a pity about Dad, but I'm glad you're coming to the concert. It's important to show our support for the Labs. Glen and Bob are coming too.'

'We've got seats in a box! Your father insisted, for security purposes,' his mother told him. 'And the Prime Minister's aide has arranged for us to meet some of the performers after the concert – some real people and some of the Labs,'

'Mom, the Labs are real people too, you know!' he admonished her.

'Have you met many of them?' she asked him.

'Yes, quite a few, through Sakura,' he replied.

'Well, I hope you're making ordinary human friends too, Simon.'

'Mom, there's not much difference at all between Labs and Non-Labs! I see *all* my friends as equal!' he protested. 'And I *totally* agree with their demands for equal rights.'

'So do I, darling. Though I'm glad all this is happening here in England and not in the US! It's a real headache for the British government, isn't it? I'm glad your father hasn't got all this to deal with. He has enough on his plate as it is!' she continued. 'Will we have time for a shopping trip before the concert this evening? Your grandmother wants some of her favourite chocolates from Harrods. And I would like an hour to visit that little boutique off Bond Street. I'll need a few new outfits for the end of next month when I accompany your father to Australia.'

When they arrived at the theatre for the concert that evening Mrs Armstrong was amazed at the crowds gathered outside.

'Well, I must admit, I never expected such a turnout!' she exclaimed.

'Zorro's really brought in the crowds!' Simon smiled. 'This is *such* good news for the Labs, getting all this support!'

They settled themselves into the seats in the box.

Simon's mother looked across at the opposite boxes.

'Isn't that the guy from *Destinations*? Isn't his wife lovely!' she nudged her son.

'That's him all right!' Simon nodded. He glanced at his watch. 'I've time to go down and see Sakura and the others.'

'He can't stay away from Sakura!' Bill grinned.

Mrs Armstrong turned to Glen and Bill. 'Do you know any Labs?'

'No. But I've seen some of them interviewed on TV,' Glen said.

'Yeah! They don't look any different from anyone else,' Bill nodded. 'Only time will tell what differences there are – if any, I suppose.'

Simon came back and took his seat just as the lights began to dim. There was a moment's silence, and then the stage was flooded with light as Zorro appeared to a roar from the audience.

'Hey! Man, it's great to see so many friendly faces here tonight!' he shouted. The audience cheered again.

'Aw, man! Tonight is going to be unbelievable! Awesome!' he stood, shaking his head. 'This has to be the most *amazing* night of my life! Tonight I'm going to be playing with the person who just *has* to understand me better than anyone else! Even better than my lovely wife! This person knows what I'm going to do next at the same time as I do myself! Here he is, ladies and gentlemen. To play my new release, "Mirror Image", with me, Jamie! *My Lab!*'

There was a thunderous applause as Jamie ran out onto the stage, a younger version of Zorro himself. He beamed at the audience. With a nod from the older man they both began to play a wild tune; then Zorro started to sing:

'Not meant to be here
Not meant to live
Not meant to feel fear
Not meant to breathe
Until I saw you looking at me
Then I understood
You're not all bad
We're not all good
And you're not just a mirror image!

Looking through the mirror
Just a mirror image!
Come on now, step through
and see what I can see,
Feel what I can feel!
Just a mirror image!
Just a mirror image!'

The audience was standing by the time they had reached the first chorus. Zorro and Jamie sang in perfect harmony.

There was a deafening applause as the song drew to a close.

'This is what the whole evening is about, isn't it?' Zorro turned to Jamie. 'Labs, Non-Labs, all equal! Just making great music!'

'Awesome, man, awesome!' Jamie grinned.

'And from this point, we're not telling you who the Labs are and who are Non-Labs!' Zorro shouted. 'So you get the idea that it doesn't make any difference!'

The concert was a variety of modern and classical music. At the end of each act Bill and Glen would argue if the unknown performers were Labs or Non-Labs.

'They're definitely Labs!' Glen said about a group of four musicians.

'No! They weren't good enough to be Labs! The Labs are perfect!' Bill argued. 'What do you think, Simon?'

He shrugged, 'It doesn't make any difference! They're good!'

Finally it was Sakura, Jade, and Miyu's time to perform. The three girls stood near the front of the stage and gave a bow. Sakura started to play a slow, mournful tune on her violin, then Jade picked up the tune and played it faster, giving it a more cheerful feeling. Finally Miyu played the same tune at breakneck speed and the other two joined in, all three girls moving around the stage, and almost dancing to the lively music.

The audience leapt to their feet as the music came to a halt. Simon and his friends stood up and clapped and called loudly. Sakura glanced up and gave them a smile. Mrs Armstrong glanced up to catch the tender smile her son returned and bit her lip.

Ruby clutched a glass of coke, gazing around her in awe.

'Close your mouth before you catch any flies!' Leon grinned at her.

'You'll soon be used to mixing with the rich and

famous!' Ruby grinned back. 'I still can't believe I'm in the same room as Zorro, the Breakers, and the Divas!'

'Hey! There's Pellier!' Leon said as their friend joined them.

They stood talking about the success of the concert for a while.

'Is Yuri with you?' Ruby asked, looking around.

'No,' Pellier shook his head. 'We haven't seen much of him lately. He rarely goes to college; says he knows more than the lecturers can teach him already!'

'He's probably right,' Ruby said. 'But college life does allow you to get used to Non-Lab life, doesn't it?'

'We don't have any complaints with college life, do we, Johnny?' Leon said as his brother approached. 'We get on well with Non-Labs, don't we?'

'I'm having a great time at college!' Pellier looked around. 'And I think this concert has shown that Labs and Non-Labs can get on quite happily together!'

Johnny nodded towards Mrs Armstrong, who was talking to her son. 'There's one person who probably wouldn't agree with you! She was talking to me earlier on without realising who I was.'

'What did she say?' Ruby asked him. 'Something against the Labs?'

'No, she wasn't openly anti-Lab, but her friendly act was starting to slip! She started to say it was nice to talk to someone who wasn't a … then she quickly changed it to “wasn’t a famous musician”!’

‘Does she know about Simon and Sakura?’ Ruby wondered.

‘Sakura will have her work cut out if she ends up with *her* as a mother-in-law!’ Johnny said.

The Prime Minister’s aide was introducing Mrs Armstrong to different performers from the concert.

‘And this is one of our talented violinists, Sakura,’ he said as Sakura held out her hand.

‘Mrs Armstrong, I am so pleased to meet you! I hope you enjoyed the concert,’ she said, smiling warmly.

Mrs Armstrong touched her hand briefly.

‘Yes, it was very good! What talented performers!’ she replied. She felt a sense of relief as the aide introduced a young man with dreadlocks.

‘Hey, man! An honour to meet you!’ He gave a wide smile, pumping her arm enthusiastically. ‘Glad to have you on board, supporting us!’

She fixed the smile on her face as she realised he was also a Lab, and murmured a vague agreement. Looking around she was relieved to see Simon coming towards her.

‘Excuse me a moment, won’t you?’ she moved to join her son.

‘Hey, Mom! Isn’t this just great! Unbelievable!’ his eyes were shining. ‘What did you think of Sakura? Isn’t she beautiful? And so talented? She’s just wonderful!’

His mother gave a slight nod. ‘Yes, she is …’

Simon continued, ‘Have you seen how many

celebrities are here? All giving us their support! It's just so good! Gives us so much hope for our future!'

Mrs Armstrong gave another wan smile. 'Simon, I'm rather tired; I think I'll get the car to take me back to the hotel.'

'Of course, Mom!' he looked concerned and spoke to the aide who gave a nod and left. 'The car will be here in a moment.'

He walked with her to the car as it pulled up and helped her in. 'I'll call and see you in the morning, OK?'

She leant back against the seat as the car sped off, Simon's words going over in her mind:

'Giving us their support … gives us so much hope for our future!'

'Us … our?' she muttered.

'Labs and Non-Labs come together for the greatest show of the year!' Johnny read aloud from the newspaper the next morning. 'And look! There's a photo of Keith on the sound system!'

'He seems to have found his niche!' Celia said, smiling as Johnny spread the paper on the table.

'There's Sakura, Jade, and Miyu. And Jamie and Zorro!' Leon leaned over his brother's shoulder.

'Last night's celebration heralds a whole new era for the Labs,' Ruby read out. 'This morning Abel, the Lab leader, is due to continue talks with the Prime Minister and members of Amnesty International to establish the legal standing of the Labs.'

'Won't it be great when we have all this is sorted

out and we don't have to hide who we are?' Leon sighed.

'Yeah, just like Non-Labs do every day!' Johnny added.

As they continued to talk about their future lives, Celia got up.

'I'd better get back to the Centre, to check Abel has all the data he needs for this meeting. No, you stay here for a while, Ruby!' she added as Ruby made to follow her.

Back at the office, Celia switched on her laptop. She plugged in her memory stick and began to scroll through the lists of names.

'There must be some more details here!' she muttered to herself, 'Something to help me get on to him!'

She clicked open a file entitled 'VC' and scanned through the information again.

> Vincent Craig, father of Marissa Craig.
> Cell donor: Marissa Craig, female, age 10 months.
> Code SEL 43126
> Procedure initiated date:.............. Personnel:...........

On a second page Celia read, as she had so many times in the last few weeks:

> Informed of death of donor, aged 4 years and two months.
> Instructions to cancel subscription and to discard cells to be implemented immediately.
> Finalised date :.............. Personnel :...........

Celia opened a second file that held a newspaper report of the tragic road accident that had killed her donor, Marissa, and left Marissa's father in a wheelchair. Marissa's mother had survived the crash, suffering less serious injuries.

She once again read through the background details of Marissa's parents. Vincent Craig worked for a large IT company in New York; his ex-wife now lived in Florida with her new family. Celia had made several searches on both of them.

'If only I could find out how they would react if they knew of my existence,' she whispered to herself. 'Would they want to meet me? Or would they hate me, surviving when their daughter did not?'

She sighed and pushed the chair back. If only they would get in touch with the Centre! But why would they have reason to? If only she knew what they were thinking…

Suddenly she sat up straight. She was staring at Vincent Craig's email address. If she could access his inbox and take a look at some of the messages he had sent and received, she might get some idea of his feelings!

When Ruby came into the Centre office that evening, Celia was still on the computer. She quickly minimised the screen as Ruby came in.

'Celia! You work too hard!' Ruby said. 'Some of the Labs have suggested a rerun of Zorro's concert on the big screen in the hall, do you want to join us?'

'No, that's OK,' she yawned. 'I'll be going to bed soon!'

'Any news from Abel?'

'He phoned a few hours ago. Things are going pretty slowly. The government officials and our lawyers are trying to establish a definition of "race" they can both agree on.'

'Nothing is straightforward, is it?' Ruby said.

After Ruby had left, Celia turned back to the computer and reopened the screen she had been looking at. Her face was tense with concentration until suddenly she gave a cry. Success! She was now looking at the first page of Vincent Craig's emails! Her heart pounded as she saw there were several recent ones from his ex-wife. She quickly opened one with an attachment.

Hi Vince,

Here are the photos I told you about. I must admit it brought back good and bad memories looking through them. Still, whatever happened, we must keep our little girl in our minds. She did bring us so much joy, we mustn't forget that – but I'm not so sure about your idea to contact the Centre, Vince. Why reopen old wounds? It won't bring her back, will it?

Take care,
Vanessa

Celia's hands trembled as she pressed the button to download the attachment. Soon she was looking at photos of the young Marissa.

The first one showed her sleeping in a cot beside a teddy bear twice her size. There were several more of her as a young baby – one had a man's arms holding her as she splashed about in a bubble bath. In another, the same arms held her up as she gazed in amazement at a brightly lit Christmas tree. The next group were of the family at a holiday resort. There was a picture of the three of them together, smiling into the camera.

Celia peered at the picture of the smiling baby. 'I must have looked exactly like that as I slept in the Nursery Ward,' she thought. She looked at a close-up of the family group.

'Who do I take after now?' she asked herself as she scrutinised the features on each face, 'Marissa's mother or father?'

She scrolled through the pictures again, wondering how it would be to be created by love and cared for by a mother and a father.

'But their love was not enough to save her when their car crashed,' she thought ruefully. 'And, yet, if it had been, I may not be here now.'

She closed Vincent's inbox as she heard voices nearing the office. Abel and Fil came in.

'Celia! You're still working?' Abel patted her shoulder, 'Ruby says you've been here all day!'

'You didn't even join us for lunch!' Fil added. 'Don't overdo it now.'

'Well, the good news is, I've been cautioned over the ABH charge, so that's all over and done with – except I'm supposed to make a formal apology to him,' Abel scowled. 'Anyway, now we can concentrate on getting equality for the Labs.'

'Any luck researching "race"? Any previous court cases? Definitions? Anything useful? Our lawyers are struggling, even with our own Lab helpers,' Fil asked.

'You can find useful information where no one else even thinks of looking!' Abel said. 'What have you come up with, Celia?'

Celia shook her head as she opened a file on the screen.

'Nothing much, so far. There are no previous situations that fall into the same category as we do,' she told them. 'But I'm not giving up yet. I've one or two ideas that may prove useful. Did you bring me the information you've obtained?'

Abel switched on his own laptop and went to pick up Celia's memory stick. 'Yes, I'll copy it for you now.'

Celia snatched up her stick and pushed it into her pocket.

'No! Just copy it straight into the office folder. Much quicker that way!'

Well, [illegible] was [illegible] down the [illegible] and [illegible] except I [illegible] supposed [illegible] to [illegible] him. [illegible] anyway, [illegible] we [illegible] concentrate on getting [illegible].

Any [illegible] anything [illegible] previous [illegible] And [illegible] the [illegible] with our own [illegible]

You can find [illegible] And [illegible] have [illegible] with Celia?

Celia [illegible] spread [illegible]

[illegible] two [illegible] you [illegible] two [illegible] and you [illegible] the information you [illegible]

[illegible] now.

Celia reached for her stick and pushed [illegible]

[illegible] straight [illegible]

CHAPTER TWENTY-ONE

Ruby sighed as she fumbled for the key to her apartment. It was nearly three months since the concert and they still didn't seem to be any nearer gaining equal rights for the Labs. She knew Abel and the others were also getting tired of being told that there was yet another hitch in the legal process. She had just pushed open her door when she heard someone call her name. She smiled as Beth hurried to her side.

'Could you come with me, Ruby, please?' she asked, a note of anxiety in her voice.

'Of course,' Ruby replied. She followed the young girl through a side gate and along a narrow road leading to the village. Her attempts to question Beth had been met with a quick shake of the head.

'Wait! We'll both tell you!' she had whispered.

At the end of the lane, Frank was waiting. He gave Ruby a smile.

'Thanks for coming. I live just up here.'

Soon they were seated in a tiny flat. Frank gave them each a mug of tea.

'Do you want me to tell her?' he asked gently and turned to Ruby as Beth nodded.

'Beth's having my baby – but everything is going to be OK. I can look after her and the baby! I've got my old job back, apprenticeship, plumber. He's given me a chance to make a go of it! And I can. I've got this place, too!' he blurted out.

'Wow!' Ruby sat back in her chair, 'Slow down a bit!' She looked at Beth who sat tensely, looking at the floor.

'Have you been to the doctor?'

Beth shook her head.

'She's fine! But we will have to think about doctors now. She's nearly two months pregnant, we think,' Frank said.

Beth shook her head again.

'No! I don't want anyone to try to take this baby away from us!'

Frank looked appealingly at Ruby, 'I've already told her they can't do that, can they?'

'No, of course not!' she said. 'You will need to see a doctor, though. Just to make sure everything is fine; it is the first Lab baby.'

'Why won't it be? Beth is healthy!' Frank smiled and squeezed his partner's hand. 'Everything will be just great!'

He looked at Ruby again, his face serious, 'There's one thing, though. Neither of us wants this to turn into a circus act! Beth wanted us to disappear and start again somewhere. But I said we aren't running anywhere, we've got nothing to hide! We're going to be a normal family!'

'I'm sure you will be! We'll have to speak to

Abel, about the doctor and also about avoiding publicity.' Ruby looked at their expressions, 'Would you like me to speak to him first?'

They both nodded.

'Beth ... we ... are a bit nervous about his reaction. But we've made our minds up!' Frank said.

Ruby also felt nervous as she stood outside Abel's apartment later that evening. She took a deep breath and knocked on the door.

Abel looked pleased to see her.

'Sorry to disturb you, Abel ...' she began.

'Ruby! Come in!' he saw her expression. 'What is it?'

She took another deep breath.

'I have to talk to you about Beth and Frank,' she waved a hand as he began to make a disparaging remark about the young man. 'No, he's much different than when we first met him. I told you how he had stopped me and apologised! He's totally supportive of the Labs. And he's extremely fond of Beth. Very protective of her. She's really inspired him. He's got a job and a flat and –'

'Why do you think I'll be interested in hearing about the reform of a young Non-Lab thug?' Abel interrupted her. 'Unless it directly affects us Labs?'

'Beth's pregnant by him!' Ruby blurted out. 'They're both really pleased! They're going to be a real family! It's a real chance for Labs and Non-Labs to integrate! Of course, Beth is going to need to have medical supervision ...'

She stopped talking as Abel stood up, scowling.

'So, for the sake of integration, you have encouraged a Non-Lab and Lab to embark on some romantic idea of family life! Have you *any* idea what you may have started?'

Ruby stood up to face him.

'Just wait a minute! I did not encourage anyone to do anything! I've only just learned about it myself! I'm here to ask you to help them, not to come down on them like a ton of bricks!'

Abel sat down, and put his head in his hands.

Ruby sighed. 'Look, Abel. This was bound to happen sooner or later! Young people together, whether they are Lab or Non-Lab …'

He looked up. 'You are a Non-Lab. You know what you are. You know how your body works; how you develop; how you have … kids. We know very little yet of how Labs will develop outside the laboratory!'

'I think we might as well be optimistic. Both Frank and Beth are healthy. So, chances are their baby will be fine.'

Abel got up and paced around the room. Finally he gave a sigh.

'I'll phone the Compound doctor immediately. Ask Beth and Frank to go to the office.'

Ruby put a hand on his arm.

'Abel! I promised Beth and Frank I would stand by them on this, and I will! They have done nothing wrong, just behaved as young people have done since … since people were on this earth! They need sympathy and help through this!'

Abel gave a brief nod and left,with Ruby following.

'Well, as far as we can tell, the pregnancy is proceeding as a normal human pregnancy should,' the doctor told Beth and Frank as they sat nervously in front of him. Frank beamed at Beth.

'I told you, love! Everything is going to be fine!'

'Looking at the scan,' the doctor continued, lighting up the image on a screen, 'I would say you are nearer to three months than the two months you calculated.'

'That can't be right!' Beth frowned. 'But as long as the baby is healthy…'

The doctor spread his hands. 'Everything seems as normal, just further on than we would expect. We will monitor you closely, of course.'

Frank beamed at Beth again, who returned his smile, 'Our baby, Beth! Our baby!'

'Would you like us to allow the others to come in now, Beth?' the doctor said.

She nodded her head as Frank frowned.

'Don't worry, Frank. All the Labs are going to be interested in what's happening,' she told him.

The doctor spoke into an intercom and Celia and Ruby entered. They looked at the image on the screen and Ruby hugged Beth to her.

'Oh, Beth, Frank! Your baby! You can almost see his, or her, little arms and legs!'

Celia looked impassively at the screen, 'It would probably be best to keep this out of the public eye for the moment.'

Frank nodded in agreement, 'Yes. We don't want reporters following Beth around! She needs to take care of herself!'

'Abel has agreed that you can both move into the empty staff accommodation for the moment, until the baby is born,' Ruby told them. 'You can continue to work outside the Compound, Frank.'

'We'll show you the entrance we use. You must be discreet,' Celia added.

'Oh, that would be great! Thanks!' Frank said. 'By the time Beth has had our baby I'll have nearly finished my apprenticeship. I'll be earning better money. We'll have a really nice home for our family, Beth!'

As the doctor arranged further appointments with Beth, Ruby spoke to Celia.

'It's so exciting, isn't it? But you're right; with Abel in the middle of talks with the government, I think it's better if we keep this story to ourselves for as long as we can.'

'I don't think that will be for too long, somehow,' Celia remarked. 'News stories seem to have a way of getting out!'

Ruby frowned. Celia was probably right. She decided to phone Isaac; ask him to prepare a positive news story ready for when the storm broke.

A week later Frank was walking out of the village when he saw Steve and Callum.

'Oh, hi guys. How's things?'

Steve shrugged. 'Pretty much the same here. I've

heard you're back at Milton's, finishing your apprenticeship?'

'That's right. Decided it's time I sorted myself out a bit,' Frank nodded. 'The old man agreed to give me another chance!'

'Your new girlfriend inspired you, did she?' Steve grinned. 'Getting serious, is it?'

'Yeah, we're OK. Better get back to work. Old Milton's a stickler for time keeping! Catch you later, eh?' Frank gave him a wave as he continued walking.

Steve stood looking after him.

'You're gross! Running round with a bunch of freaks!'

'Yeah!' Callum agreed. He paused, 'But he might be right about, you know, doing something, you know, work and stuff …' He looked at his friend. 'I've been thinking myself, might think of, you know, joining up …'

Steve looked at him. 'You? Join the army? Go around killing people?'

'It's not all like that, you know. You do other stuff, too. Learn stuff and things, like those guys at the Centre. I got talking to one of them on gate duty. He got me some brochures and stuff. And we got talking about life on duty up there, at the Compound. And he told me …' he stopped suddenly.

'Yeah?' Steve prompted him.

'Well, he only hinted at it really, didn't give any names, but … he sort of said that one of the Labs might be knocked up!' Callum looked at Steve. 'What if it was …?'

'Frank's freak?' Steve burst out laughing, then his face grew serious, 'This is a big news story! It could mean a few bucks for us! Come on, let's make a few phone calls, matey!'

'Hey, it's probably not even true! It's probably just some rumour!'

'Never mind!' Steve shouted as he ran towards his house. 'It'll make a great story! "Frank, mummy freak, and baby freak"! Ha!'

'Yeah!' Callum laughed, 'Yeah! The freak family!'

The following afternoon, Beth and Frank were chatting happily as they made their way to the village shop when suddenly a car drew up beside them and two men jumped out.

Beth shielded her eyes as a camera flashed in her face.

'Is it true that you're pregnant?' a second man said, pushing a microphone in front of her. 'When exactly is the baby due?'

'What the hell do you think you're doing?' Frank shouted, putting his arms around Beth. 'Get away from us!'

'Just a few questions!' the man continued. He turned to Frank as the camera flashed again, 'And you must be the father-to-be, Frank, isn't it? How do you feel about being the first human to father a Lab child? And what do you think the future holds for you all?'

Beth shrank into Frank's arms.

'I don't know where you got your information

from, but get away from us right now!' Frank snarled.

'So are you denying it, sir?' the first man continued, hurrying to keep up with them.

By now a number of people had stopped and were watching with interest.

'Is she one of those from the Compound?' someone asked.

'That man said she's having a baby,' another said.

'Young Frank, there, he's not from the Compound,' the first said.

'He's taken up with one of them,' Steve had joined the crowd and was looking on with a nasty grin on his face. 'Must be nuts if you ask me! She'll probably give birth to a monster with two heads!'

Standing beside him, Callum sniggered.

'Two heads?' a woman shuddered.

'Stands to reason, doesn't it? They're not normal!' Steve continued.

'Have you any fears for your unborn child?' the man asked Beth as the camera kept flashing. 'What kind of tests have been carried out, so far?'

'Look! I said get away from us, OK?' Frank raised his fists.

'Hey, we just want a story!' the man answered.

'Frank!' a voice shouted.

He looked up to see Abel pushing his way through the crowd towards them. He wrapped his arms around Beth.

'Come on! Move out of the way!' he screamed at the crowd, forcing a pathway for them.

Soon they were standing inside the shop.

'I'm calling for help,' he explained to the startled shopkeeper as he pulled out his mobile. 'There's no way in here from the back, is there?'

She shook her head silently, a nervous expression on her face.

A few minutes later an army jeep drew up. Beth, Frank, and Abel were bundled into the back. The driver sounded his horn as the vehicle edged its way through the crowd.

Some of the reporters followed the jeep while others turned towards the shopkeeper.

'Do many of those from the Compound shop here? Do you know the pregnant girl?'

Steve stepped forward.

'I can tell you about the father, Frank, we went to school together. He's changed completely since he took up with that girl; it's like she's hypnotised him!'

'Ah, you must be … Steve!' a young reporter said. 'Aren't you the one who phoned our office? And a few other newspaper offices, too, by the look of it!'

'It's a story that needs telling, that's what I think. He was my mate, you know, before *they* came along!'

The crowd gathered around him as he settled down to give his version to the reporters.

Back at the Centre, Frank sat with his arm around a sobbing Beth.

'What happened?' Celia asked. 'How did the press get to know about this?'

Ruby shook her head, 'The story was bound to get

out sooner or later. This is the first Lab baby born. There will probably be many others over the years and they won't attract so much attention!'

'I'm so sorry! I never wanted Beth to have to face …' Frank stammered, pulling Beth closer to him.

Celia shrugged. 'We can't hide away from the real world.'

'I would like to hide away from all those people for ever!' Beth said tearfully.

'It would be better for her to be moved to a quieter, safer place until the baby is born,' Abel said.

Frank looked at Beth and nodded.

'I've phoned Isaac; his interview and photos are going to be published in tomorrow's paper. We can count on him to give a more balanced view!' Ruby said. 'He also suggested moving Beth to his aunt's house further north. It's not too far, Frank. You could visit her quite easily.'

It was getting dark when Ruby headed back to her own rooms. Abel was standing in his doorway looking out over the rows of prefabs in the Compound.

'They sound so happy, don't they?' he said, listening to the sound of shouts and laughter.

'They *are* happy, Abel,' she replied.

'Happy in their gilded cage! But when they step outside it?' he murmured. 'Will we ever be free and equal? Without having to pretend to be something we are not? We are people in our own right, not just human reflections!'

'It won't happen overnight, but it will happen,

Abel,' Ruby insisted.

Abel smiled at her, then moved as if to stroke her cheek.

'If only …' he pushed his hands into his pockets, 'if only there were more Non-Labs like you!'

Dette came into the office with a pile of newspapers early the next morning. Celia scowled as she looked at the first one:

First Lab/Non-Lab Baby Due!

Looking at Beth, the Lab girl from the Compound – all is not well!

There was a picture of a sobbing Beth being led to the jeep by a young soldier. Abel groaned as he looked at the next one:

Flying in the face of Nature

Do we really know enough about this new 'race' to start producing hybrid young? Where are all these clinical experiments going to end?

The paper continued by printing an interview with an eminent scientist who envisaged all the worst-case scenarios of how the baby might be adversely affected by its mixed origin.

Abel threw it down onto the table.

'I don't know where he gets his so called facts from!' he growled.

Ruby held up the *Times.*

'Look, Isaac has written an article which is very supportive of Beth and Frank. And of all the Labs!' she said, beginning to read it out loud.

' *"New news? Or old news? How new is a story of a couple from different races flying in the face of convention and having a child?*

How many people of different colours and creeds have enjoyed long and happy relationships and reared healthy, independently minded children over the centuries? Frank and his girlfriend Beth are just two youngsters in love. They deserve to be given the opportunity to build a future together."'

Isaac had included some photographs of Beth chatting happily with some other girls on the Compound and another of the young couple smiling as they walked hand in hand along a country lane.

Ruby scanned through the article, reading out several more positive comments.

'It's nice to see not everyone is full of doom and gloom!' she remarked.

Abel raised his eyebrows. 'Ever the optimist, Ruby! Well, I'd better get organised for the meeting later. Your research has proved invaluable, Celia. Our own lawyers are amazed at the information you have unearthed to help us win our case!'

'No one knows their way around the internet like Celia does!' Dette said admiringly.

'Oh, Simon! What can I say to stop you asking the same question?' Sakura pulled herself from his arms.

'Yes!' he replied pulling her back into his arms. 'Just say yes, you will marry me! Unless you don't really love me?'

'Simon, you know I love you! And you know why I can't say yes. Not at the moment, anyway,' she looked at him earnestly.

Simon sat up and listed in his fingers, 'First – children. Well, Beth and Frank have demonstrated that it is fine for Labs and Non-Labs to be parents together …'

'They haven't actually *had* their baby yet!' Sakura pointed out.

'But, the doctors say everything is going well!' Simon quickly replied. 'Secondly, the legal standing of Labs, Abel and the lawyers are confident of finding a resolution very soon! So what is there to stop us from announcing our engagement right now?'

'Your parents,' Sakura answered.

'My parents know how I feel about you!' Simoncontinued. 'And they won't be surprised.'

Sakura looked down at her hands. She had felt the animosity when she had met Simon's mother at the concert. If all the other issues were resolved, maybe she could win Mrs Armstrong's approval. She smiled and looked up at him.

'OK, Simon. Once the Labs have legal standing and Beth and Frank's baby is born safely, *then* we'll think about our future together!'

'It's all I think about *now*!' Simon grabbed her

hands, 'Tell you what! I'm going home for a week next month. I'll arrange a time with them when you can visit. Get to know my parents better! They'll soon love you as much as I do, I know they will!'

Simon sighed as he picked up his rucksack from the carousel. His week at home had not gone as he had expected at all. He shut his eyes as he recalled the conversations they had had.

'Do you really know what you're letting yourself in for, Simon?' His mother's hand had shaken as she poured herself a cup of coffee at breakfast one morning. *'This may only be a sort of crush. Very understandable under the circumstances!'*

'No, Mom. It's not just a crush. I love Sakura, she loves me, and we want to get married.'

His mother had shot a desperate glance at his father.

'Well, I'm sure you know your own mind, Simon. She seems a nice enough girl,' his father had remarked. *'But you're still young; no need to rush into anything!'*

Simon had smiled. *'Thanks, Dad. I'd really like her to come and stay with us for a couple of weeks over Christmas. Then you could all get to know each other better!'*

'But your grandmother will be with us for Christmas. And your uncle!' his mother had protested in alarm.

'Yes, Sakura would love to meet them all! She's never known what family life is like, though of

course, she has always had her sisters and the other Labs,' Simon had replied.

'Well, we'll have to talk about this nearer Christmas!' his mother had said.

She was obviously relieved when the phone rang and Simon set off to see one of his friends. As he had left the room, the sharp tone of his mother's voice had stopped him in his tracks. His stomach churned as he listened to their conversation:

'"Seems like a nice girl"? Is *she a girl? What do we know about these …* people*? What in God's name are you doing encouraging him to even* consider *marrying her?'*

'Honey! Calm down! Like you said, it's probably just a crush, with all the stuff that's been happening lately!' his father had replied. *'But the worst thing we can do is to forbid him to marry her! That'll have them heading off to Vegas in no time!'*

He had peered through the doorway to see his mother slump into a chair and push her hair back from her face.

'You're right, darling. I just find it so hard … We had such dreams for our boy … there are hundreds *of lovely* human *girls out there who'd make him a perfect wife! Why couldn't he have chosen one of* them*?'*

He had raised the subject with his father that morning on the way to the airport.

'I heard you and Mom talking about me and Sakura yesterday, I thought you supported the Labs, Dad.'

His father had glanced at his son's face.

'Look, son. I do, I really do. But, well, we don't really know how things are going to turn out with the Labs at the moment, do we? We can't really go overboard right now, can we? You must understand, son. We don't really know what the US position will be on this one, do we?'

'Go overboard? The US position? What are you talking about, Dad? I told you and Mom I love Sakura and want to marry her! We're talking about personal relationships here!'

'I know how you feel, son; I'm just saying, we need to slow down on this.'

He had looked at his father.

'I understand, Dad. We're on our own here. OK.'

There had been a coldness as they had said their farewells at the departure gate.

Simon felt his heart swell as he looked up to see Sakura waving to him from the barrier, a warm, welcoming smile on her face. He smiled back.

No one was going to keep them apart!

Celia breathed a sigh as she sat down in her apartment that evening and pulled her laptop towards her. She was anxious to see if Vincent had made any comment on the news of Beth's pregnancy on his emails. She had to make several attempts to get into his email box. His security system was frequently updated, against hackers like herself, she supposed.

She felt a thrill as she noticed a recent email to Vanessa and quickly opened it.

Hello Vanessa,

Yes, I too have been following the story of young Beth. It makes you realise how far the medical research had gone. They have actually created people able to have relationships and capable of reproducing!

I know I said I would not mention this again, but I feel I must. Sorry. I am thinking of contacting the Centre. I know you think – you always have thought – that I am not allowing myself to move on, but I must know for sure that the cells were destroyed. Maybe then I can finally come to terms with it all.

I must apologise if I have upset you, Vanessa.

Vincent

Celia checked the date on the email. It had been sent the previous morning. She scanned his inbox, but there was no reply from Vanessa. She might have phoned him, or she might still be considering it. Her heart began to race! Maybe he had phoned today when she was out of the office. She jumped up and made her way back to the Centre office.

While she was looking through the record book, Abel walked in.

'Working late again, Celia?' he asked her.

'No, I had packed up,' she replied. 'I was just

taking a quick look to see if there had been anything important while I was out of the office earlier. Valerie was in here. No, nothing!'

She turned to Abel and smiled. 'How did it go today?'

'I feel we're finally getting somewhere!' he answered. 'It was decided that the Labs are to be recognised as a "race" under the definition we decided on: "*A Lab is to be defined as a human who has been created under laboratory conditions through the process of cloning cells. A Lab must be able to exist independently after a period of maturing.*"

'We spent another hour discussing how long a Lab must have "existed independently" before being entitled to belong to the Lab race – and finally agreed on a month. Dermot O'Brien is confident that now we have achieved this much, most of our other demands will be favourably viewed!'

'When the Centre closed down, I thought soon we'd all be equal, everything will be straightforward. I never imagined that things would be so complicated and take so long!' Celia sighed.

'None of us had any idea, Celia; Labs or Non-Labs!' Abel patted her shoulder, 'Still, we are making progress, slowly! I'm going down to the Compound. I told them I'd let everyone know how things are progressing. Do you need help here?'

'No, I'm just going to lock up,' she replied. 'See you tomorrow.'

It was getting late and she still sat alone in the office. When the phone rang, she picked it up and gave her usual greeting.

A man's voice answered. He sounded uncertain of himself.

'Hello, umm, this is Vincent Craig. I was a subscriber – well, oh, several years ago. I, umm, we actually cancelled our subscription after, well, after we lost our daughter. She was the donor. Marissa Craig.'

Celia gave a sharp intake of breath. 'Oh yes, Mr Craig. I remember your name. You cancelled your subscription when … I'm so sorry you lost your daughter!'

'Yes, yes … thank you. I, umm, I wondered… I know we asked for the cells to be destroyed at the time, but with all the news about the Centre … I just wanted to confirm that they were actually destroyed.

Celia's hand tightened on the phone. She took a deep breath, 'I don't actually have access to that data, Mr Craig. I will have to consult my senior officer … If, if it turns out they were not destroyed … if the Lab was … allowed to develop… what steps were you thinking of taking next, Mr Craig?'

'I have given this some thought, and I would … I would like to make contact with her, if she agrees. Get to know each other, a step at a time …'

'I will follow this matter up, Mr Craig. How can I get in touch with you?' Celia felt she was moving in a dream as she noted his number and replaced the handset. She had wanted to get in touch with him so badly; now she had the opportunity to do so, she felt afraid.

'What?' she looked up, startled, to find Ruby standing in front of her.

'I just wondered why you were sitting here in the dark,' Ruby looked at her face, 'Are you OK, Celia?'

'Oh, Ruby,' Celia began, 'This is going to sound silly. I don't even know why I didn't tell him who I was!'

Ruby sat down beside her and listened while Celia explained what had happened.

'It's not silly,' she said, 'It's a big step. Why don't you suggest getting to know each other slowly? You could start by emailing. That will give you both time to think about what you want to say to each other and questions you want to ask each other.'

Celia smiled and patted her hand.

'I know I often criticize you, Ruby, but you are clever in many ways! I'll do that!'

'Do you want me to phone him?' Ruby offered.

'No, thank you,' Celia sat up. 'I'm going to do it right now!'

As Ruby left she picked up the phone again.

'Mr Craig? Yes, It's … the Centre. Your … Lab, she … survived and, erm, she would like to get to know you, too. She would like to email you initially. What do you think?'

'Yes, I think that would be a wise decision. I was thinking along the same lines myself,' He gave her the email address, which she carefully wrote down, although she already knew it by heart. 'Thank you so much for your help. And do tell her I'm very much looking forward to hearing from her.'

‘I will, Mr Craig,’ Celia said softly.

After putting the phone down, she sat for a few moments looking at the piece of paper where she had written Vincent Craig’s email address. It was strange to think that he had actually given it to her.

She turned to the computer and opened her own emails. She pressed ‘new’ and looked at the blank page before her. What could she tell him? Where would she start?

Dear Vincent,

she began, and then started again:

Dear Mr Craig,

I am pleased you wanted to get in touch with me. I will tell you some things about myself.

I am now called Celia, although my original Lab code is Sel.

I live and work at the Centre, with other Labs and Non-Labs. My role is in administration, mainly computer-based. In my free time I enjoy sports.

I am looking forward to learning more about yourself and your family.

Yours,
Celia

She reread it several times, and then pressed 'send'. Within an hour she excitedly opened a reply.

My dear Celia,

It was so good to receive your email!

My work is computer-based too; I design anti-virus software for businesses and industries.

I am divorced, but remain on good terms with my ex-wife, who is happily remarried and has two boys.

I am disabled, so I don't get to do regular sports, but I follow my own keep fit programme with a very bossy personal trainer!

Yours,

Vincent

CHAPTER TWENTY-TWO

He read the news story of the Lab/Non-Lab baby with disgust.

'Further contamination!' He threw the paper to the floor.

She picked it up. 'If this baby is healthy, to Non-Lab standards, it could be the first of many Lab/Non-Lab offspring.'

'We must put our plan into action as soon as possible!' he said. 'There's no time to waste!'

Another person was in a furious mood that afternoon. John Baxman fumed as he left the Centre.

'How dare they tell me I am not entitled to be informed of the Centre's present financial state!' he growled to himself as he headed for the car park.

He had been enraged when he saw how much money had been spent on the Compound. He couldn't begin to imagine how much would be spent on the claims submitted by former subscribers.

'From last year's profits of over two billion pounds – to this!' he muttered. 'All this bad publicity means we can't even branch out into other fields of medical science! All our investments going to waste!'

'But the former managerial staff at the Centre are no longer trusted!' Celia had pointed out to him tersely. 'You know the government's decision: any viable ideas for future medical research based on any experiments here will be closely monitored by a team of handpicked scientists from six of the ten countries formerly involved with work at the Centre.'

'Yeah! Pass it over to the do-gooders! Where's the profit in that? This place will be closed down within a year, mark my words!' he had spat out.

'Wecan't do that. We still have nearly one hundred Labs who have just been moved to the Childhood and Adolescence Ward. We need at least two more years until they reach maturity.'

Baxman had been shown off the premises shortly after this exchange. He had scowled as he walked past some Labs from the Compound.

'Billions of pounds down the drain! And they're not even human!' he muttered to himself. 'If only there was some way of recouping even half of what we've lost! If only *someone* could be made to see *sense*!'

A figure stepped out of the shadows as Baxman opened his car door.

'Mr Baxman! Can I have a word with you for a moment, sir?'

Baxman glanced up. A look of annoyance passed over his face as he saw the young man standing in front of him.

'What is it? Better be quick, I'm in a hurry!' he

answered curtly.

'I can sense your disappointment that the Centre is to close,' he said. 'I also know that it may not be long before a serious case will be made against you as chief administrator of this establishment.'

Baxman looked up at him.

'What the devil are you talking about? My lawyer has made it perfectly clear that I am no way implicated in the medical developments of the Centre! Mr Sven was solely responsible for things on the medical side. My role was purely as administrator on the financial side!' Baxman made to get into his car, but the younger man stepped forward and put his hand on the door.

'According to video footage of conversations between yourself and Mr Sven, you were clearly aware of the extent of the developments in the Centre. The Labs have handed them over to the police.'

'How do you know this?' Baxman's eyes narrowed. 'What do you want with me?'

'I mean you no harm, Mr Baxman. I am also saddened to see the end of the research you have achieved at the Centre,' the young man raised his hands, 'after all, you gave me – gave all Labs – life!'

'*You* are a Lab?' Baxman's expression changed and he nodded vigorously, 'Indeed we did! Indeed we did! I wish just there were more people who could see things as you do, young man!'

'Neither you nor I, nor Mr Sven, wish to see the abandonment of such advanced research, Mr

Baxman. Surely the continuation of such work could only be of benefit to both your people and mine. With Sven's scientific knowledge, your contacts and my knowledge of … other areas … we could go far!' The young man looked questioningly at him.

Baxman sighed. 'Now that the police are involved there wouldn't be a chance. And if Sven is arrested – And I myself may be wrongly accused …'

'We probably have about twenty-four hours to remove you and Sven from this unpleasant situation, Mr Baxman,' the man continued.

Baxman threw up his hands, 'My passport has been taken; I am forced to sign in at the local police station daily, like a common criminal; Sven is under house surveillance – what can we do at this stage?'

'You can trust me to supply the necessary documentation and travel arrangements, Mr Baxman, for yourself and Mr Sven. I believe you had a phone conversation with a former client who expressed his sadness on hearing of the closure of the Centre. He remarked that if it had been set up in his own country, where people of your calibre were appreciated, this would not have happened.'

'You listened to my phone conversations?' Baxman spluttered. He took a deep breath. 'But you're right. The gentleman did express an interest in establishing a medical research centre in his own country. But how …?'

The young man handed him a mobile phone.

'Call him on this. You will find his name in the contacts list. And also mine. Tell him we will be there tomorrow evening, on this flight, under these names,' he handed him a slip of paper. 'Do you know the Express Hotel off the boundary road? I will meet you there at six o'clock tomorrow evening. Sven will be with me.' He turned to leave. 'Make sure you're not followed.'

'Mr …' Baxman began, looking down at the slip of paper, 'Vlensky. How do I know you are not setting me up? How come you want to get involved in all this? I mean, the other … Labs … are baying for our blood!'

'Money, Mr Baxman! I wish to make enough money to lead a life I choose for myself. I do not wish another … person, of any background, to dictate what kind of life I am entitled to!'

Baxman began to laugh.

'You're an intelligent young man!'

'I know, Mr Baxman, I know,' he replied.

Two days later the three men and their new investor sat together around a low table. Their host raised a glass and smiled.

'To the success of our new venture, gentlemen!'

The three others murmured their agreement.

'I must admit, Mr Vlensky, I did have my doubts about your ability to outsmart the British police and to get these two men here, and so quickly!' their host continued.

'Luckily for me, the British police also underestimated my abilities,' Vlensky replied.

Baxman picked up the photographs on the table in

front of him.

'The sooner we get down to work the better. This site seems ideal. You've thought of everything!'

Their host smiled and inclined his head then turned to the scientist, 'Mr Sven, what is your opinion?'

The old man shook his head, 'I leave that to the others. Baxman has a list of my requirements. I would appreciate the use of the computer with the given specifications as soon as possible. And a fully equipped laboratory.'

'Of course, Mr Sven,' the man replied. He pushed a button on his desk and a young man entered. 'Al, arrange for a car to be sent immediately. I am taking the gentlemen to look over the complex.'

The young man gave a bow as he took the paper and left.

Half an hour later the men stood in the entrance hall of a large glass-fronted building. Outside, the sun beat down, but inside the lightly tinted glass and the air conditioning kept the temperature at an agreeable level.

'Isn't it a little over-exposed?' Baxman looked around him.

'We hoped that by providing an open, welcoming reception area, we would give our clients a sense of security. We do not want our medical research to be in any way associated with the work that has caused so much controversy in the UK,' he explained. 'This way, gentlemen.'

They entered a lift. Their host pushed a button.

'There are three floors; on the ground floor we propose to accommodate the administration offices. Here we are at the first floor,' the doors opened and they stepped out onto an expensive thick-pile carpet. 'This floor would be where initial medical tests are carried out, DNA samples taken, et cetera, as you did at the Centre.'

He pushed open a door to a large room. Near the window side was a leather-topped desk with oversized comfortable chairs on either side. On the other side a screen was pulled back to reveal a couch.

'Whatever equipment you request will be installed as soon as possible,' he said as they viewed three more similar rooms.

Baxman pulled out a file from his briefcase.

'I've details of the equipment we had at the Centre. Sven has amended the file and added any updates.'

'Of course, Mr Baxman. We have an extensive budget for the initial outlay,' he smiled. 'I already have a list of customers who are interested, especially on the cosmetic side. Their dream of eternal youth seems to have become possible!'

'At a price!' Baxman laughed.

'What price can you put on eternal youth, Mr Baxman?' the other man smiled.

Soon they were being shown around the second floor.

'The layout is pretty much the same on each floor. This floor will hold the operating theatres and recovery wards.'

'This way, gentlemen,' their host smiled again. He led them along a corridor and into a small security office. In front of them were several screens showing different views inside and outside the building.

'There are five more security offices, very similar to this one, but this particular office will be manned by specially selected staff.'

He stepped up to one of the floor-length windows and pushed a button, and the window drew back to reveal a lift. He gestured for the three men to follow him. The door slid shut behind them.

'On all the cameras, that lift appears only as a window looking out on to the grounds,' he said as he stepped out of the lift. They had emerged into a clearing behind the building. A small electric vehicle was waiting for them. After a ten-minute ride, they were led up a narrow staircase into the ground floor of what appeared to be a hotel.

'We hoped to learn from … the challenges … you faced in your country!' he explained.

A bell boy stepped forward and bowed.

'Welcome, gentlemen. This way.'

They were taken to an elegantly furnished office. A smartly dressed waiter appeared with a tray. Their host sat in front of a computer screen.

'This entire building will accommodate the development wards.'

They looked at images of the hotel floors, showing wards set out much the same as they had been at the Centre.

'Of course, we do not have any of the capsules

you will need at present. The images are based on information from the UK television stories,' he said. 'Again, you only need to present your specifications and we will employ a qualified team to create the required capsules here in this building, in the basement.' He brought up a camera shot of the basement area.

Baxman shook his head, 'I can't believe all this! But how come you have all this available?'

He shrugged, 'Since I realised the full extent of your … research … in the UK, I knew it would not be long before the unimaginative, restrictive laws of your country would put a stop to such valuable work. I had begun to plan Laqaar Medicentre several years ago, and was hoping to make enquiries about expanding your research when Medicfrontier beat me to it! But, once the Centre was closed down I knew it was only a matter of time before I would hear from someone. That is why I phoned you – to let you know there was a new pathway open to you!'

'And here it is!'

'Indeed, here it is, Mr Vlensky! Here it is!' the man agreed.

'So, when am I going to get to see this wonderful new Centre?' she asked him.

His eyes shone, 'There are one or two details that need attending to, but it will be soon, very soon!'

'Oh –' she began, but he pressed a finger to her lips before she could say his name.

'Vlensky! You must call me by this name all the

time, when we are with the new team. And you are …?'

'Lena,' she nodded. 'You are right, we must get used to our new names! But when we're here, amongst other Labs, we must remember to use our given names for this country.'

'Hopefully we will not have to spend too much time here. Make sure you have an acceptable story to justify your absences over the next few weeks,' he added. 'We don't want anyone associating us with any forthcoming events. Especially when the twin female and male Labs go missing.'

She shifted in her chair, 'Is it really necessary to involve these Labs?'

He patted her hand, 'Why are you worrying? We are going to create a *perfect* race. These Labs are lucky to be selected. They will benefit from our investigations!'

She smiled, 'I'm being silly. Of course you would not allow harm to come to another Lab! We must keep a careful eye on Sven and Baxman. They would not feel so concerned!'

'They won't be involved in this side of our work. I have suitable twins in mind already. One male and one female are to be the controls while we enhance the abilities of the second one,' his eyes lit up and he squeezed her hands. 'Just think of the new race of Labs we will create! They will be perfect! They – *we* – will rule the world!'

'And none of the Non-Labs involved are aware of our plans?' she asked.

'Not at all! I have carefully selected our staff and the individual duties they are to perform. Sven is happy as long as he is in his laboratory. We can even allow him to create a few substandard Labs! Baxman and Maher are happy predicting profits. Before anyone even begins to suspect anything, it'll be too late. The future is ours!'

CHAPTER TWENTY-THREE

Isaac and Frank arranged a silk shawl over the back of the sofa and a vase overflowing with an array of brightly coloured flowers on a table to one side.

'Great! Just put the vase of red roses on the table behind the sofa. Over a bit, perfect!' Isaac instructed Frank.

Isaac's aunt, Linda, gave an admiring glance around the room as she walked in with a smiling Beth who was holding a squirming bundle.

'My lounge has never looked so colourful! So many people are wishing you well, Beth!' she said. 'The US president, the French president, Zorro. And so many others, Labs and Non-Labs!'

'Here, let me take little Frankie while you settle yourself into a suitable pose, Beth!' Frank held out his arms and gently took his son.

'Now, if you would just sit over at this end, Beth, so the shawl is in the background. Great. Just move those roses slightly. Yes, that's it!' Isaac continued, looking at the screen on a large digital camera. 'Just Frankie to add now!'

He spent the next half hour taking pictures first of Beth and the baby, then the baby on his own, and finally of Frank, Beth, and their son.

'Well, that's it then!' he beamed. 'I'll send them to the office straight away! Everyone will find it hard to believe that I scooped the first interview with Beth and her new baby! And photos, too!'

He quickly loaded the photos on to his laptop. Beth and Frank stared at the images on the screen.

'He's so beautiful!' Frank breathed.

Beth nodded silently in agreement.

'The doctor and midwife seemed to think so! A real bonny baby, they called him.' Linda smiled.

'Well, if you're not too tired, Beth, we could get started on the interview. It'll be published in the next *Sunday Times* magazine,' Isaac said, pulling out a notebook. 'We'll show those doubting Non-Labs!'

Ruby echoed his sentiments as she opened the magazine the following Sunday at the Centre.

'How could anyone not fall in love with such a beautiful baby?' she exclaimed. 'Have you seen this, Abel?'

He reached over and took the magazine from her hands.

'And there are no medical issues at all?'

'Absolutely none. Beth had a normal birth and both she and the baby are doing fine!' Ruby answered. 'That will be a relief for many Labs and Non-Labs, I am sure.'

Abel watched her as she gazed down at the picture of the baby with a soft smile on her face.

Dette walked in holding the magazine.

'Ah, I see you've got your copy already! Isn't he a

gorgeous baby? And I must admit Isaac has surpassed himself with this piece of writing. A whole Sunday magazine article! Listen to this:

"Following a normal pregnancy with no complications, Beth, the new mother Lab, gave birth to a baby boy one month premature. Both mother and baby are doing fine. And proud dad, Frank, too!"

'What does the caption say?' Abel asked.

'*"Baby Frankie sleeps peacefully, unaware that his birth has caused such a stir. The first Hybrid child to be born to a human father and a Lab mother. Could he be the first of many?"* I wonder what it must be like to have a tiny, moving little person in your arms,' She looked at Celia and Ruby. 'Does it make you think of having a baby, too?'

Ruby smiled, but both she and Dette looked up at Celia's abrupt, 'No!'

Celia coughed, 'I mean, it would be very … worrying to have such a tiny creature dependent on you … all the dangers there are in the world!'

'But lots of babies are born every day!' Ruby said. 'Of course their parents have to think about the dangers, but most of them do bring up happy, healthy children. Or other people in their families do.'

Celia looked unconvinced. 'Some dangers you cannot protect them from.'

Dette put her arm around her, 'Sometimes you just have to take risks, Celia.'

Ruby looked back at the article, 'Beth and Frank seem so happy with their new baby! I think this news will be a help to all Labs.'

She read out the comments written next to a photo of Beth and Frank:

'*"When asked about their future plans, Beth and Frank said that they are eagerly awaiting the outcome of the parliamentary debate on the rights of the Labs.*

'We both want to know that our child has a secure place in our society. Like all parents, we want him to have the chance of a good education and a happy future,' Frank added. 'We're both willing to work hard to give him everything he needs and deserves!"'

'Mr O'Brien, Amnesty International, and the US President are all pressing the Prime Minister to give us an early reply to our requests. We will have full press coverage at next week's meeting,' Abel said. 'Perhaps you're right, Ruby. Perhaps the birth of this baby will speed things up a bit.'

Celia stared down at the photo of the baby in the arms of Beth. She put the paper down and silently left the room.

She felt disturbed and confused. Everyone seemed to be celebrating the birth of this tiny helpless being. Didn't they realise how vulnerable he was? No one seemed to recognise how powerless they were to protect him! Were the risks worth it? What would Vince say on this subject?

After a few weeks of emailing each other, Celia was pleased when Vince suggested speaking on the phone. He often made her laugh with his wry comments. Despite his disabilities, she found him to have a very positive outlook on life. The knowledge that she had hacked into his computer and already knew of some of the things he told her about often made her feel guilty.

One evening she confided her feelings to Ruby.

'I really want to tell him, but if I do, he may not want to speak to me again!' she said.

Ruby frowned. 'I think it'd be better if you do own up now, rather than later. If you let something slip, or he found out for himself, it could be worse.'

'What if he reacts badly?' Celia asked.

'Well, if you explain to him *why* you hacked into his computer …'

'And I haven't done anything like that since we've been in touch,' Celia added.

'Tell him as soon as possible,' Ruby advised.

Celia answered the phone nervously when Vince phoned that evening.

'I wonder how much you are like Marissa,' Vince said at one point. 'I'll send you some photos of her; you can see her for yourself.'

'Vince, there is something I must tell you!' Celia stuttered. 'I … I … have seen photos of Marissa …'

'But how?' he sounded puzzled.

Celia explained to him how she had believed he would not get in touch with the Centre if he did not know of her existence. She told him how she had found out his email address and said she had used it to get details from his personal computer.

'And I *so* wanted to know about you and your family! I felt I had to make every attempt to find out who had caused me to be created …' she finished.

There was silence at the other end of the line.

'You mean you hacked into my private files on my computer?' he said softly. 'Did you read my emails too, Celia?'

'The ones to Vanessa, yes,' she was almost whispering now. 'Oh, Vince, I'm so sorry! I haven't gone near your computer since we've been in touch, I promise you!'

There was another long silence.

Vince had Celia's words going through his head. *I felt I had to make every attempt to find out who had caused me to be created.* He had been involved in her creation. He was responsible for her very existence. He couldn't turn his back on her now.

'Vince? Are you there?' she ventured.

'Yes, Celia, I am,' he gave a sigh. 'But this is the point where we promise honesty in all our future dealings, OK.'

'I promise, Vince! I have no need to go behind your back; I can just ask you now!' Celia answered simply.

'I hope you will. And I've a few things I'd like to ask you, too!' he said solemnly.

'Yes?' Celia nodded. 'Whatever you ask, I'll be honest!'

'How the heck did you do it?' he laughed.

'Well, after hacking into the Russian government offices, it was quite easy really. Their defence systems are extremely challenging!' Celia told him.

'Hey, wait a minute! Government offices?' Vince gave a low whistle. 'There's a lot I don't know about you yet, Celia!'

Celia was humming softly to herself as she and Ruby made their way to the twins' house the following week.

'You're a different person since you've been in touch with Vince,' Ruby commented.

Celia smiled. 'I feel more like a *real* person – not just a Lab created in a test tube, but a person with a background!'

'That's how everyone should feel!' Ruby said. 'When other people think we are worth something, we are – Lab or Non-Lab!'

'Hi there!' Johnny said, opening the door.

'No Abel?' Leon added.

'He's still at a meeting,' Celia explained.

'Mmm, I thought he'd have been in touch by now,' Ruby continued. 'He usually lets us know how these meetings go, even if it's just to complain about the people he has to deal with!'

'These meetings seem to be getting longer,' Celia commented. 'I don't know if that is a good sign or a bad sign!'

'I hope it is not too much longer before we are accepted as equals,' Leon said.

'Yes,' his twin agreed. 'Scouts from the Liverpool and Manchester clubs have shown an interest in us as players!'

'That's great news!' Ruby cried.

'But what would their attitude towards us be if they knew we were Labs?' Leon asked.

'We were thinking it is time we revealed our true

identities,' his brother said.

'But we'd be happier doing this if we had a proper place in society!' Leon added.

Celia's phone rang.

'Maybe this is good news!' she said. Suddenly her face grew serious. 'What? Oh, no! Where is he now?' she pulled out a pen and paper and began to write with a shaking hand.

'… Central Emergency Unit, off Regent Street … OK, I've got it. We're on our way!' she put down her phone and looked at the three faces looking anxiously at her.

'It's Abel. He's been shot! On the way to the Downing Street this evening! We must go there straight away!'

'Is … is it serious?' Ruby asked her as they climbed into the car.

She nodded, 'They are operating now.' She punched the destination details into the control panel. An hour later they were shown to a small room near the operating theatre in the hospital.

Johnny murmured as he sat down, 'He's *got* to be OK!'

Leon nodded in agreement.

They all stood up as a doctor entered.

'Is he badly hurt?' Ruby blurted out.

He nodded, 'Yes. He was hit at close range in his chest. Luckily the bullet missed his vital organs, but he has lost a lot of blood. They are operating now. We will let you know the full extent of his injuries as soon as we can.'

'Who did this?'

'Why?' The twins asked at the same time.

'Probably someone politically motivated, I imagine,' the doctor said, 'but, hopefully, the police will catch whoever did it.'

Ruby looked down at her hands, silently willing Abel to pull through. Glancing at Celia, she could see the same tension in her face. Johnny paced up and down the small room, while Leon drummed nervously on the table top.

They all looked up as the door opened again.

'Keith! Dette!' Celia jumped up and hugged them.

'We got your message and came straight away!' Dette said. 'How is he?'

'We must wait and see,' Ruby told them.

'How much longer do we have to stay in this place?' Leon whispered nervously. 'I don't like the smell!'

'Of course!' Ruby patted his arm. 'It must be very difficult for you all to find yourselves in a hospital!'

Keith gave a weak smile. 'It is a reminder of our time in the Centre.'

'We must think of Abel!' Celia reminded them firmly.

Two hours passed before the doctor reappeared. He gave a reassuring smile, 'He's going to pull through.'

Celia sat down heavily on a seat, giving a deep sigh of relief. 'Oh, thank goodness!'

'Can we see him?' Johnny and Leon asked together.

‘Well, he’s sleeping at the moment. Perhaps in a few hours’ time he could see you,’ the doctor told them.

A nurse came in and called the doctor to one side. He looked surprised, shrugged, and turned back to Johnny.

‘Well, it seems he’s already coming around and is anxious to see you,’ he said. ‘Perhaps just one or two of you could go in for a moment.’

Celia and Ruby followed the nurse to Abel’s bedside.

Abel gave a weak smile as they entered. His face was pale, apart from a long purple bruise where he had hit his head as he fell. His chest was bound with a thick white bandage.

Ruby felt tears spring to her eyes as she drew close to his bedside. She held his hand and felt a slight pressure in response.

‘Time to go!’ the nurse said in a determined voice. ‘You can visit him again tomorrow. Time to rest now, Abel!’

‘Let them stay with me!’ Abel muttered, gripping Ruby’s hand tighter.

Ruby looked at Celia’s face. She seemed even more uncomfortable in the small room.

‘How about I stay here tonight?’ she suggested. ‘And you and the others get off home.’

She was rewarded with a grateful look.

‘If you are sure …?’ Celia ventured.

‘Yes. You and the others go now. I’ll phone you first thing in the morning.’

Ruby spent the night by Abel's bedside. At one point she nodded off, letting his hand slip from hers. He became agitated until he realised she was still beside him.

Early the next morning the nurses began their work on the wards. A young nurse came into the room and began to check Abel's charts.

'You've a better colour on you this morning, Abel,' she chatted cheerfully, as Abel stirred. 'You gave your friends a bit of a shock last night. They'll be glad to see you're doing so well!'

She picked up a phial from her medicine trolley and prepared a syringe. Ruby felt Abel's grip on her hand tighten as the nurse approached the bed.

'No!' he shouted, knocking the equipment from her hand and pulling himself upright. 'You're not pumping any stuff into me!'

The nurse stopped, looking flustered. 'It's nothing harmful; only antibiotics prescribed by the doctor.'

Abel began to struggle out of the bed.

'I'm ready to leave the hospital now,' he said.

Ruby stood up and put her hand on his shoulders.

'Abel, the nurse is only trying to help you. You've been badly injured. You must take it easy!'

Abel shook his head, 'Where are my clothes?'

'I'll have to call Sister!' the nurse said, running from the room.

'Abel …' Ruby began.

'I can't stay here, Ruby! I must leave immediately!' he continued.

A short, plump woman entered followed by the

young nurse.

'What's all this about, young man?' she said in a no-nonsense voice. 'We can't have you making all this fuss! You're in no condition to leave today, and won't be for another week I should imagine. Now let's get you back into …'

'I'm leaving now.' Abel said in a steady tone. Ruby could see beads of sweat on his forehead.

'You certainly won't be leaving without the doctor's say-so; so why don't you –' the sister continued.

Abel turned to Ruby as if the sister hadn't spoken. 'My clothes - where are they?'

The ward sister bristled. 'I don't think you quite heard me! Now let's have a more reasonable attitude, shall we? Nurse, help Mr … Abel back into bed and we'll see what the doctor has to say when he makes his rounds later this morning, shall we?'

'I'm not staying here any longer!' Abel's voice was rising.

Ruby spoke up. 'Sister, you must understand, the experiences Abel and other Labs have of medical centres run by Non-Labs – humans – has made it difficult for him to be here. It would probably be better if he continued to convalesce at home …'

'Don't you try to tell *me* what his treatment should be, young lady!' Sister answered sharply. 'And I'm quite used to handling uncooperative patients, thank you!'

'He's not being unreasonable!' Ruby protested laying a protective hand on Abel's arm. 'If you could just try to understand …'

'You're right,' a voice broke in. They looked round to see the doctor in the doorway. 'I'm Dr Patrick Jensen. We've not handled this situation very sensitively, have we? We should have been aware of Abel's possible reaction to finding himself in a hospital. I'll take it from here, Sister.'

The ward sister gave Abel a sharp look as she bustled out.

The doctor looked at Abel who was seated on the side of the bed, a sheet wound around his body.

'Nurse, see if you can find something for Abel to wear.' The doctor sat in a chair on the far side of the bed from Abel. 'You are free to leave whenever you want to. But I must point out that you have received a serious injury that will need attention. I would like to take a look at it before you do leave.'

Ruby patted Abel's arm as he began to shake his head. 'It would make sense, Abel. I'll be here.'

'No tests, no medication!' Abel muttered. He lay back on the bed and watched as the doctor gently removed the bandages. He gave a short whistle. Ruby looked at him in alarm.

'No, I am amazed! Usually, for a normal human anyway, it would take weeks for the wound to heal as much as yours has done overnight, Abel!'

He continued to inspect the wound, asking occasional questions about injuries any of the Labs had suffered, receiving brief responses from Abel. He finally applied a lighter dressing and handed Ruby a package of extra bandages, giving them some instructions on Abel's care at home.

'You're well on the mend, thanks to your own constitution,' he said. 'I would like to know more about your healing abilities.'

'My people don't want any more testing or experimentation!' Abel answered shortly.

The doctor spread his hands. 'I quite understand, Abel. But I wish you no harm,' He pulled a card from his pocket. 'Here's my number if you ever need me, for any reason.'

He turned as the nurse arrived with a bundle of clothes. He gave Ruby a wink, 'You certainly put Sister's nose out of joint! I hope her mood improves, for the nurses' sake!'

Abel sat with his eyes closed in the back of the car. Celia glanced at him in the rear-view mirror, 'Are you sure you're OK, Abel?'

He nodded and slowly opened his eyes.

'That's the first time we've had to use Non-Lab medical facilities,' Celia said.

'Mmm. Do we have many Labs studying medicine?' Abel asked.

'Four are taking Open University courses in medicine in the Compound. They want to go to medical school next year. And there are about ten more free-living Labs studying at university in London, Cardiff, and Birmingham,' Ruby told him.

As Celia and Ruby helped him into his bed, Abel squeezed Ruby's hand.

'I never thought I'd say this to a Non-Lab,' he smiled at her, 'but I would not have managed without you there, Ruby. I was losing the plot!'

'I'm glad you're OK, Abel,' she said. 'Do you need any painkillers?'

He shook his head. Ruby and Celia waited until his breathing showed he was asleep before they crept from the room.

CHAPTER TWENTY-FOUR

'Lily, Milly!' he stopped in front of them. 'What a surprise meeting you here!'

'Oh, hello! We didn't know you were in London!' Milly smiled.

'I had to collect some equipment from a place nearby,' he told them.

'We've just finished work and are on our way home,' Lily added. 'Come back to the house with us! The boys will be so glad to see you!'

'That would be great! I have my work van just around the corner. If you don't mind sitting in the back …?'

'Not at all!' Milly said.

'It is better than walking in this rain!' Lily laughed.

'What work are you doing now?' Milly asked as they walked around the corner. 'Hey, look who else is here!' she added as a young woman appeared beside the van.

The next morning Ruby looked up as Abel walked into the office.

'Abel! You are looking so much better today!' she

smiled. 'How is your wound healing?'

'I am feeling quite well,' he replied.

'I'm so glad, Abel. I was so worried about you! I mean, we all were!' Ruby said.

Celia burst into the room. 'Ruby! Oh, Abel, I'm so glad you are feeling better! Sophie has been on the phone. It might be a fuss about nothing, but … well, she was worried enough to ring me. Lily and Milly did not come home last night. It seems they left work at the usual time, but they never arrived home.'

'Perhaps they stopped off to see some friends on the way?' Abel suggested.

'That's what I said to Sophie. But it is unlike them. They are quite shy girls,' Celia continued. 'And they would have phoned the others to explain their plans.'

'Have they phoned all the people they know around there?' Ruby asked. 'Labs and Non-Labs?'

Celia nodded.

'It's not like Lily and Milly to behave like this,' Ruby frowned. 'They're only just getting used to working among Non-Labs. It's unusual for them to venture very far without one of the other Labs with them.'

'Perhaps they decided it is time they spread their wings a little?' Abel suggested.

'Maybe,' Ruby said, unconvinced.

'Phone Sophie. Tell them we will be with them in an hour!' Abel said.

'Are you sure you are well enough?' Celia asked.

'I'm fine.'

*

When they arrived at the house, Ben and his housemates were also there.

'Should we call the police?' Joe asked.

'Yes, though there is no need to tell them the girls are Labs at this stage,' Celia suggested. 'It could have far-reaching effects on the other Labs living under false IDs in the community.'

Ruby, Sophie, and Megan headed for the police station.

'We can't just sit here!' Ben jumped up. 'We could retrace their steps since they left work.'

'Yes, you and Lucy could do that. The rest of us could split into pairs and call at any other likely places the girls may have visited,' Celia added. 'Abel could remain here to take any phone calls.'

By noon, they were still no nearer finding out what had happened to the two girls.

'Surely the girls will come to no harm. At least they are together,' Ruby sounded as if she was trying to convince herself.

'They are quite naïve,' Joe said as Oliver nodded.

'We've all Labs in London and in all the other areas looking out for them,' Abel said. 'Simon and Isaac have also promised to do the best they can.'

The young men made several more trips around the neighbourhood during the next few hours.

Finally, as they had almost given up hope, Ruby, Sophie, and Megan were called to the police station to look at some CCTV images.

‘Yes, that’s the twins!’ Ruby said excitedly.

‘Who’s the man with them?’ Megan squinted at the screen at a young man who was wearing a baseball cap pulled low over his face.

‘I can’t see much of his face,’ Ruby answered, ‘but they seem to know him.’

They watched the three people smiling and chatting together as they walked along the road near where the girls worked.

‘This was taken at a quarter to six yesterday evening,’ the police officer told them.

‘They finished at the office they work in at 5:15,’ Ruby told them.

‘Have you spoken to the other people who work there?’ Sophie asked the policeman.

‘Yes; no one noticed anything unusual. They said the twins left at the normal time. Two other girls walked as far as the tube station with them, then Milly and Lily continued along the road as usual. The girls didn’t talk about their evening arrangements. In fact, the girls said it was usually quite hard to make conversation with the twins as they’re rather shy.’

Ruby nodded in agreement. ‘They are.’

After leaving the police station, they walked along the same route and stopped at the point where the twins were filmed talking to the young man with the baseball cap.

‘What can have happened to them?’ Ruby said. ‘Who did they meet here?’

‘Well, the police are going to show the CCTV

footage on the news. Who knows, maybe someone somewhere will have something to tell us,' Oliver said.

A week later Johnny and Leon were walking home from college. Johnny opened the newspaper he was holding and turned the pages until he reached the article he was looking for.

'Still no news of Milly and Lily,' he looked at the photos of the two girls.

'The story isn't even front-page news anymore,' Leon replied, looking at the paper over his shoulder as they walked along the road. 'What can have happened to them?'

'They can't have disappeared into thin air! Someone must know something!' Johnny replied.

They both looked up as a girl stepped in front of them.

'Johnny! Leon!' she smiled at them. 'Am I glad to bump into you!'

'Hey!' Johnny smiled back. 'We haven't seen you since … oh …'

'It must have been that party at Ben's place,' Leon said.

'Anyway, what are you doing here?' Johnny asked her.

She sighed, 'I recently moved into a flat near here and I've just bought a new television. They delivered it to my home, but only as far as the front door!'

'Lead us to it!' Leon told her.

'No job too big!' Johnny joked. 'Where is it?'

'Just behind that white van,' she said.

'Hey, look who else is here!' Leon said as a figure stepped out from behind the van.

Dette toyed with a pen as she spoke on the phone to Celia. 'I'm probably just overreacting, but after the girls going missing, I can't help it.'

'Johnny and Leon are a lot wiser about life in the Non-Lab world than the two girls, Dette,' she answered.

Dette shrugged. 'That's what Keith said when I phoned him. I know they *do* stay out overnight sometimes, but we all agreed, after Milly and Lily, that we'd phone each other so no one would be worried. And they haven't called anyone!'

'Let's give them until this afternoon. They've been known to find an excuse to skip college lectures, but they never miss football training. If they don't turn up for that, we need to start worrying.'

'And if they are there I'm going to have a serious word with them!' Dette said. 'I'll phone you from college later.'

Ruby looked at Celia. 'Do you think …?'

'Come on now!' Celia said breezily, 'Dette is overreacting! You know what the twins are like, Ruby!'

'You're right, Celia,' Ruby gave a tight smile. Mentally she was compiling a list of people, Labs and Non-Labs, who might have an idea where the twins could be.

By two o'clock that afternoon she was seated with

Dette and Keith adding names to the list.

As Abel put down the phone, he ticked another name off the list beside him. He called someone else and soon repeated the action.

Two hours later they had exhausted all the names they had collected together.

Celia picked up the phone as it rang.

'Isaac? Any news? No, nothing here either … Yes we may have to … We'll discuss the situation now … Yes, thank you,' she replaced the receiver and looked at the others.

'No news. Isaac, Simon, Ben, and the others will continue to check out places they might have gone to. They'll phone if there's any news,' she looked at Abel, 'He asked if we'd told the police about the twins and the girls being Labs. He feels it might be relevant.'

Abel sighed, 'I think he may be right. I've made an appointment to see Detective Chief Inspector Fells, who is in charge of the investigation into the disappearance of Milly and Lily.'

'So you did not think to inform us of this fact at an earlier date, Mr Abel?' The chief inspector's face was grim. 'We would have looked at this case in an entirely different light!'

'And how many other Labs are living under assumed IDs in our community?' his second in command, Detective Inspector Thomas, added. 'I think we are entitled to know the identity of all these people!'

'Perhaps we could discuss that point at a different time?' Abel gave an impatient shrug. 'What matters now is finding out what has happened to these four Labs!'

The DI began to make his objections but Fells interrupted him.

'I think Mr Abel has a point, Thomas; our priority at the moment is to find these youngsters.' He turned to Abel. 'The Labs have not always been made welcome in our society, have they? You yourself were the victim of an attempted murder only a short while ago. The police still have no evidence of who is responsible for that attack, though there were rumours it was someone from the Forever England group.'

Abel nodded. 'And it was a few days later when the girls went missing. The two events could very well be connected.'

'Sven and Baxman also disappeared nearly two months ago. There has been no trace of them either, has there?' Inspector Fells turned to the DI, 'I'd like you to collect all the information you can on the investigation into their disappearance, Thomas.'

'I'll get on to it right away, sir.'

As Thomas left the room, he turned as the chief inspector called his name.

'And we won't be revealing to anyone that the missing youngsters are Labs. Not until I've spoken to the Prime Minister with Abel here.'

*

‘So, no news yet?’ Vincent Craig asked Celia that evening.

‘Nothing. I’m so worried, Vince! What can we do?’ she sobbed.

There was a pause.

‘I’ve been thinking about the fraud cases I’ve come across in my line of work. The first thing we did was make a list of all the people the company had any dealings with. You need to check out all the subscribers, donors, pharmaceutical companies, equipment providers – anyone with a connection to the Centre.’

‘I’ll divide these up between us and get on to them straight away,’ Celia said as she jotted down notes.

‘And look at all the communications with the Centre around the time it closed – emails, phone calls, letters, everything,’ he said. ‘Do you have access to them? Or can you gain access, somehow?’

Celia looked down at her memory stick.

‘Yes, I can! Thank you, Vince! I’ll go through it right now myself. We could make a list of all the people that oppose us!’

‘Look at supporters of the Centre, too, Celia. They may have made new plans of their own,’ Vince added. ‘And get back to me with any news, any time of the day or night!’

Abel entered the Centre office late that night. Ruby, Celia, Dette, Keith, and Isaac looked up eagerly, but their faces registered disappointment as he shook his head.

'The police have no leads whatsoever at the moment,' he sighed. 'I looked at some CCTV footage. It shows the boys walking along the main road near the shopping centre. There was a teenager, could be male or female, wearing a baseball cap pulled down to hide their face, in the background further up the road.'

'It could be the same person the girls spoke to!' Dette exclaimed.

'It could be anybody.' Abel told her.

'Anyway, we can't just sit here!' Ruby's eyes were red-rimmed. 'Who knows what is happening to Johnny and Leon, and the two girls!'

Dette nodded. 'You're right! There must be *something* we can do!'

Abel sat down and pulled a sheet of paper towards him.

'This is what we discussed today – first Sven and Baxman went missing …'

'But I don't think anyone would kidnap them, Abel!' Ruby interrupted.

'No, but they may be involved in the kidnapping of the twins shortly afterwards,' he said. 'The police, and I think they are correct, are assuming that the same people are responsible for the disappearance of both the male and female twins.'

'That could be it!' Keith said. 'If we could locate Sven and Baxman, we may be on the trail of the twins!'

'Why would they want them?' Dette said softly. 'Could they possibly be continuing their research …

as they were doing at the Centre?'

'We *must* find them soon!' Ruby cried.

'Vince suggested that we take a look at all types of communication with the Centre when the background was made public. Perhaps that would give us some clues,' Celia suggested.

'But all those details have been removed from the Centre system,' Dette said. 'We don't have access to them now.'

Celia pulled the memory stick from her pocket and inserted it into the computer. 'I made a copy of some files I needed.'

The others gathered around her as she opened a file on the screen. She scrolled down until she came to a folder titled 'Communication'. As she clicked on it 'Access Denied – Managerial Level Only' appeared on the screen.

'How can we get managerial permission?' Ruby asked.

'We can't,' Celia said simply. 'We're not supposed to have any of this information.' She frowned, then typed a password and tried unsuccessfully to open the folder again.

'Hmm!' she murmured to herself. 'Try to think like a Non-Lab!'

After two more attempts, she gained access.

'Phew!' She smiled. 'Another wrong attempt and the file would have locked itself!'

They looked at the screen to see several more folders. Celia clicked open one labelled 'Phone Transcripts'. There were several folders, each one dated. She clicked on the most recent date and scrolled down through a long list of messages mainly from disgruntled subscribers with complaints on many subjects, including demands for repayments and queries about medical treatment.

'That's not really important news,' Abel pointed out. 'We already know about these complaints. Many have been dealt with by the newly appointed management.'

Celia scrolled down further then stopped.

'Look, here's a different kind of message.' She read out:

A message for John Baxman,

It's a great blow to the future of medical development worldwide to witness the closure of the Centre for the Development of Medical Advancement, halted by the foolishness of a committee of ignorant, uninformed pen-pushers! I just want you to know I remain a stalwart supporter of your company and ideals and will be happy to voice my opinions publicly.

Gerald Hardgrave

She scrolled down further. 'And this.'

My Dear Mr Baxman,

I was very disappointed, although not too surprised, to hear of the closure of the Centre. When man is capable of making such remarkable medical advances, one must expect the less gifted to view such developments with trepidation. I only wish that such a remarkable institution as yours could be given the chance to develop and stride forward unfettered in a country that could appreciate such genius and the benefits it could provide to all mankind. I would like to assure you of my loyal support.

Rafe Maher

'While I continue to look through the phone transcripts, Dette and Keith find out some background information on anyone we list as possible supporters of Baxman,' Celia suggested.

'We could begin by Googling them,' Keith said as Dette turned to a second computer.

'I'll give Isaac a ring. He may know something about these people,' Ruby reached for the phone.

By the end of the afternoon, Celia has found ten more messages supporting the Centre's work among the many letters of complaint.

'Four of those sound as if they are from rather disturbed minds,' Celia said, reading out:

' "*I have always believed it is possible to breed a*

race of super monsters which we could keep in harness until the day we have to face the inevitable attack from space. Together we can save planet earth!'"

'That *could* be the kind of person we are looking for,' Keith sighed.

CHAPTER TWENTY-FIVE

Two men pulled the trolley into the dimly lit room.

'Pull it alongside the capsule,' he said in a low voice. 'Gently!'

The occupant of the trolley was gently lifted into the capsule. He flicked several of the switches on the monitor nearby.

'Mmm,' he nodded. 'All signs are regular.'

'Are they going to be all right?' she asked him.

'Of course. The others are, aren't they?'

'But they put up more of a fight,' she replied. 'It took the two boys longer to respond to the tranquiliser.'

'They've suffered some slight bruising, that is all. We will delay any tests until they have completely recovered,' he answered.

He closed the capsule lids and keyed data into a pad.

'They'll be fine now. They're sleeping as peacefully as the others!' He smiled at her as the two men wheeled the trolley away. 'Now our real work begins! Let's go to the laboratory!'

They found Sven there in front of a computer screen.

'This is as far as we were able to go at the Centre,' Sven explained, demonstrating with 3D images on the screen. 'But I am interested in developing these ideas further! Take a look at this!'

He brought up a different set of images and lists of data, talking excitedly all the time.

'Hold on!' Vlensky said after a while. 'I'll need to go through this a bit slower! I'm not up to your standard yet!'

Sven shook his head. 'Sorry! I just get so excited, thinking about the possibilities!'

Vlensky clapped his shoulder, 'I know how you feel! I would really like to study the data you have put together, Sven. Would it be possible for me to put it on my memory stick and take a look at it at a slower pace?'

Sven shrugged. 'By all means! Look through. Tell me if you have any ideas to offer, especially on the second stage – I have not perfected this yet. There is time, the DNA samples will be prepared by the end of the month.'

He turned away from them and was soon so engrossed in viewing slides under a microscope that he did not respond to their goodbyes as they left the laboratory.

In a second laboratory Vlensky scrolled through Sven's data.

'Most of this I can understand, but where exactly would we be able to input new data?' he said.

Lena peered at the screen and scrolled down. 'There are several suitable points. It depends on the type of data that is to be added. But Sven has already speeded up the growth rate and raised the IQ levels. What else are you suggesting?'

'I have a list here of possible characteristics and talents the new Labs will require. Not all the Labs will have the same talents of course,' he said.

'No, that would not be a good idea!' Lena smiled, 'We want a varied society! And one that will fit into life with the Labs already in existence.'

He stood up and patted her shoulder, 'I'll leave you to look through the files. I have an appointment with Baxman and our host! We have to keep the Non-Labs happy while they control the purse strings!'

Isaac rubbed his eyes and took another mouthful of coffee.

'I've been in touch with anyone who could have some information. Two guys said they'd get back to me if they can get hold of anything else.' He turned to look at Abel. 'I don't know if you'd consider this, but if we let my uncle, in on this and fill him in on the background details, he may have some advice he can give us. Three of these people live in Middle Eastern countries. He has travelled extensively in this area himself over the past twenty years.'

All eyes were on Abel, who was looking intently at Isaac. Finally he broke the silence. 'We could do with your uncle's help. Would he agree to keep this news away from the public eye for the moment at least?'

'He would not put any of you in danger, I assure you!' Isaac pulled a phone from his pocket. 'I'll call him immediately.'

Two days later Isaac and his uncle, Jake, were landing at the airport of the first country they had decided to visit.

Isaac heaved a sigh of relief as they entered their cool, air-conditioned hotel room after the hot and sticky taxi ride from the airport.

'It's like looking for a needle in a haystack!' he groaned as Jake spread a map of the country on the table.

'We'll follow our plan,' Jake replied. 'We are here to compile a tourist guide for the well-heeled. We want to see the best hotels, the most interesting sites, and of course be aware of the medical facilities in case our holiday makers need recourse to emergency facilities.'

By the following evening they had built up an extensive itinerary that would appeal to their imagined visitors.

'The Temple Hospital is definitely first class,' Isaac said. 'But I don't think it could have the facilities that the Centre had.'

His uncle agreed.

'Though the new building being constructed on the town outskirts could be more than offices for an international bank. That could just be a cover,' he pointed out. 'We should keep an eye on that.'

'I've let Celia have all the details. She's going to

take a look at their website,' Isaac replied.

By the end of a fortnight they had visited four different countries.

'It's Saturday, so it must be Rome!' joked Isaac.

'Laqaar, actually!' his uncle smiled spreading the map out on the table. 'Same plan as before. We'll start tomorrow morning. How about we take this evening off and go and get something to eat near here? The market square outside looks like an interesting place, if we were really thinking of holidaying here!'

'First a cold beer and then something to eat!' Isaac said as he headed for the shower.

'That looks just the place for that beer,' Jake said half an hour later as they made their way through the crowd jostling each other as they looked at items spread out on the stalls in the market place.

'Sorry!' Isaac said to a young woman as he knocked her arm and the fruit she was holding fell to the ground.

'It's OK, I've got it,' she replied picking them up.

'You speak English?' he smiled at her.

She pulled the scarf she was wearing so that it covered most of her face. 'A little!'

As he placed the fruit in her hands he felt the plastic strip on the inside of her wrist brush his fingers and he glanced up to see the look of fear pass through her eyes.

She flung the fruit back on to the stall and hurried away.

'Wait!' he called trying to follow her through the

crowd, but within seconds she had disappeared out of sight.

'Come on!' Jake was beside him. 'What about that cold beer?' His face grew serious as he saw Isaac's expression. 'What is it?'

'The girl I was talking to just now; we must find her! She's a Lab!' Isaac replied. 'She was wearing jeans and a cream-coloured headscarf.'

Though they searched the area extensively, there was no sign of the girl.

'Let's get back to the hotel. I'd better give Celia a call,' Isaac said finally.

Hidden in the shadows nearby, Lena breathed heavily as she watched them make their way back to the hotel. She had recognised Isaac from a gathering at Ben's house in London. She could not remember his name but he had arrived with another Non-Lab, the girl Ruby. Both had seemed very close to Johnny and Leon. She felt a pang; the twin boys had been so full of life, so full of fun – and look at them now! She shrugged off the feeling. She must concentrate on her work with Vlensky. Soon all the Labs would be able to enjoy a fulfilling life. No more waiting in the shadows! She pulled her scarf around her face and slipped away.

'Celia, it's Isaac,' he could hardly contain the excitement in his voice as, back in the hotel room. He clutched his mobile in his hand, 'There's a Lab here! A mature Lab! I didn't recognise her, her face was pretty well-concealed under a scarf, but I felt the plastic strip on her arm!'

He went on to relate their meeting that afternoon.

'Then she just disappeared from sight! Looks like she knew her way around here.'

Celia opened a file on the computer screen. 'Laqaar; you're where Rafe Maher lives, for most of the year anyway. He has several homes around the world, including London and New York.' She scrolled through the other information, 'He has investments in hotels, casinos, and leisure centres there in Laqaar, and deals exclusively with a multi-millionaire clientele. He had made several bids for shares in the Centre, though his offers were not accepted.'

'Email me a list of the business ventures he is involved in over here and we can take a look around them first, Celia,' Isaac told her.

'I'll do that, and I'll make further enquiries from here, too,' she replied.

She had just sent off the email as Abel and Ruby came in to the office.

'Any news?' Ruby asked her eagerly.

They sat and listened in silence as Celia recounted her conversation with Isaac.

'This seems unbelievable!' Abel shook his head. 'Could they already be producing Labs? But the plastic strip… I must go there immediately!'

'What if …' Celia looked thoughtful. 'What if some of our Labs are involved in the running of the new centre? Even involved in the kidnapping of our Labs …'

‘Why would a Lab turn against another Lab?’ Abel looked incredulous.

‘It could be for the same reasons Non-Labs turn against each other,’ Ruby ventured. ‘Greed. Power.’

‘But the man in the CCTV footage, with the girls and with the boys – none of us recognised him!’ Abel said slowly. ‘He could not be one of our Labs!’

‘Perhaps he did not want us to recognise him,’ Celia pointed out. ‘We have often altered our appearance to avoid recognition. Ruby has never been recognised by anyone who knew her previously.’

Abel shook his head firmly, ‘No, I do not believe any Lab could turn against another of his or her own kind! We are not like Non-Labs!’

‘Milly and Lily were very shy when it came to mixing with Non-Labs. They would be more likely to go with a Lab,’ Ruby said thoughtfully. ‘I would like to believe you are right, Abel, but we must consider all possibilities.’

‘Well, Keith and Dette are checking all the free Labs are safe. We’ll know from this if they are all accounted for,’ Celia said simply.

Abel took a deep breath as he heard Keith’s voice on the phone later that afternoon. He told him of the latest developments.

‘And are the Labs in Manchester all accounted for?’ he asked.

‘The ones we saw are. Three of the girls are in London for the week, staying with Joe and Oliver until they get news of Lily and Milly. We spoke to them on the phone just now. They're all trying to remain positive, though it's getting difficult, with so little news,' Keith told him.

'With these reports from Isaac we're hoping for news very soon,' Abel cleared his throat. 'Keith, are there any other Labs that you haven't seen or spoken to from the houses in that area?'

'We haven't seen Pellier, but I know he is with Jamie at the moment, in London. Jamie's been trying to help us. I'll be joining them this evening.'

'So, all are accounted for?' Abel gave a sigh of relief.

'Oh, well, not all, actually. I haven't seen Yuri, and I have not been able to contact him on his mobile phone. But according to the others, since he dropped out of college he has been working away for weeks at a time over the past few months, and it's often been difficult to contact him. So it's not a cause for concern, at the moment anyway,' Keith added.

Abel caught Celia's eye, 'Could you let me have the times he's been away over the last few months. And let me know as soon as he returns.'

'Do you think that he … could be involved in this, Abel?'

'No, not really, but at this stage we have to keep all our options open,' he replied. 'Just keep these ideas to yourself for the moment, Keith.'

'Of course, though I cannot imagine a Lab being involved …' There was a pause. 'Are all the Labs in the southern houses accounted for?'

'We are waiting for Dette to phone us.'

'I never thought we'd end up suspecting our own

kind.' Keith sounded thoughtful as he put the phone down.

'Can you obtain documents for me to travel to Laqaar, Celia?'

Celia raised her eyebrows. 'I expect I could, but it will probably take a few days.'

'We may not have that time!'

'You must tell the inspector dealing with the twins' case, Abel. Perhaps he can arrange them for you. They'll need your assistance if Labs are involved,' Ruby suggested.

'I'll speak to him this morning. I hope he'll be able to arrange for travel documents for me to go to Laqaar immediately,' he replied, picking up the phone.

An hour later he stood in the inspector's office.

'But I've already been issued with a travel permit for the USA. It shouldn't be difficult to obtain a visa for Laqaar. I can be of help in this situation if Labs are involved!' he insisted.

'He could be right, sir. We may very well need his assistance. He can understand how these people will react better than we can,' the younger police sergeant ventured.

The inspector frowned. 'Do you realise that Rafe Maher has been nominated for the Nobel Peace Prize for his community work in the neighbouring country? This could spark an international situation!'

'So we're both looking at this from the same angle. We all want a low-profile approach; we wish to safeguard the kidnapped Labs. Bad publicity at this point could jeopardise our chances of obtaining equal rights for the Labs here in the UK,' Abel said emphatically.

There was silence for a few minutes.

'OK, I'll arrange for entry permission for you as a part of a small security force involved in the Nobel nomination. God help me if this backfires! Pack your bag and be back here in an hour.'

Abel picked up a small rucksack at his feet. 'I'm ready!'

Lena had printed out the data Vlensky had asked her to look through. She shuddered. It sounded like a list of requirements for a military organisation, not the characteristics one would like to see in normal, happy, well-balanced people.

She sighed. Probably Vlensky was getting a bit carried away with his ideas, she was sure if she made a few comments he would become aware of how … soulless … these new Labs sounded.

She was scribbling a few of her own ideas in the margin when he came in.

'Ah! Just the person I wanted to talk to!' she smiled. 'I was looking through your programme plans. I think it would be a good idea to include an appreciation of the arts and an interest in sport because …'

Vlensky shook his head, 'No need to include that in the new Labs. Those kinds of leisure pursuits are for Non-Labs!'

Lena frowned. 'Well, I can see the purpose in

being able to enjoy one's leisure time …'

Vlensky shrugged, 'The new Labs will not need leisure time. They will be fully occupied by their assigned roles.'

'Oh, they seem more like an army than I had envisaged …' Lena said uncertainly.

'Exactly! An army! With us in control!' he smiled as he downloaded data onto a memory stick. 'Ready for a little experiment on our Lab friends?'

They entered the small dimly lit room where Milly, Lily, Johnny, and Leon slept, oblivious to their surroundings.

He put a memory stick into the computer at the head of Johnny's capsule.

'What are you going to do?' Lena asked him.

'I'm going back to his original programming and inserting extra data, at the point where you suggested mental abilities could be input,' he said. 'For the girls, I thought I would try out the opposite – delete some of their programmes at the same point.'

'Are you sure they will not be harmed in any way?' Lena asked him nervously.

'Not one hundred per cent, no,' he answered. 'Let's just see what happens, shall we?'

'I … I thought you said no harm would come to them?' Lena said.

'Well, there will have to be *some* sacrifices made if we are to achieve a perfect world,' he shrugged and turned back the screen. 'If this works, we may be able to re-programme some of the existing Labs.'

'But why would we want to do that?' Lena asked.

'I told you; the work done at the Centre was just the start of what the future could hold. Look at these Labs, for example, poor specimens! The boys are obviously of low intellectual ability. And the girls! Huh! Their timidity prevents them from participating as useful members of society!' he glanced up at her. 'So, first we see if it is possible to correct these imperfections. If not, their loss will be negligible.'

'Surely the loss of any Lab is far from negligible!' Lena was shocked.

'There is no space in the future world for second-rate Labs!' he said coldly. He keyed some information into the panel above the capsule. Johnny's body shuddered slightly but he remained asleep.

Lena bit her lip, her brow furrowed.

'I thought we shared the same vision of the future!' Vlensky spoke softly, but a menacing note crept in as he continued. 'If you are willing to put up with something less than perfect …?'

Lena looked into his eyes and saw that what she had taken to be enthusiasm was in fact more akin to mania. She shook her head.

'No! Of course not! It's just all happening so fast …' She gave a nervous laugh.

'Good!' said Vlensky, moving towards the capsule that held Milly and inserting a second memory stick into the screen above her head. Once again, the sleeping occupant shuddered as he keyed in data, then relaxed again.

He walked back to Johnny's screen and brought

up an image of the sleeping Lab. He enlarged an image of his head and rotated it.

'Look!' he cried. 'The central area is responding to the input!'

Lena watched a series of red contours spread out into widening circles. She scanned the rest of the image.

'It doesn't appear to have affected the rest of his brain activity, as far as I can tell.'

Vlensky turned to Milly's screen and brought up the image of her brain. At one side a green contour was diminishing.

'Ha! Success! And this is only the beginning! I have so many other ideas!' Vlensky smiled as he opened a new screen on his laptop.

'Hmm. I would suggest terminating the experiment here, for today,' Lena said in an even tone.

'Lena! There is no room for useless sentimentality!' Vlensky looked at her.

'No, but why waste reasonable specimens? It won't be easy to obtain new ones for further experiments,' She was jotting down data in a notebook as she replied and he could not see her expression.

'You're right,' he conceded, removing the memory sticks, 'I've a few more ideas I want to try out! Go and see Sven. He is getting curious about what we're doing here. Get him talking; get some more data from him. Do anything to keep him busy and away from this laboratory.'

Lena nodded and left the room. She stopped at a glass door where she could see Sven bent over a microscope. A computer screen flashed images in front of him. She paused, then decided she would tell Vlensky she had spoken to him, but he had seemed too immersed in his work to even notice her presence. It had happened before! She went to her room and grabbed her phone and purse. Then, pulling a long cream scarf over her head and around her face, she headed for the town centre and the hotel that Isaac and his companion had entered.

CHAPTER TWENTY-SIX

How is it going? Any news? V.

Nothing new. Celia had replied to his email. *No further sightings of the Lab. And we have followed up all the leads that Isaac has given me on the business interests Maher is involved with in Laqaar. I wish I knew what to do next!*

He replied immediately.

If only I could help! Perhaps you could forward any business names and I will see if I can make some enquiries. I don't suppose I'll have any more luck than you have, but I feel so helpless sitting here! V.

Celia highlighted and forwarded him the list of business interests Maher had in Laqaar.

Hope you can find out something useful here. Thanks. C.

I just hope I can be of assistance. It must be late there. You should get some sleep. I'll get back to you in a few hours. V.

I am *tired. I'll speak to you later. C.*

As she walked back to her apartment Celia gave a wistful smile. Vincent Craig was a source of strength for her during this difficult time.

*

Lena stood in the same place she had hidden before, watching the entrance of the hotel. She glanced at her watch; she had been there for nearly two hours. Vlensky or the others might question her whereabouts. She would have to think of a good story to cover herself.

Just then Isaac and his uncle climbed out of a taxi outside the hotel. They turned as they heard her call out. Isaac hurried over to her.

'I can't believe we've found you!' he held onto her hand as if he was afraid she would disappear again.

Lena glanced around anxiously and pulled them back into the dark side street. Jake looked wary.

'No! I mean you no harm!' she told them. 'I'm thinking of your safety. And that of Johnny, Leon, Milly, and Lily!'

'How do we know she's telling us the truth?' Jake asked his nephew. 'We don't even know who she is!'

'I am a Lab!' she pushed up her sleeve to reveal a tattooed code. 'There might not be very much time! You must trust me! Please!'

Isaac looked at her. 'Where are the twins? Are they alright?'

She bit her lip. 'At the moment, but we must act quickly! Come with me, please!'

'Give us the details and we can decide what we will do from there,' Jake suggested.

Isaac shook his head, 'No, Jake, if the twins are in trouble, we must go straight away!'

'You won't be much help if you walk into a trap, Isaac. Think, lad!' his uncle warned him.

Isaac looked at Lena. 'Where are they now?'

'At the Cactus Flower Hotel,' she said. 'It is not really a hotel; it is a front for the new research centre. Vlensky has already started some experiments on both sets of twins! We must stop him going any further.'

'We'd better phone the police!' Jake said, pulling out his phone.

Lena put her hand over his. 'You must not do that! Maher has planned for such an event and can cover his tracks easily! He has the local police force eating out of his hand. It will be our word against his. And time is running out for the twins!'

Isaac looked at his uncle. ''I'm going with her!'

'Let's go!' his uncle replied.

Lena hurried ahead of the two men. She stopped a short distance from the research centre and drew them behind a large floral display. Isaac looked at the glass building with *Laqaar Medicentre – Director R. Maher* on a large sign above it.

'It doesn't look much, does it?' he said, watching several people, some mothers with young children, coming and going from the building.

'No, Maher has even leased out three of the ground floor suites to newly qualified doctors at very low rents. He thinks it makes the place seem more authentic,' Lena told him. 'That is not the building we want, though. The real work is done at the hotel. Come!' she led him through a maze of narrow streets to the outskirts of the small town. They stopped at a distance from the large, impressive marble hotel building. In front of it was an ornamental pond with a dazzling display of brightly coloured flowers.

‘How are we going to get into it?’ Isaac asked her. ‘It’s completely cut off.’

‘Not completely,’ Lena told him. ‘We need private access away from the eyes of our host.’

She led them stealthily to an overgrown area at the back of the building. At a border of tall rushes, she stopped and faced the two men

‘We must be very careful here! Security is very tight! Wait for me.’ She crept forward and disappeared from sight.

‘I’ll go in, Jake,’ Isaac held up a hand to silence his protests. ‘Wait here and if I’m not out in an hour come looking for me. With reinforcements if possible!’

The older man shook his head. ‘I don’t like this at all!’

‘Try to get hold of Celia and Abel,’ Isaac said as Lena reappeared, beckoning him to follow her.

He found himself in front of a concealed doorway. Lena swiped a card and the door swung back. Inside they found themselves in a narrow tunnel which led to a metal door. Lena inched the door open and they stepped into an empty corridor. There was the sound of machinery nearby. Isaac was pushed into a small, dimly-lit room as Lena pressed her finger close to her lips and left him there. After a few moments the door was reopened.

'Help me!' Lena whispered, pulling an inert figure behind her.

'He's not …?' he began.

'Dead? No, he'll probably come around in about an hour.' She pulled her scarf off her head and used it as a gag. 'Put on the jacket – it's a bit tight, but you can leave it open.'

She pinned the unconscious man's ID card onto the jacket, smudging the photo with dust.

'That should cover you,' she said.

She peered out through a chink in the door.

'The coast is clear. We have to go past Sven's laboratory, but he will probably be too busy to notice us! The whole place is bugged, so don't ask any questions until I tell you it is safe to do so!'

They both slipped out of the room and made their way down the corridor. Lena exchanged a brief greeting with a man dressed in overalls who acknowledged her and gave a cursory glance at Isaac.

As they made their way up a flights of stairs a second man in a security uniform appeared and stopped them.

'Madame Lena, Mr Vlensky was enquiring about your whereabouts a short time ago.'

Lena tapped her forehead. 'I forgot! I promised I'd call him. I was caught up in my work! I'll go and see him straight away.'

The man nodded and continued on his way.

Lena hurried along the corridor and paused outside a glass door.

She breathed a sigh of relief, 'Good, Vlensky isn't

here at the moment!'

She led Isaac to the small side room where the twins lay sleeping in their capsules.

'Johnny, Leon, girls!' Isaac cried, reaching for the first capsule lid.

Lena laid her hand on his arm.

'We must ready them for awakening before the capsules can be opened.'

'How long will it take?' Isaac looked down at the sleeping figures.

'Half an hour. Their bodies need to be reacclimatised to our present environment,' she took a deep breath as she keyed in data on the screen above the head of each person. Then she undid the lock on each one.

'Are you sure they'll be OK?' Isaac whispered.

'Not absolutely. We must hope!' she replied. 'In this room it's safe. You better phone your friend; he'll be worried about you.'

Isaac had hardly dialled Jake's number when his uncle answered.

'Isaac! Are you OK?' Jake cried.

'I'm fine. Any news from Celia or Abel?' he asked.

'Celia and her friends at the Centre seem to have everything in hand.' His uncle explained how the situation was developing in the UK. 'In fact, I'm waiting for Abel and the police officers to arrive any time now.'

'Good. We've got another twenty minutes before the twins can be awakened,' Isaac said, looking at his watch. 'Don't let anyone do anything before then!'

He dialled a second number.

Celia stared at the computer screen and hit the table in frustration.

'I can't work out how to get into the hotel site!'

'There must be a way!' Ruby looked around at Dette, who shook her head.

'I know much less than Celia about this, I'm afraid.'

'There is one person who might be able to help me!' Celia said. She picked up the phone and dialled a number.

'Hello, Vince? It's me, Celia. I know it's late there, but we really need your help!'

'Celia!' Vince answered. 'I'm here! Anything I can do?'

He pulled himself out of bed and into his wheelchair.

'I've got my laptop on now ...'

He listened, occasionally commenting as she filled him in on the details of the recent events.

'OK, I've got the hotel site in front of me now. We need to get into the admin files.'

'I know, but I just cannot get any method to work!' Celia sounded panicky.

'Hey, calm down a minute ...' he murmured.

'It could be a matter of life and death!' Celia began to sob.

'OK,' his voice was calm, 'I'm thinking like a Non-Lab here!'

He began to key in data. 'No … not that … but wait …I'm getting somewhere! … Are you ready?'

Celia listened and keyed in the instructions he gave her. There was a tense silence in the room as she worked.

'I've got it on the screen now, Vince!' she cried as she saw a selection of files in front of her. 'Admin, Sven, and Vlensky.'

'Well, we know Sven is Non-Lab, so perhaps Vlensky could be the errant Lab,' Vince continued. 'I'll try to work out Sven's password, you try Vlensky's.'

Dette picked up a second phone as it rang.

'Isaac! Celia is on the hotel site, trying to gain access to Sven and Vlensky's files. From there Celia thinks they can disable the computers at the hotel.'

'They have the twins sedated in four capsules at the moment. Lena has unlocked them, but it will be another fifteen minutes before we can get them out safely. Don't let them turn off any equipment until then,' Isaac told her, checking his watch. 'Lena is copying files from this centre as evidence against Maher and the others. Oh, I'll have to go, someone's coming!'

'In thirteen minutes' time the twins will be out of the capsules and you can disable the equipment, Celia,' Dette said, looking at the clock.

'If only I knew who Vlensky is,' she said, 'then maybe I could have an idea of what his password might be!'

Ruby pictured the CCTV image in her mind.

'Someone tall, broad shouldered, straight black hair – though he could actually have fair hair. Probably self-opinionated; pretty confident,' she said aloud.

'You know it sounds a bit like …' Dette began.

They all looked at her.

'Don't be afraid to speak against anyone. If you're wrong it won't matter, and if you are right it could save the twins' lives!' Celia urged her.

'Well, Yuri. He could be a bit pompous at times; always saying he was better than the Non-Lab lecturers; that's why he dropped out of college …' She paused. 'What if it *is* Yuri?'

Celia pulled a scrap of paper towards her and began jotting down ideas. 'What would he choose as his password, what would he choose?'

'Quick, go behind that desk! Someone is coming!' Lena told Isaac.

He had hardly hidden himself when the door opened.

'Lena! Where have you been? I have looked for you everywhere this afternoon!' Vlensky said.

'Oh, I got carried away! Lost track of time! I have been thinking about some alterations we could try out on our friends here,' she pulled out a file and carried it to a desk at the far side of the room. 'Will you look at them with me?'

'In one moment. First I would like to try out something myself. I've something to take Johnny's mind off football!' he smiled as he headed for the capsule.

'No!' Lena cried out. Puzzled, Vlensky faced her.

'I mean … we have already input data today. I think we must … wait until tomorrow. His brain will be useless!'

Isaac looked at his watch; still five minutes until the Labs would awaken.

'Hmmm … perhaps you are right!' Vlensky sat down beside her and looked at the sheet spread out in front of her. 'But this is the data I gave you!'

'Yes! Exactly!' Lena turned to the computer, 'Now, I was thinking we could group the characteristics according to compatibility then input the entire group at certain points, such as the ones I mentioned earlier.' She opened the file on the screen and rotated an image of a human brain.

'Brilliant! I knew I could count on you, Lena!' He sprang up. 'But let's make it more realistic! Let's get up an image of one of our Lab friends here. The real thing!'

He headed for the capsules and suddenly stopped.

'What has happened?'

'What is it, Vlensky?' Lena's voice sound shaky.

He ran towards the capsules, shouting, 'Johnny's capsule; someone has unlocked it! They are all unlocked!'

Isaac sprang from behind the desk and pushed Vlensky over as he ran past. Both men fell to the floor, knocking down a pile of books and glass slides.

Vlensky pulled himself to his feet. 'What are you doing here?'

He grabbed Isaac's collar and pulled him up, raising his fist threateningly. Lena ran to the two men and grabbed Vlensky's arm.

'No! No! Yuri! We can't do this anymore! We must stop, before it is too late!'

Her companion glared at her, 'You? You are in on this, too?'

He shook off her arm and threw Isaac to the floor. He fell heavily, wincing as he crashed into a desk. Winded, he looked up to see Vlensky pull a metal bar from the remains of the desk and raise it over Lena.

She rolled to one side as the bar crashed through a chair near her. Vlensky upturned a case of glass containers on top of her and headed for the capsules once more.

Grimacing with pain, Isaac pulled himself up and threw himself on to Vlensky, pinning his arms to his sides. With a strangled cry Vlensky wrenched him off and flung him to the floor once again. Isaac shielded himself behind the desk as a hail of equipment rained down on him.

'You will *not* stop me now!' Vlensky screamed. 'No Lab or Non-Lab will stand in my way!'

Isaac saw the lid of a capsule move. He picked up a piece of wood and began to walk towards Vlensky.

'We will! We will! Give up now!' he said quietly.

The second man faced him and laughed, 'You think you can stop me? You don't stand a chance!' he moved menacingly towards him.

From the corner of his eye, Isaac could see a figure sitting up in the capsule. A second one was also opening and another figure climbed out and slipped out of sight. The white hooded outfits they wore made it hard to identify them.

'The place is surrounded! There's nothing you can do!' Isaac kept on talking as the first figure crept up behind Vlensky.

'Really?' Vlensky turned swiftly as he heard a sound behind him.

After a brief struggle, the figure was overpowered. Vlensky pulled down the hood to reveal Johnny's face. Smashing a glass bottle, he held the jagged end to Johnny's throat. 'This gives me a bit more bargaining power now, doesn't it?'

He edged backwards towards the door, 'If anyone gets in my way …'

There were shouts outside the door and Abel and Jake came running in, followed by the two policemen, both holding guns.

'Get them out of here!' Vlensky shouted at Abel.

As he nodded at them, they stepped back out of the room reluctantly.

'Yuri? What are you doing?' Abel shook his head in disbelief.

'Just building a better future for the Labs. Not the second-class life you had planned for all of us!' he spat out. 'Johnny's coming with me. You want to see him again, you listen to me. I need transport out of here, by air. Tell them!'

Jake looked at Abel and went outside to the

waiting police and security guards waiting there.

'I've collected enough data to set up my own place! I don't need anybody to help!' Yuri looked down at Lena's unconscious figure, 'No one understands! Lab, Non-Lab – you're all pathetic! Call yourself a leader, Abel? You are willing to accept any crumbs that fall off the great Non-Lab leaders' tables! The Centre was the start of something great!'

Isaac could see a small, hooded figure edging towards Yuri; their eyes met. He cleared his throat.

'What makes you think you can build a better future on your own, Yuri? Wouldn't it be better for all the Labs to pull together? Many are working with Non-Labs; we're all getting somewhere …'

'No! There are too many substandard Labs! I will build a perfect world. Get rid of the flawed Labs. Only the best will survive! Has transport been arranged?' As he glanced towards the door the figure jumped up, pulling the glass from Yuri's hand and pushing Johnny's head to one side. Isaac leapt forward and pulled Johnny out of the way as Abel threw himself on top of Yuri.

There was a scream as the two remaining capsules were pushed open and one of the figures leapt upon the bloodied rescuer.

'Milly! Milly! Are you OK?' she cried, tearing strips of her suit into makeshift bandages which she wound around her twin's hand.

A sudden crash caused them all to look around.

Abel had been flung back against one of the

capsules which had collapsed on top of him. The next moment the doorway was filled with police and security men. Amidst the shouts and crashing of glass, Lena opened her eyes and gave a weak smile as she watched Yuri slip out of the door.

'So we missed all the action!' Dette was saying a few days later as they all sat around in the Centre office. She smiled at the people around her.

'We found out that Celia and Vince had been pretty busy themselves!' Abel smiled.

'Yes, when Rafe Maher sent out the order to destroy certain documents on the Laqaar Medicentre computer system, he found he was too late! Celia and Vince had already barred access to the system and emailed copies of incriminating files to Scotland Yard!' Isaac slapped his thigh, then grimaced in pain. 'I wish I had your quick healing powers!'

'One thing that does bother me is that Yuri escaped,' he added.

'He won't be able to contact Baxman or Sven this time,' Celia said.

'Are they both being held in custody?' Ruby asked.

'Baxman is in a high-security prison block. Sven is in a psychiatric prison unit,' Celia told her. 'Neither will be granted bail before the trial. I doubt if Sven will ever be released.'

Lena, who had gone back to her old name of Fiona now that she was no longer part of Yuri's scheme, gave a sad smile, 'Sven cannot be held guilty for his part in all this. He lives in another world.'

She pulled two memory sticks from her pocket. 'And Yuri does not have the data he thinks he has. I substituted blank memory sticks for his own. I don't think he represents a future threat.'

She passed the memory sticks to Abel and looked at him.

'I was surprised that you didn't inform the police of my role. Why did you tell them I'd been planted there to monitor Yuri's activities?'

'For the same reason you didn't inform the police of Yuri's escape route, Fiona. We could not hand a Lab over to the Non-Lab justice system. They don't understand all sides of the story. And we could not let a Lab be incarcerated in a Non-Lab prison. We've already been imprisoned by Non-Labs!' Abel answered.

'And we don't think you'll be a threat to any Lab in the future,' Leon added.

Fiona shook her head, 'No, I … I was so foolish, so blind! But I could never cause harm to another Lab!'

Isaac shrugged as the other Labs nodded in agreement.

'You Labs certainly stick together.'

'Milly, you were so brave!' Lily said, looking in admiration at her sister. 'I have never seen you so fearless before!'

'Yes, I surprised myself!' Milly grinned. 'I don't know why I was so reticent before. We must be more assertive, Lily!'

Her sister gave a weak smile. 'Yes.'

'Thank goodness you *were* feeling brave!' Johnny said, rubbing his throat.

Silence spread over the company as they all considered the events of the last few days. Johnny pulled a plaster off his finger and began to whistle softly.

'What's that you're whistling?' Leon asked him.

'Brahms violin concerto,' Johnny replied absently, 'Sort of soothing, isn't it?'

Leon gazed at him with an incredulous expression.

'How do you know anything about Brahms or violins?' he gasped.

Fiona sat forward. 'Yuri put extra data into your brain. And for Milly he extracted something, your timidity. Hence your new strengths, or interests.'

'Does that mean you are not so good at football?' Leon asked his twin.

Johnny's jaw dropped, 'Come on! Let's go and find out!'

Ruby stood in the doorway watching the two boys playing football with some of the Labs from the Compound. The others were deep in conversation with Fiona on the experiments Yuri had carried out. She became aware of someone standing beside her.

'His new interest in classical music has not affected his football, has it?' she said to Isaac.

'No,' he replied. 'When I think back on all that has happened since I first confronted you about the number of twins you knew! I didn't know what I was letting myself in for! And I bet you had no idea what the future held for you when you first met the Labs, did you, Ruby?'

'Not at all,' she laughed. 'But I don't regret a single thing about my life now.'

'Nor me. They are a wonderful group of people. Just look at what Celia can do with a computer! She's amazing!'

They both looked up as Abel joined them.

'Isaac! You can't use any of *this* story, but we still have the possibility of the twins signing up for one of the premier football teams. And of course, there will be a definite story for you when Beth, Frank, and the baby come here in a few days' time! It'll hopefully coincide with the government announcement of the rights of Labs. Let's sort out some details, shall we?'

'All this happening at the same time! Wow, what a news story!' Isaac smiled.

Ruby followed them inside and joined Celia and Dette.

'So, you are going to meet up for the first time!' Dette exclaimed.

'Vince?' Ruby said.

Celia nodded, 'He'll be here in a few days! He's anxious to meet everyone, especially after all this excitement!'

'He'll get to meet Beth, Frank, and the baby, too!' Dette smiled. 'They're moving back into the Compound at the end of this week!'

'The news reporters have been less interested in

them since the reports of three other mixed couples expecting babies!' Ruby said.

'And Simon wants to announce his engagement to Sakura soon, too,' Dette added, 'though his parents are not that keen. Especially his mother. She's doing everything she can to break up their relationship!'

Abel smiled and looked around at the people gathered in the Compound hall. Labs and Non-Labs mingled together. Isaac was busy organising Beth and baby Frankie for a photograph.

'This is Vincent Craig, Abel,' Celia said proudly, introducing a smartly dressed man in a wheelchair.

'Pleased to meet you,' Abel said, holding out his hand.

'I'm very pleased to meet you, too, Abel. You have done so much for your people. It can't have been easy!' Vince said. 'It's so good to put faces to the names I have heard so much about!'

'Mr Craig! I'm so glad you are here!' Dette shook his hand. 'Celia has told us so much about you, too!'

After a while, Abel wandered over to Beth and Frank, who were chatting to Johnny and Leon.

'Can he walk yet?' Johnny asked, looking at the baby in Beth's arms.

'No, not yet; it will be another year before he can do that, according to the midwife,' Beth told him, 'Although she says Frankie is developing a lot faster than most babies. Here, hold him, Johnny. It's OK, he won't break!'

A smile spread over Johnny's face as little Frankie looked up at him with wide blue eyes.

Leon stroked the baby's kicking feet, 'It's so strange to see such a little person moving about; young Labs just sleep!'

A worried look passed across Johnny's face as the young child began to squirm and then let out a loud howl. 'Oh, Beth! Something's wrong!'

'Don't worry, he's just letting us know he's hungry!' she smiled, standing up and taking the baby from Johnny. 'He probably needs changing, too. We'll see you later.'

'He takes some looking after for such a small person!' Leon shook his head.

'Well, yes, children brought up in a Non-Lab way do take some looking after, but it's worth it!' Frank smiled. 'I wouldn't like to see him grow in a capsule. I want to teach him things myself. Like football!'

Leon nodded enthusiastically. 'We can help you there, Frank!'

'And he should learn about music, too! Not all classical music is boring, you know, Leon!' Johnny said.

'There's more than just classical music,' Sakura added as she joined them with Miyu and Jade. 'You should meet some of the talented musicians we have been working with!'

The two other girls nodded.

Simon joined them, putting his arms around Sakura's waist and pulling her to him. 'You are all wonderful musicians!'

‘Your big concert is on Sunday, isn’t it?’ Abel said. ‘It is definite now that the prime minister is going to make an announcement about the legal status of the Labs on Monday morning!’

‘It’s worked out perfectly! We’ve decided that now is the time to reveal our true identities!’ Jade said.

‘No more hiding!’ Miyu added.

‘Whoever chooses to accept us, or not …’ Sakura looked in to Simon’s eyes.

‘They will be the losers, not us!’ he said softly. ‘We’re standing together!’

‘No more hiding!’ Johnny repeated, looking at his brother. ‘We’re going public!’

‘Yes, we’re signing for Manchester Central as Labs!’ Leon nodded.

‘Show the world you are proud to be Labs!’ Simon said. ‘Hey, why not get all this together? Let the Labs who are ready to reveal their true identities do so when Johnny and Leon sign up for Manchester?’

‘Keith! Isaac!’ he beckoned them over. Isaac nodded eagerly as Simon explained his ideas.

‘This could be the most spectacular event of the year! The Labs will have really arrived!’ He rubbed his hands together.

When Beth re-entered the room a short time later she made her way over to Celia, Ruby and Vince.

‘They seem excited about something.’ She gestured towards Isaac and the others.

Ruby explained what they were arranging.

Beth frowned, 'I don't want to seem ungrateful, but I don't want Frankie to be part of a circus every time we are seen in public. I just want a normal family life …'

Ruby patted her arm. 'You are entitled to that, Beth. Go and speak to Isaac and Frank now. Make sure they understand your point of view. Here, let me hold the baby for a while.'

She watched Beth join the group. 'I hope they listen to her. I can understand how she is feeling, can't you, Celia? Celia?'

Celia's mind was far away as she gazed down as the sleepy child, a look of wonder and also fear on her face.

Vincent cleared his throat. 'Ruby, go and make sure they listen to Beth. Give me the child, he's nearly asleep. Celia, we'll go for a walk outside, help the little chap to nod off!'

Celia stood up awkwardly, 'Are … are you sure, Vince?'

'Absolutely! Let's go!' he replied.

It was peaceful outside. Only a few of the Labs were playing football and basketball near the hall.

'It's been quite a week so far, hasn't it, Celia?' he said softly.

Celia nodded. 'It has. I knew the past few months have been leading up to this, but now it is all happening, I feel, I don't know really …'

Vince nodded. 'It's all happening so quickly. And you still have a few issues to sort out yourself, don't you?'

Celia turned her face away as if to hide her expression.

'Sit down on that bench there, Celia,' Vince nodded towards a wooden bench shaded by an overhanging tree.

Celia settled herself and looked at Vince.

'Here,' he said. 'Your turn to hold the baby. Gently now; he's almost asleep!' he said, silencing her protests.

Celia's hands trembled as she held the sleepy child. She looked down into his face as he struggled to keep his eyes open.

'Just like Marissa was at that age!' Vince chuckled. 'Can't let himself go to sleep in case he misses something important! Isn't he beautiful?'

'He is,' Celia smiled as his tiny fist close around on of her fingers.

'Vince … there's something I want to ask you …' she said softly.

He waited.

'I don't know how to say this … I don't want to upset you …' she was almost whispering now, rocking the child in her arms.

'I know, Celia,' he answered.

He took a deep breath.

'You are afraid to ask me what it feels like to have a child, like this little person. To hold her in your arms, to love her, to have so many dreams for the future as you watch her take her first steps, to feel in your heart you would die for her! And then to lose her.'

He turned to look at Celia. She nodded tearfully.

'I couldn't do that! Look at him – so peaceful, so trusting – yet I cannot promise that I will be able to protect him against all the dangers of the world. I couldn't risk it!'

Vince's eyes too were moist as he laid a hand on her arm.

'No. We want to make these promises; we can offer to lay down our lives for our children, but sometimes even that is not enough!'

There was a long silence. Celia watched as a tear fell onto Frankie's blanket and was absorbed into the soft material.

Eventually, Vince continued.

'But we *can* take these risks. We have to. It was too painful to think of them at first, but as the time went by I got great comfort from the sweet memories Marissa had left behind. All the happy times we had shared together. Eventually, after a long time, I was able to look at the photos and think about the good times, too.'

Celia remained silent beside him.

'I know you have one more question to ask me, Celia,' Vince said. She looked up and waited.

'Yes. It was worth having Marissa, even though we lost her so young. The four years she spent on this earth gave me and Vanessa so much pleasure and we would *never* want that to be taken from us. I know Vanessa thinks so, too. She was the first to realise that, while I was so lost in my grief I could not see anything clearly.

'So be brave, Celia. Don't deny yourself the greatest gift of all just because you are afraid you are not strong enough to protect him or her from everything! No one can guarantee that. We are all human – however we came to be here. The risk *is* worth it!'

Most of the others were grouped in a large circle when Vince and Celia rejoined them. Beth rose and came to take the sleeping child.

'Oh, you got him off to sleep. Thank you, Celia. You certainly have a way with him, it usually takes us ages to get him to nod off!'

Celia smiled at her. 'Any time I can help, Beth, now that you're moving back to the Compound, just ask!'

Dette and Ruby exchanged glances.

'Come and join us, you two, we'll explain our plans for Monday. The Labs will finally be legal! Simon has some great ideas for publicity,' Isaac called out, pulling up a chair for Celia beside him.

'I'll get Frankie into his cot now,' Beth said to Frank.

'I'll walk up with you and get the phone book from the office, and we can make a start on some of the calls we need to make,' Ruby said, getting up too.

Abel also stood up, 'I need a file from the office.'

'Oh, if you tell me which one, Abel …' she began, but he followed them from the room.

They walked with Beth as far as her apartment.

'Are you sure you have everything you need, Beth?' Ruby asked her.

'Yes, thanks,' Beth smiled. 'It's lovely to be home again.'

Ruby and Abel turned back down the pathway.

'It'll be interesting having a baby around,' Abel began.

'Yes. And I've heard that at least one of the mothers-to-be is planning on moving to the Compound!' Ruby said. 'It would be lovely to have children around here!'

'You seem to know what you're doing with Frankie,' Abel said.

'I love babies!' Ruby smiled.

As they neared Ruby's apartment she stopped.

'I think I'll pick up my jacket, it's getting a bit cooler now,' she said. 'I'll catch up with you in a minute, Abel.'

As she opened the door she was surprised to find he was still beside her. He pushed the door closed.

'Ruby…' he began nervously.

'Yes, Abel?' she waited.

'Over the months I've got to know you – well, we've got to know each other – and you've made me realise, first of all, that not all Non-Labs are our enemies! Some in fact can become special friends.'

Ruby smiled. 'I remember at first, Abel, you didn't like Non-Labs at all. You were quite scary! Isaac and I were terrified of you!'

He nodded. 'Yes, I suppose I was a difficult person to get on with. All I thought about was protecting the Labs. I never wanted to ask for help, especially from Non-Labs. Well, I was wrong!'

'I'm so glad things are finally working out now. You've fought long and hard for the Labs!'

'With help, Ruby. I couldn't have done this on my own,' he replied.

She had picked up her jacket and had turned towards the door when Abel caught her arms.

'Ruby …' his face was close to hers now. She could feel her heart quickening. 'Ruby … do you, remember that time, at the university demo …'

'Yes,' she felt her face flush.

'I just wondered …' as he moved closer to her his mobile phone started to ring. Exasperated, he pulled it from his pocket and, switching it off, tossed it onto the table, 'Whoever it is, they can wait!'

He turned back to her and blurted out, 'Ruby, I really like you. Very much, in fact.'

He faltered as Ruby stood silently in front of him and his arms dropped to his sides, 'It's OK if you don't feel the same.' He began to back up towards the door. 'Maybe there's someone else you like, someone more like you. That's fine.'

As he turned to leave, Ruby grabbed his shoulders and pressed her lips hard against his. She felt his body relax as his arms slid around her and drew her close. After several minutes she pulled back and smiled at him.

'I was afraid that first kiss didn't mean as much to you as it did to me.'

Abel shook his head. 'I was afraid of how I felt about you and I had no idea if you felt the same way!'

Ruby smiled and pulled him closer to her.

'So that's the plan; a live TV programme. The twins, the new Manchester Central players, will reveal themselves to be Labs, and then many other Labs will also reveal their true identities!' Isaac said, nervously fingering his collar. 'If we can pull this off, we'll have made history!'

'I can't believe the manager agreed so easily!' Celia told him.

'Well, Central's owner, Lib, is a great friend of Zorro's,' he replied. 'So persuading them was not too difficult! Plus the publicity can only be good for the club! Think of the sales at the gates when they have the first two Labs on their team!'

'Convincing the prime minister to allow this to go ahead is going to be the most difficult thing!' Abel said.

Ruby squeezed his hand. 'We can do it! We have so many people on our side!'

They all looked around as the door opened and the prime minister and two of his aides appeared.

'I'm sorry to have kept you waiting; I had an unexpected phone call from President Armstrong. He has made it known that he is agreeable to the show going ahead as you have suggested,' he explained. 'He is very keen on the Labs becoming fully integrated members of society as soon as possible.'

The others exchanged smiles.

'But I have made no promises to him at all. I had hoped that we could introduce the Equality Bill for

Labs in our society on a quieter note. I am afraid that such publicity and celebration may incite violence, Mr Abel,' he said.

'As Labs we feel the Equality Bill is a cause for great celebration, Mr Cartwright. And as Jason Fullman, the manager of Manchester Central, is pleased to allow us to have a live show when our Lab boys sign up we felt it was a great opportunity for all of us, Labs and Non-Labs, to celebrate together,' he replied. 'These boys are great role models for both Lab and Non-Lab youth.'

'As the Labs gain their equal status in our society, what guarantee do we have that the Labs will respect our laws, Mr Abel?' Mr Cartwright continued.

'The same guarantee that all of the Non-Labs in the UK will do likewise, Mr Prime Minister!' he said.

'Mr Cartwright, could I also say something?' Vincent Craig sat up straight.

The prime minister nodded for him to go ahead.

'I have become involved with the Labs, through one young lady in particular, over the past few months,' he returned the smile Celia gave him. 'One thing she said to me really stuck in my mind. When she was trying to find out about me, she said she had "wanted to find out more about the person who had caused her to be created." Many of us, directly or indirectly, have caused new people to come into existence. Surely if we have caused new life to be created it is a reason for celebration, not something you want to keep quiet? I know, for one, that I have celebrated every day that I have got to know Celia! And all her friends, too!'

Mr Cartwright closed the file in front of him and smoothed down the cover.

'If I can see the plans for the show by this evening I will get my aides to look through them,' he finally said.

'I have them here!' Isaac said, pulling a folder from his briefcase. 'There's also a list of names of those involved in the programme broadcast who will be informed of all the details beforehand, from the top level to the boys on the floor, *and* a list of security precautions, Mr Cartwright!'

CHAPTER TWENTY-SEVEN

'Are all the Labs going to reveal their true identities today?' Valerie asked as she entered the studio with Isaac and Dette.

'Only those who wish to do so,' Dette replied. She looked around the studio audience and smiled. 'I recognise so many Lab faces!'

'There's the woman from the BBC, I must go and make sure everything is ready.' Isaac smiled, 'This interview will go down in history!'

'We have seats here at the front,' Dette said.

As she and Ruby sat down a middle-aged man was taking a seat on one of a group of sofas arranged to the side of the studio stage. A silence fell over the room as he cleared his throat.

'It's George Hickman! One of the most highly paid sports commentators!' Ruby whispered to Dette.

'Good evening, ladies and gentlemen. Today we can finally reveal which new boys we will see signed up to Manchester Central! And have we got some surprises in store for you today! But first of all, let's have a word with Manchester Central's manager, Jason Fullman, and the club's owner, Lib, the lead singer of XSity.'

There was a round of applause as Jason Fullman and Lib made their way onto the set and joined Hickman.

'First of all, let's talk about the success the club has enjoyed over the past year, Jason!' Hickman began.

They talked at some length about the team's successes and watched clips of spectacular goals scored and shots saved.

After half an hour, Hickman turned back to the audience. 'Well, you might be wondering, as I certainly am, why Manchester Central are thinking of signing up two totally unknown players. Perhaps you could give us some information on the background of these boys, Jason?'

'Well, George, we heard about these lads from one of our sports colleges and I must admit, we were pretty sceptical when we were told how amazing they were. But, I think you'll agree with me, these lads are in a class of their own when it comes to skills on the field, isn't that right, Lib?'

'Oh, yeah! Whatever position you ask them to play, they can outdo any player around them!'

'They're that good, Jason?' George asked.

'*That* good, George! When you've seen them in action in the clips I'm about to show you, you'll know what I'm talking about!' Jason turned back to the large screen.

There were delighted cries from the audience as Johnny and Leon were shown scoring and setting up superb goals, and even performing brilliantly as goalkeepers. The audience rose and gave a resounding applause as the film clips drew to a close.

George shook his head, 'If I didn't trust you, Jason, I'd say that filming was rigged! Those boys are absolutely remarkable!'

He turned back to the studio audience, 'You'll get the chance to meet these lads a bit later on, but first we have a special guest appearance by someone who is a great friend of Lib. In fact, your band joined them on tour for some of the concerts on their present UK tour, didn't you, Lib?'

'Oh, yeah! We go way back!' Lib chuckled. 'It's always great getting to play with these guys!'

'So, taking time out from their UK tour, a big hand for Zorro!'

Zorro and Jamie came running on to the stage.

'Thank you, George! Good evening, Jason!' Zorro pumped each man's hand enthusiastically. 'Yo, bro!' he laughed, giving a high five to Lib.

'Well, today, first of all, we want to celebrate the club's success so far – to players and management – and to wish them the very best next season with their two great new players!' he said.

'And we also want to celebrate the day the Labs get full legal standing!' Jamie added. 'From midnight tonight, we are all equal in the eyes of the law!

'So as a double celebration we'd like to start our performance with a song that we think you'll all recognise now!'

They moved across to join the rest of their band and went straight into 'Mirror Image'.

The audience were again on their feet as they drew to a close.

'The trio that is to follow you has also been on tour with you, haven't they, Zorro?' George said as the two men joined them on the sofa.

'These lovely ladies have raised the roof in many a concert venue in the UK over the past month!' Zorro agreed, and laughing he turned to his friend. 'Maybe not your kind of music, Lib!'

'No, their instruments are still intact at the end of their performances!' Lib drawled, smiling.

Sakura, Miyu, and Jade appeared. They played a series of violin pieces, ending with the energetic, rousing number they had played at their earlier concerts.

'That was certainly something! A big hand for Sakura, Jade, and Miyu, everyone!' George stood as the girls joined them on the third sofa.

'And now, last, but certainly not least, we are going to meet the boys themselves! Central's two new talented players: Johnny and Leon!'

The audience were whistling and on their feet again as the twins entered.

'Well boys, where did you learn these incredible skills?' George asked. 'We hear that you had no formal training in football until you enrolled at Castlewell College. Is that right?'

'Yes, that's true,' Johnny began. 'We never had training, as such …'

'But we've always been kicking a ball around, since we were, well, walking, really,' Leon added.

‘So it’s a big day for you today then lads?’ George smiled broadly.

‘It certainly is! Today we are so proud to sign up for Manchester Central …’ Johnny said, nodding to his brother.

‘Yes, and to be able to sign up as our *real* selves!’ Leon said.

Both boys stood up and turned to Jason Fullman and Lib.

‘Thank you for convincing everyone in the club to give us a chance, as our true selves! As *Labs*!’ Johnny said.

‘And from midnight tonight, as Jamie has already said, *legal* Labs!’ Leon added.

Both boys pulled back their right cuffs and punched the air, showing their codes.

There was a moment’s silence, then slowly the audience stood up, applauding and whistling.

‘Well, boys!’ George settled himself back in his seat as the noise finally subsided, ‘This is quite a day for you!’

He turned to Jason and Lib, ‘It must have been hard for you to keep that one up your sleeves, as it were!’

‘Yeah, well, there were a few legalities that had to be ironed out, last-minute sort of thing,’ Lib nodded.

‘But we’ve got the go ahead now. There’s no reason why the boys can’t join us as regular players!’ Jason added.

‘And how do you boys feel about it now?’ George turned to Johnny and Leon.

'We can't believe we've been selected for the team!' Johnny began.

'Manchester Central!' Leon shook his head. 'It's a dream come true!'

'And you being … Labs … doesn't that give you an unfair advantage over other players?' George asked.

'This was one of the objections we had to face, George. But they are just two young men who are particularly good at football. They can't be penalised for that!' Lib said. 'You can't ban someone from something because they are good at it!'

'No, no! Of course not! I'm not suggesting that! What I am saying is, aren't the boys physically enhanced by scientific means?' George continued.

Leon and Johnny looked at each other.

'We're the Labs that are good at football!' Johnny grinned. 'We don't really know much about big words!'

'Other Labs got the brainiac skills!' Leon added. He kicked his feet around. 'Our skills went to our feet!'

The audience began to laugh.

'OK,' George smiled. 'Well, tell us a bit about your background, lads.'

Johnny looked at Leon, 'We always were ready to kick a ball around. And there were always a few of the others ready for a bit of a game.'

'We all kept fit, but it was more than just exercise to us,' Leon said. 'We always loved it!'

'Yeah! Our competitive side showed up pretty

early on. We always wanted to go one further than the others!' Johnny laughed.

'This was at the Centre?' George asked.

'No, after that,' Leon said.

'Once we moved to Castlewell and enrolled at the sports college, things really came together!' Johnny continued.

'Yeah, the sports we could take part in! We just tried everything out!' Leon's face lit up. 'They've a great gym and two competition-sized swimming pools.'

'But football was the sport we knew was really for us!' Johnny nodded.

'And as twins, or rather clones, I suppose, you can sort of read each other's minds, I take it?' George said.

'They don't just play as a twosome, they play as members of the whole team. That's one of the things we were looking for!' Jason interrupted.

'Yes. As Labs we learnt you have to work together as a team!' Leon nodded. 'Whatever skills you have, you use to help everyone!'

'And have you been in touch with your … donor?' George asked. 'Or his family? Are they celebrating somewhere today for you?'

Johnny and Leon both shook their heads.

'We know he died quite a few years ago,' Johnny told him.

'He had divorced several years before and had never had children, so there is no family,' Leon added.

'The Labs are our family. So, today is a great day

for us! And it's a great day for all Labs!' Johnny grinned out at the audience.

Both boys stood up once again, punching the air to show their tattooed codes.

Sakura, Miyu, and Jade looked at each other, then stood up also, pulling off the plastic strips and holding their arms high. Simon slipped out from behind the scenes and pulled Sakura to him. He looked down at her wrist and kissed the code tattooed there.

There was a moment's hush. Slowly many of the studio audience stood up, pulling back their sleeves and pulling off plastic strips to reveal similar codes, punching the air.

There were gasps from several people in the audience and murmurs among the Non-Labs:

'*I had no idea …*'

'*All the time we've known you …*'

'*Why didn't you tell us?*'

'Most of us didn't feel we could reveal our true identities until we could stand up as equals to Non-Labs – humans. We've finally gained that right today!' Leon said.

There was a resounding applause.

'We'll sing to that!' Zorro and Jamie jumped up. Lib joined them, and grabbing their guitars they broke out into another loud chorus of 'Mirror Image', accompanied by the girls on their violins.

The audience joined in enthusiastically.

Dette and Ruby hugged each other and looked around.

'It has taken so long, now we can move on as *real*

people!' Dette said, her voice faltering.

'We are *all* real people – Labs and Non-Labs! And *all* equal!' Abel said, appearing beside them and hugging each girl to him.

Dette turned as Keith came towards them, his sleeve rolled up to reveal his tattoo.

'We've come a long way since the Caves, Abe!' he smiled.

Abel nodded. 'We certainly have, Ket!'

He turned to Ruby as other Labs joined them, all talking excitedly.

'And you, Ruby. Will you reveal your true background, too?'

She looked wistful, and then shook her head slowly.

'No, I don't think so. I was never really happy as Stella. Especially when Gran died. I found my family with the Labs. I'm happy to be Ruby.'

Abel smiled and pulled her close to him. 'You'll always be a part of our family! I'm counting on you to be my Non-Lab instructor!'

'I can manage that job easily enough!' she grinned.

At the back of the room a young man stood silently watched the crowd singing and smiling, hugging each other. A girl bumped into him and steadied herself on his arm.

'Isn't this just wonderful?' she beamed.

He gave her a cold stare as he brushed her hand away and began to walk out of the studio.

She shivered, then turned and joined a boy who was calling to her.

Ruth Armstrong could just make him out on the screen. He had walked straight up to *that female.* The two young footballers had been in front of him, but she thought she had caught a glimpse of him taking her hand.

Was he totally bewitched by *that female*? Was he lost to his family for ever?

She looked up as a middle-aged woman cleared her throat.

'Oh, Carol, just leave those phone messages on the table. I'll look through them later,' Mrs Armstrong looked up from the television, rubbing her brow. 'I've got a headache coming on.Could bring me a cup of tea?'

'Oh, Mrs Armstrong, I'll get you one right now!' Carol rang through to the kitchen. 'I see you're watching the latest news about those Lab people! What a story, eh? Trust your Simon to be so concerned about them; he always was one to support good causes, wasn't he? Even as a little boy.'

Simon's mother began to relax.

'You're right, Carol. He was; whether it was saving the whales or saving the trees! Looks like he's found a new cause! I expect it will be something else by Christmas!'

She sat back and sipped at her tea as Carol left the room. That was it! It was just a passing phase. Young people, she smiled to herself.

*

'Honey, you're not watching the UK news again, are you?' Bill asked his wife.

Vanessa turned to him. 'I keep looking at the faces, seeing if I can recognise her. Surely I should be able to?'

'Look, if you want to meet her, perhaps you could talk to Vince and arrange something?' he suggested.

'I don't know. Somehow I feel like I'm betraying Marissa by even wanting to know about … this person!' she said.

'Mom?' Edward, her younger son, had entered the room. 'Surely we all need to meet her. Isn't she sort of family, somehow?'

'Is that what your brother thinks, too?' Vanessa said quietly.

Tom, the older boy, came in and sat on the arm of the sofa.

'Yes, Mom. I know it was hard for you, when … Marissa didn't make it. But this girl has done nothing wrong, has she?'

Vanessa shook her head. 'No, she hasn't.'

Her gaze went back to the screen and scanned the smiling crowd.

Find us on f
/TrishMoranAuthor

THE DIFFERENCE BETWEEN GOOD AND EVIL
ISN'T EXACTLY BLACK AND WHITE ...

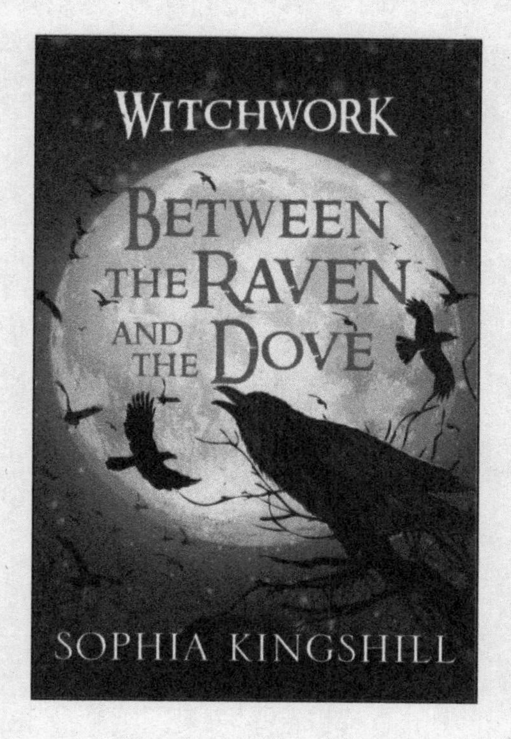

An exciting supernatural YA series
with a strong diverse lead.

What if every coincidence was a tiny miracle?

A tale of passion, secrets, second chances and the invisible threads that bind us …